BOMBERS' MOON

Recent Titles by Iris Gower from Severn House

DESTINY'S CHILD
EMERALD
FIDDLER'S FERRY
HEART ON FIRE
HEART IN ICE
HEART OF STONE
PROUD MARY
A ROYAL AMBITION
SEA WITCH
SPINNER'S WHARF

BOMBERS' MOON

Iris Gower

This first world edition published 2009
in Great Britain and in the USA by
SEVERN HOUSE PUBLISHERS LTD of
9–15 High Street, Sutton, Surrey, England, SM1 1DF.
Trade paperback edition published
in Great Britain and the USA 2009 by
SEVERN HOUSE PUBLISHERS LTD

British Library Cataloguing in Publication Data

Gower, Iris
  Bombers' Moon
  1. World War, 1939-1945 - Evacuation of civilians - Wales -
  Fiction 2. Agricultural labourers - Wales - Fiction 3. Wales
  - Social conditions - 20th century - Fiction 4. Love
  stories
  I. Title
  823.9'14[F]

ISBN-13: 978-0-7278-6765-0   (cased)
ISBN-13: 978-1-84751-139-3   (trade paper)

All Severn House titles are printed on acid-free paper.

Typeset by Palimpsest Book Production Ltd.,
Grangemouth, Stirlingshire, Scotland.
Printed and bound in Great Britain by
MPG Books Ltd., Bodmin, Cornwall.

One

I might die tonight. The thought came to me as I was sitting under the table in our house waiting for a bomb to fall on me. The Germans had missed me in last night's raid though a house down the road had vanished into the night in a big pile of rubble, all the people inside killed, crushed or burned. I saw that bit of news in the local paper; the date on the paper was February 1941, and even though I tore it into shreds and screwed the paper up for the fire, I couldn't get the picture of the poor family, who had died so horribly, out of my mind. I cried for them even though I didn't know any of them very well.

I used to see Mrs Griffiths in Taylor's greengrocer's shop, which always smelt of damp earth and potatoes; she always had a shawl wrapped round her, Welsh fashion, with a bald-headed baby hidden in its folds. She had a few other little ones hanging on her skirts, all girls I think. Their dad, like mine, was away fighting the war. He would come home on leave with his kitbag on his shoulder and find his house gone and his family all dead.

I tried to think of other things and, looking down, I noticed how crumpled my school skirt was; the pleats were spoiled and needed ironing but if I died I'd have no need of a school skirt anyway. And then I noticed how bony my knees looked glowing red in the firelight. I hated my knees.

I looked up at the underside of the table in an effort to distract myself from thoughts about my shortcomings and about bombs killing people and touched the screws holding the table in place; they were shining like gold as the flames of the fire licked patterns of red and yellow light across the room. I hoped briefly that the blackout curtain was safely tucked into the windows in the holes where the draughts came in and the light sneaked out.

There was a bit of writing on the underside of the table. I could only just make out the numbers, but for the rest it, it was too dark to see properly. And then my hair seemed to stand on end as I heard the first eerie drone of the bombers coming for me.

I looked quickly into the fire and concentrated, eyes half closed.

Trying hard I could see two faces in the fire, mine and John Adams'. I liked John Adams but I wouldn't admit that to anyone not even my best friend Sally Bevan. Our faces, mine and John's, were close together in the picture in the flames, perhaps kissing. I'd never kissed a boy but I heard all about it from Sally. She'd kissed lots of boys, so she said.

Unmistakably, the noise of the planes was getting louder. I got goose pimples that were nothing to do with the cold of the February night with frost on the ground and a bright silvery moon overhead, a bomber's moon, as the old people called it.

I felt the hard wood of the table rough under my fingers. I suppose there was a point in having the protection of the table but if a bomb dropped and the house fell on your head it wouldn't matter much if you had a table or not, you'd still die from smoke and fire, that's what I heard Tom Potty saying and he should know, he was an ARP warden. So I faced it; tonight if the German bombers came to our house I might die.

Worried with thoughts of dying I looked at the world of the parlour outside my hidey hole; all I could see were legs and feet. I could see old Mrs Evans's slippers – one of them had a hole through which her big toe poked obscenely, like a big nose with chilblains. Alongside the worn slippers rested Kate Houlihan's red shoes. Kate's feet were small and neat but I'd heard her say the red shoes were too tight for her. Still, she'd wasted good coupons on those shoes and she'd wear them if it killed her, which was a funny thing to say; bombs killed you, shoes didn't.

I could see Kate was proud of those shoes, the uppers shone with polish, but through the sole there was a bit of cardboard pushed inside to cover the holes.

And then pride filled me. I could see the lovely legs of my big sister, painted down the back with a line of black meant to look like the seam of a stocking.

Nylons: I'd heard the word and I knew that Hari longed for a pair of the gossamer stockings; but the big girls warned that American soldiers, when they came, would want to go 'all the way' in exchange for those wonderful nylons. I briefly wondered what 'all the way' meant and I opened my mouth to ask but just then something screamed like a banshee overhead and all the grown-ups huddled to the floor except Mrs Evans, who seemed to be asleep though one eye kept opening like the eye of a wary cat. Faces all around me were white and strained and I knew something awful was going to happen.

I was frightened and tried to pull old Mrs Evans down with the rest of us on to the floor but she wouldn't move from her chair; stubborn was Mrs Evans with her hair in curlers under a bright scarf. Mrs Evans shook me off and declared in a loud voice she wouldn't move from her chair not even for the Luftwaffe.

Suddenly the walls were flying apart. A great big wind engulfed the house and I couldn't breathe. A brick hit my leg and I suddenly felt angry, the table was supposed to protect me but it looked as if I was going to die anyway. And then I went to sleep.

Two

Hari sat on the bed in Mrs Evans's house and stared at the unfamiliar pictures on the walls. They had been placed more to hide the damp patches than for any aesthetic desire to enjoy the wonders of scenic Italy. She held a cup of weak tea in her hands, wrapping her fingers around the warmth for comfort. She would have liked some sugar in her tea but Mrs Evans had used up her ration. Well, the poor old soul would have no need of ration books or tea, come to that she would be laying on a slab somewhere.

Hari shivered; she would have to find somewhere permanent to stay for Meryl and herself, she couldn't impose on old Mr Evans much longer. It was only twenty-four hours since the bomb had dropped, flattening her home; it was a miracle that everyone, except stubborn old Mrs Evans had survived. In such a short time, everything had changed and yet the air raid seemed distant now.

Hari wanted to put the horror of it out of her mind and yet she was reminded of the helpless feeling of lying beneath the rubble, dust in her eyes and mouth, every time Mr Evans chewed at the subject, his eyes begging Hari for some titbit of information about his wife, some talisman he could hold on to for comfort. Now, his voice penetrated her thoughts.

'Tell me, girl, what did my Maud say, what were her last words, did she give you a message for me?'

Hari couldn't remember Mrs Evans speaking at all, all she could see was the older woman's slippered foot with one toe poking out of the hole.

'My sister tried to pull her down on to the floor but Mrs Evans wasn't having any of that.'

She could see that wasn't much help. 'But we were together,' she said, 'Mrs Evans wasn't on her own when . . . when the bomb fell. It would have been quick, you know, she wouldn't have suffered.' She had no notion if she was right or not but some of the strain eased from the old man's face.

Mr Evans rubbed his eyes. 'That's one bit of comfort I suppose – but if only I'd stayed in that night, let other buggers do the firefighting, she might have been all right. They would have let me off, see, one of the younger men, you know that boy from the mines, Tommy Trinder we called him because of his big chin. He said to me, "Granddad, why don't you go home, put your feet up," he said, "you've had your war."'

His Adam's apple bobbed up and down in his thin throat as he tried to control his tears. 'His mate Dai Thresher offered to take over my duties but I felt sorry for him; "He'll have enough to do when he goes back to sea," I said. A sitting target he'll be out there alone with the water all around him. Still, being a lighthouse man he won't go to the front, not like my boy, Billy. Dai is in a "reserved whatdycallit".'

'Reserved occupation, Mr Evans.' Hari took his hands. 'Perhaps they'll let your Billy come home now on compassionate leave.'

'Aye, perhaps so –' Mr Evans' voice was dull – 'not much hope of that though is there? What with my boy being in the thick of it like.' Abruptly the old man began to cry; he held his gnarled hands over his face and the thick veins stood proud, the brown liver spots almost joined so plentiful were they. Hari hesitated for a long moment and then put her arms awkwardly around the old man's bony shoulders.

'It's bad, I know it's bad but it will pass, you'll see. They say time heals don't they?' She was mouthing platitudes and she knew it but the words seemed to help and Mr Evans rested his head against her breast and she patted his back as though he were a child.

'Go to bed, Mr Evans,' she said softly, 'try to get some sleep. Meryl went up hours ago, I don't think she's recovered from the shock of the . . . well you know.' She moved away from him decisively. 'I'll tell you what, I'll make us a nice drink of Ovaltine, how about that?'

'Aye girl, you do that, it'll have to be mostly water mind, there's not much milk left.'

While the kettle boiled, Hari stood in the doorway of the house and stared at the road, her road. There was a gaping black hole where her home had once been, 'The Big House' as it was known in the neighbourhood. Jagged pieces of stone and timber looked like tombstones in the moonlight. Hari stared up at the moon, willing it to go behind a cloud so that the enemy bombers couldn't see what was left of Waterfield Road. She fe' like calling out to God to 'put that light out' but it was too late en for divine help for already she could hear the drone of engines and knew the enemy were on their way again.

Three

I was to go and stay with strangers, I was an evacuee on account I had no mother and my father was away fighting the Hun. Paul Houlihan sitting in the bus beside me dug me in the ribs and began to grin. I got to my feet impatiently – why couldn't it be John Adams sitting with me? But he was further down the bus sitting with Sally. How I hated my friend in that moment. I swayed down the aisle of the bus clinging to the backs of seats for support. I must have caught Sally's hair because she howled like a wounded wolf.

I looked at John; he winked at me and, embarrassed, I stared through the grimy windows of the bus as though my life depended on it. The buildings were giving way to countryside and I thought about what I'd left behind. The wide roads, the bustling streets, the neighbours popping in and, most of all, my sister Hari.

Hari had seen me on to the bus. I had a label round my neck and a gas mask in a box clutched to me like it was gold, frankincense and myrrh. Mind I was never sure what myrrh was, apparently it was very precious, and so was my box with its ugly gas mask in it.

Someone had given me a tin of cocoa to take with me. I offered some to John. He shook his head; his arm was stretched across the back of Sally's seat. Disconsolately I dipped my finger in the tin and sucked; it was sugary and sweet – it was lovely. I went back to my seat and let Paul Houlihan have a dip too because he was only ten and now the reality of the situation had sunk in.

'Remember what your Kate said?' I plumped down beside him forcing him to move into the window seat. He shook his head.

'She said you were nearly a man and big enough to look after yourself.' He looked doubtful. Big sisters talk a lot of scribble sometimes.

The bus grumbled into sudden halt as a cart pulled out of a lane beside us. I jerked forward hitting my head against the seat in front of me.

'Bugger it!' I said, and Paul stared at me in admiration.

'Bet you wouldn't say that in front of Hari.'

'Bet I would.'

'Say it to the driver then.'

I hesitated and the bus lurched forward again and I bumped my head a second time. Through the window I saw miles and miles of green grass with tiny cows and sheep dozily standing still like toy farmyard animals. This then was the country and I knew at once I didn't like it.

'BUGGER IT!' I screamed as, thirteen years old, I peed my pants.

Four

'You have lovely golden hair, pet.' The air force pilot leaned over Hari, in an attempt to dance the waltz with her. His eyes were glazed, his breath smelling of whisky. The pilots liked to live high on the hog, Hari noted with resignation.

'Well, don't get too close, *pet*.' Hari edged him away from her and took a deep breath of the cigarette smoke that was marginally better than close-quarter whisky fumes.

'Don't push me away, you know I love you.'

She looked up into his face: he was handsome and broad-shouldered, with thick, severely brilliantined hair that shone like shoe black under the lights; and he had a dimple in just the right place on his chin. She didn't even know his name.

'I love you, I really do.' He nuzzled into her neck, his lips sucking at her skin. Irritated, she pulled away from him and left the dance floor.

'I've got some fantastic stockings,' he called after her. He was swaying where he stood and for a moment Hari felt sorry for him, tonight's mission might be his last. She was sorry, but not sorry enough to surrender her virginity to him.

'I hope they suit you,' she called back, and made her way outside the hall to take a deep breath of clean air. She looked up at the sky – the clouds were scudding like large black pillows edging and pushing past a watery moon. She shivered. It was a sudden cold snap come early in November reminiscent of the February night when her life had been torn apart by the three nights' heavy bombardment of Swansea. Below her the town was in darkness, the only lights,' shining dimly, were from the dock's emergency lights that would be extinguished only if there was an air raid.

'Sorry about Stephen.' A voice spoke close to her ear and she turned around, startled. Framed in the doorway was the slim figure of an airman. 'He's lonely and afraid.'

He held out his hand. 'I'm Richard Squires. I'm based at Fairwood so I get into Swansea quite often.'

She took his hand. 'Hari, Angharad Jones, and don't worry about your friend, as you say, he's just a bit drunk.' She rubbed her hands together. 'How can he possibly fly a plane the way he is?'

'Shoving your arms into your flying jacket and preparing to take off soon clears the head. Up there you're on your own, no one to rely on but yourself.'

'I suppose you're right.' Hari turned away from him. She didn't allow herself to make friends with the men from the airfield as inevitably, one night, one more of them would fail to return from a raid.

Kate came out of the Glyn Hall giggling and clinging to the arm of the airman Hari had been dancing with.

'He loves me, so he does – at least that's what he tells me.'

'Me too, Hari said dryly. 'Any minute now he'll tell you about his stockings.'

'These you mean?' Kate dangled the fine stockings from her fingers. 'If he's good I might even try them on for him.'

'He's scared, apparently,' Hari said. 'The poor chap is frightened of dying without knowing what it is to have a woman – that's the new way of making a pass these days. It's anyone, anytime, anywhere – so don't encourage him.'

Kate held up her hand. 'No lectures, Hari, I'm a big girl now, remember?' She rested her hand on Hari's shoulder. '*I'm* scared. I work with them damn shells all day; I could be blown up at any time and *I* don't want to die without "knowing" too.' She clutched the pilot's arm.

'Come on, *pet*, we've got to go.'

Reluctantly, Hari remained silent. If Kate was old enough to risk her life in the munitions factory she was old enough to make her own choices in other ways. She looked up at the man at her side. 'Well, Richard, I'm off home.' She held out her hand and he took it.

'Can I see you again?'

'Why not? I'll be here at the dance again next week.'

'I might not be here next week.' Richard smiled down at her. 'What about a walk around the bay tomorrow night?'

'All right,' Hari said, 'I'll see you at the ice cream parlour by the slip about seven. It's just a walk mind.'

'I know – a walk it is. Where's the slip?'

'On the sands near the bridge.'

'Could I walk you home?'

Hari hesitated. 'Best not, there might be an air raid.'

'All the more reason—' She didn't allow him to finish the sentence.

'No.'

She walked away from him briskly, but as the music from the dance hall faded away she wondered if she would ever see Richard alive again.

Kate lay down in the grass and Stephen lay down beside her. He was just like a puppy, uncoordinated and foolish. She wanted to kiss him. She leaned over him and touched his cheek. 'There, there, my little man, everything will be all right, so it will, Kate says so.'

Stephen curled into her arms. 'Hold me, Kate,' he said softly, 'just hold me.' He began to cry and Kate rocked him in her arms the way she did with her baby brother, the youngest one, Sean, two years old and 'into everything' as her mother often complained.

She felt a moment's pang of loss for her other brother, Paul, gone to some funny place to live with strangers, begging to come home in every letter he sent. Soon, she knew her mother would give in and fetch him back to Swansea from his place of exile. Evacuation they called it but she called it a cruel shame.

She looked down at the airman in her arms, his eyes were closed, incredibly long lashes swept against his thin cheek, he was nothing more than a boy, little older than her Paul; her heart ached for him. Fascinated, she touched his skin; she could feel the stubble on his chin. He was a hero, flying into danger whenever duty called. He was so different from every other boy she knew. They lay together for a long time and then Kate shivered and shook him awake.

'We've got to go, Stephen, it's cold enough out here on this hill to freeze the backside off me.'

Stephen was awake in an instant. 'And the balls off me! Sorry, pet, it's not right to swear in the company of a lady.'

Kate was touched by his humility. She kissed him and his response was immediate and unexpected. 'Let me, Kate, let me.' He rolled over until he was on top of her, she could feel his hardness against her belly and then he was kissing her, drowning her in kisses. He pushed her skirt up and slid his hand to her thigh. The most absurd thought that her stockings would be torn flitted through her mind and then he pulled her knickers aside and he was against her, flesh on flesh, he, hard and yearning, and Kate bewildered – did she want this? Was it wrong to give comfort to a man going to war in the skies? But he was pushing against her, tearing her under-clothes in his eagerness.

'I won't hurt you,' he gasped and Kate gave in and took him in her hand and guided him to her. She almost screamed when he came into her, he was so big, but then perhaps all men were the same. She'd heard some of the more racy girls in the factory talk about it and the giggle always came at the end and the phrase 'bigger is better'.

It didn't seem so to Kate; it hurt, by Mary and all the angels it hurt, but she bit her lip and let him have his way. It was all over in a few minutes and he lay on her gasping. Kate felt only relief.

He adjusted his dress and then led her back to the road, thanking her with his dark puppy eyes, looking down at her with some-thing like awe. 'I love you, Kate,' he said softly and, at that moment, she knew he meant it.

Five

'This girl's got a head full of nits!' Mrs Dixon pushed me away and stared at me as though I had the plague. She fetched the scissors from a drawer and began to chop at my hair without minding what she was doing.

'I didn't have them when I came here,' I said with venom. 'I probably got them from your precious Georgie Porgy – he's always sitting by a scruffy girl at school.'

I'd come to hate Fat George with every bit of me. When I first set eyes on him I nearly burst out laughing; he had queer trousers that were tucked into his socks and pouched out around his legs like big bloomers. He also wore a cap on his scraggy hair and he talked so funny I could hardly understand him. He was two years older then me but he acted like a child. Even after all these months I hadn't got used to him. He reminded me of Podgy the pig in one of my Christmas annuals.

'Ow, you're hurting me!' I pulled away from Mrs Dixon and slapped her hand so hard that the scissors fell on to the floor. In retaliation, she slapped my legs, a stinging slap that had me hopping about like a wounded chicken. Georgie laughed and, forgetting the pain in my leg, I ran to him and pushed him hard. Taken by surprise, he fell on to his fat backside and stared up at me mouth open. I'd never seen such an ugly sight.

I couldn't help it, I just had to say it: 'You look just like one of them pigs you're so fond of – all bristly and red and ugly. I hate you George and your mother's a cruel witch!'

'That's it. You're no longer welcome in my house.' Mrs Dixon took me by the shoulders and shook me until my head buzzed. 'You're a horrible, no-manners town girl and I knew you were trouble the moment I set eyes on you. I've tried to tame you but I give up, you're a wicked, wicked girl.'

When she let me go I flew out the door and began to run. I had no idea where I was going but I wanted to put as much distance between me and the horrible Dixon family as I could.

I ran until I was breathless and then sat down on a flat stone at the side of the road and wondered what to do. There were fields all around, winter-bare, hedged and looking just the same as the next lot of fields. Without houses and bus stops and shops and all the things I was used to I had no focus, no way of finding out where I was. Still, I wasn't completely stupid, it was obvious Mrs Dixon would tell someone about me, the police most probably or whoever it was who arranged places for the evacuees in the first place. They'd learn a thing or two about Mrs Dixon if I had anything to do with it.

I couldn't sit here all day though, the road was narrow without a signpost in sight. I'd been sent to somewhere called Carmarthen; what I needed was to find a big road leading towards Swansea where I could be picked up easily.

I found a hill – there were plenty of them – and I stood up as high as I could to look around. Over to my left, I saw a farm cart, the big horse plodding along head down. This, as far as I could see, was the only traffic I would find.

I began to cross the field towards the other road and halfway over the cold ground the cart came swinging towards me. There was a man on the cart who looked older than me – about the same age as my sister Hari. He drew the big horse to a halt as near to me as he could get, which wasn't very close because I kept edging away from the great creature whose loose mouth, filled with huge teeth, was a bit too near for comfort.

'What you doing here?'

'What does it look like?' I wrapped my arms around my skinny body realizing my jersey wasn't doing much to keep me warm.

The man leaned forward, his big-booted foot resting on the edge of the cart. 'I don't know,' he said, 'you'll have to tell me.'

'You're a foreigner.' He had the faintest accent and it wasn't Welsh.

'Very quick of you. Come on, what you doing out here on your own? Where have you appeared from – you're not a mirage are you?'

'I'm running away. In any case they only get mirages in the desert, haven't you ever been to school?'

He smiled. You don't look like you're running away. I thought real runaways had a stick over their shoulder with a lump of old clothes tied to it. Where's your stick?'

I had to laugh then. 'You're not so bad for a grown up,' I conceded.

He looked at me for a long time. 'Get on the cart,' he said, 'I can't leave you here, can I?'

'Why not? And what if I don't want to get up on to your scruffy cart?'

'So many questions.' He raised his eyes to the sky as if he was looking for planes. 'Well, let's consider,' he said, looking at me again. 'The cows will be down here soon from the top field, they'll need milking and they come down very quickly when they need milking, don't care who they trample the old cows don't.'

'Bit like Mrs Dixon,' I mumbled. Then what he'd just said sunk in and a field full of huge dirty cows coming for me was frightening. I scrambled up on to the cart.

'I'm Michael,' he said.

'So what? Want a medal or something?'

'Just being polite, even townspeople are polite, aren't they?'

'I suppose so. I'm Meryl Jones.' I could have bitten out my tongue; I'd fallen right into his trap. Now he knew my name anything could happen. Then I brightened up – anything, like being taken home to Hari. My sister wrote to me every week; she hadn't yet made it down to the country to see me but then she was very busy looking for a new home for us. I was going home to Swansea soon, I was determined on it.

Michael stopped the big horse outside a farmhouse. It was big and scruffy inside even though from the outside it was posh: big windows, tall walls and a weather cock on the roof among all the chimneys. It was a bit different from the rows of terraced houses near where I lived. It was full of old, stuffed, splitting furniture and loads of books and papers that littered the floors.

A big lady led me into the kitchen without any show of surprise. 'Another one of those evacuees run away is it?'

'Aye,' Michael said, 'the third this year.'

'A lot of kids been staying with Mrs Dixon then have they?' I sounded brazen but I didn't care and if I wasn't mistaken Michael stifled a laugh and shut up only when the big woman stared at him.

'We'll have to deal with it,' she said, looking me over carefully, 'awful haircut – new fashion is it?'

'Mrs Dixon said I had nits –' I knew my tone was indignant – 'she cut my hair all off and it's not even cut straight. She slapped my legs hard.' I pulled aside my skirt and, satisfyingly, a big red mark bore out the truth of my statement.

'Humph.'

'Are you Michael's Mam?'

She avoided my question. 'You can call me Aunt Jessie for now, until we get you sorted.'

'I don't like the sound of "sorted".' I felt like crying.

Michael went out and he seemed to be gone a long time. I followed Aunt Jessie around the house while she made some food for the evening meal. I could see bits of chicken in a pot surrounded by vegetables and I watched fascinated as the big lady took a handful of dry things from a jar and put them in the pot with the chicken. The things began to unfold and the smell of onions filled the kitchen and my mouth watered.

Then I stood and watched as the big woman sat in a chair, pushed off her slippers and held her feet out to the fire. I was reminded then of old Mrs Evans, her big toe hanging out of her slipper, and I began to cry.

All at once, the big lady became Aunt Jessie as she scooped me up and cuddled me to her bigness. 'There there, it's hard on you little ones leaving your mother and all.'

'I haven't got a mother,' I moaned, 'and my dad's away fighting the Hun!'

'Shush, don't say that too loud some person might be hurt by it.' She brushed my hair away from my forehead. 'Look, about Michael, his father . . . well . . . his father was a German gentleman –' she hesitated – 'well, now Michael is with me and he's real Welsh, speaks Welsh and everything. I knew she wasn't telling me the whole truth because of my age. I came across a lot of that from so-called adults.

'Well, when the war started,' Aunt Jessie went on, 'Michael was too young to join up; in any case, he reckoned he would do more good helping me on the farm so he stayed here.' She smiled a lovely smile. 'The dear boy didn't want to leave poor Jessie alone.'

She looked serious then. 'You mustn't mention a word of this mind, not to anyone.'

I nodded, but I knew I would tell Hari as soon as I saw her.

'If he's a German, he might kill you in the night and run away with all your money,' I suggested.

'Bless you, I haven't got any money to speak of. In any case, how could he run away? You found it hard enough making your way here and if Michael hadn't picked you up you could wander over the fields for the rest of your days without finding anyone to help you.'

'But Germans are fiendishly clever.' I'd heard the words somewhere and they sounded good. 'He could fly in a plane.'

'Maybe, if he could find a plane and if he could, he might get shot. And why would he want to run away when he's been here since he was ten. Think about it.'

I thought about it. 'You're right,' I said.

'Glad you agree.'

When Michael came back he had a stern-looking man and a kindly looking lady with him. The lady smiled and I smiled back feeling like a grinning ape. Still, I knew it was important to be pleasant and well mannered to people who were clearly from the 'authorities'.

'Well, young lady,' the man said, 'what's the story then? Why have you run away from Mrs Dixon's house?'

My mouth fell open. 'That was quick! You told them everything, Michael.'

'I didn't have to. Mrs Dixon had already reported you as a runaway.'

'Please sir –' I used my best wheedling tone – 'can't I just go home?' His mouth became a straight line of disapproval. I turned to the lady, looking for sympathy. 'See how she chopped off my hair? And she slapped me, hard.'

'You attacked her son.' The lady had a hard voice in spite of her kind face and her expression didn't change even as her voice condemned me.

'He was 'orrible to me ever since I came. Look, I won't be any trouble if I can just go home.'

'Get that thought out of your head at once, young lady.' The woman spat out words like the hard glittering pieces of anthracite coal we put in the stove at home. 'You are here for your own safety. Whatever happens, you are not going home.'

My heart sank to my boots; I knew when I was beaten. I was in Carmarthen to stay – for the whole of the buggering war.

Six

Hari folded the letter and stuck a stamp on it wondering how Meryl was enduring her life in the countryside. Her young sister's letters were chatty enough but there was an underlying sadness in her words.

Hari looked around. 'Home' was a bedroom and a tiny sitting room. The bathroom and kitchen were shared with Mrs Cooper, the owner of the house, a tiny lady who dominated her huge husband. Together the Coopers ran a public bar that was little more than a room at the front of the house.

At first, Mrs Cooper told her proudly, they'd only had an opening into the narrow street of terraced houses, serving beer by the glass from a window. Slowly it had evolved into a sitting room bar with solid benches around the walls and sawdust on the floor. 'Now it's a *real* public house,' Mrs Cooper said, waving her hand to encompass the tiny space.

The small, yellowed room was always thick with pipe smoke and beer fumes but it was a hub of much-needed humour for the men, too old for war, left at home.

Dai Cooper sometimes played the accordion, his still-adept hands sweeping over the keys, the gasp of the instrument sounding like lungs in torture.

From her room Hari could hear the sounds from the bar room; sometimes she peeped in when she passed the front room door and was struck that there were never any women there – the spurious emancipation war brought to women hadn't penetrated this far into Swansea.

But Hari had plans and she was saving her wages from the Bridgend munitions works. It was a little way out of Swansea but the wages were good and she'd got a good position in the tiny signals room there. Soon, she would buy a house, her own place on the outskirts of Swansea, away from the centre of the bombing.

At the moment the houses were cheap enough but no one knew if they would still be there in the morning.

Now she sat on her bed and picked up a book, listening to the wash of voices downstairs. Hari was lonely and wished Kate was here or even Meryl with her endless chatter. Hari's troubled thoughts dwelt again on her sister, stuck in the country with cows and sheep and creatures she detested.

Meryl was a town girl. She loved the lights, the shops, the little Italian cafés; she loved the beach front with its swings and ice cream stalls. Hari knew in her heart that, however much she didn't want to believe it, Meryl was unhappy in the country. It was only a matter of time before trouble erupted in the peaceful valleys of West Wales.

Meryl was a bundle of energy, sometimes it was difficult to harness the fire – that spirit – that made Meryl a personality even at a young age. Meryl was one of life's reporters, seeking, eager for a story, quick to condemn but just as quick to shed tears of pity. But above all, Meryl found trouble wherever she went.

In the morning Hari was proved right. An official-looking letter came for her with the early morning post. Mrs Cooper looked at it suspiciously as she handed it over. 'I know you're on your way to get your breakfast, my *cariad*, but this 'as come for you, and trouble it is if you ask me.'

Hari took the letter, refraining from telling Mrs Cooper that she wasn't her sweetheart, she wasn't her anything except a lodger and she didn't appreciate Mrs Cooper scrutinizing and anticipating the contents of her mail.

'Thank you,' she said stiffly. 'I'm late. I'll have something to eat at work.'

She grabbed her coat from the overloaded hallstand in the little hallway that was reeking with the smell of stale ale and hurried outside. A light rain was falling, the air seemed misty, unreal, heavy, yet nothing deterred the German bombers, they would be back whatever the weather. She stopped at the bus stop fingering the letter, knowing instinctively it concerned her sister.

The bus lumbered into sight and with a sigh of relief Hari climbed aboard the metal platform, clinging to the rail as the bus, hardly stopping, chugged on its way towards town. She went upstairs where she would meet Kate at the next stop.

Hari slit open the letter and read it quickly. A smile quirked her lips as she read about the contretemps between the Dixon boy and Meryl, she'd apparently called him an ugly pig and Meryl was nothing if not observant. The smile vanished when she read that the authorities were uncertain what to do with Meryl.

Hari looked up as Kate breathlessly slumped into the seat beside her. 'Nearly missed the bus so I did!' – Kate was out of breath – 'again'.

Hari looked out of the window in surprise. 'You should have got on at the last stop,' she said, 'what on earth are you doing here in Oxford Street?'

Kate looked defiant. 'I stayed over with Eddie,' she said. 'It's all right, his sister was there and his mother.' She paused and a glimmer of a smile touched her lips. 'Eddie's lovely, Hari.'

'Kate! How many is that and when are you going to stop all this nonsense?'

'It's all right, this time I'm in love.' Kate's face was awash with happiness. 'The others were airmen, off on a mission, fighting back the Luftwaffe. Since those three nights of Swansea bashing the bombers have laid off a bit but our poor boys are still doin' their bit, some still dying for it.'

'Quite a speech, sure you believe it?' Hari's voice was dry. She felt a bit like her little sister, blunt and a not a little sarcastic.

'Oh, read this.' She hastily handed Kate the letter. Kate gave her a funny look but took it anyway.

'Aw, Jesus, Mary and Joseph that Meryl of yours is the limit! She can even go to the countryside and find trouble.'

'The woman cut her hair out of spite, told Meryl she had nits!' Hari relented and joined in Kate's laughter. 'You're right though, Meryl would find trouble in the ruins of Pompeii.'

'Where's Pompeii?' Kate asked. Hari just shook her head as the bus jerked to a stop.

'At last. Come on we'll have to run for the train if we're to catch it.' Hari pulled at Kate's arm. 'I don't want to be late, I've got a lot of work to catch up on.'

'Aye,' Kate said mournfully, 'and I got a few buckets of powder to carry over those rickety boards to put in the shells. Even my bloody knickers are turning yellow with that powder.'

Hari peered at her friend. 'Your face looks all right.'

'Only because I plaster it with petroleum jelly before I start. The other girls laugh at me but I know what I'm doing, my face is as pale as the day I was born. Do you know the girls from Bridgend call us Swansea lot "Yellow Daffodils". Well, I call them lot "Yellow Pee the Bed Dandelions!"'

Hari paused. 'Joking aside, what do you think of that letter, should I go and fetch Meryl home?'

Kate looked thoughtful. 'Wouldn't that spoil your bit of night life?'

'What night life? I spend most of the time studying signals and things.'

'That's your fault you swot.'

'I know. Anyway, I am worried about Meryl.'

'Forget Meryl, she can look after herself.'

They parted at the gate and Hari was happy to step inside the warmth of the signals room. As soon as she sat down Colonel Edwards came to her desk and leaned over her. 'I have some special work for you, clear your desk.'

An hour later Hari was in a small side room with a bank of radio receivers before her, intimidating her. The Colonel looked down at her, an old man but upright still with a strong military bearing.

'I've been watching you these past months and I'm impressed with your sharp intelligence and I've decided I need help with the signals.' He took a deep breath. 'I think you are capable of learning quickly how to use these.' He waved his hands at the machines, radios and Morse code transmitters.

Hari was fearful; she wished she had his confidence. The Colonel went on talking.

'I've had very encouraging news this morning – the Germans are being cornered at Stalingrad. If the Russians force the enemy to retreat it will be a turning point for the whole war, but there will be months of fighting ahead yet before anything as good as that happens to us.' He turned at the door and smiled. 'Now get on with your work, miss, and for all our sakes reward my faith or I will be the first one in the firing line.'

Seven

The 'authorities' were back and were insisting I must go to live with the Dixons again. I cried until I was nearly sick and at last Aunt Jessie took charge, fixing the tigress of the woman official with cold eyes.

'Mrs Preston, the child will be staying with me.' She gathered me towards her. 'Can't you see she's hysterical?'

The woman blustered. 'Well! I'm the one who must decide where Meryl Jones goes.'

'You'd best decide she goes here with me then, hadn't you?' – Aunt Jessie's big frame seemed to fill the room – 'or I might be having a strong word with Jimmy, you know, Jimmy Clark, head of the services department, your boss I believe.'

The next minute the 'authorities' were gone leaving a gust of wind as the door banged shut after them.

I still clung to Aunt Jessie, my arms wrapped around her big, reassuring body, my head against her broad bosoms. I liked the sound of the word 'bosoms', it was more descriptive than 'chest', which sounded like a flat wooden box not a bit cosy and comforting as Aunt Jessie's bosoms were.

At last I calmed down and began to hiccough; my melo-dramatics weren't all put on – I'd been truly afraid I'd be taken to a 'home' and everyone knew that 'homes' treated you cruelly and wouldn't give you more if you asked for it.

'There, sit down, love, I'll make us all a cup of tea.' Michael, who'd been silent throughout the shenanigans, ruffled my hair. Usually, I hated that but when Michael did it, he was so, well what-ever he was, I didn't mind him ruffling my hair one bit.

Aunt Jessie sank into her chair and there was a sound like air coming out of a cushion but it was air coming out of Aunt Jessie's lungs.

'That was a right battle royal and if that old hatchet-faced biddy thought she was going to get the best of me she had another think coming.'

Aunt Jessie's face was red. I was sorry for upsetting her and I cuddled her and kissed her cheek. 'Thanks for sticking up for me,' I said humbly.

Michael brought a tray with a brown pot on it and some cups and I thought I could see some rich tea biscuits on a plate and brightened up.

I stared at Michael: no one would take him for a German. Well, he was half Welsh or English or something but he *had* lived in Germany for a time when he was young and he spoke the language very well. Secretly, he'd begun to teach me to speak German. We both knew Aunt Jessie wouldn't approve so we didn't tell her.

He was too young yet to go to war and, anyway, which army would he join? It was a strange thought and it gave me a bit of a pain in the middle of my tummy.

I ate most of the biscuits and Aunt Jessie wagged a finger at me. 'I've got soup on for our tea, mind,' she said sternly. 'I don't want you wasting good nourishment by filling yourself up with rubbish.'

She didn't know what an appetite I had – my sister Hari called me a gannet and that's a bird that eats everything in sight. When I thought of Hari I felt like crying again. I wanted to go home, to look out of the window and see lights, dimmed by the blackout curtains, but there behind the windows. I hated the endless darkness that was the countryside but then that's why we were never bombed here, the Germans couldn't see us. I'd stopped calling them 'the Hun' in respect for Michael.

I looked at him now, he was falling asleep, his long legs spread out before him, his toes reaching for the warmth of the fire. His hair was over his eyes and his mouth was open. He looked very handsome.

Aunt Jessie was dozing as well, her big hands idle for once in her lap. I felt the warmth and the comfort of the room, the coals falling in the grate and suddenly I was peaceful. If I couldn't be home, here with Aunt Jessie and Michael was the best place to be in all the world.

I woke to the sound of voices and realized the awful Mrs Preston and her meek male assistant were back yet again. I pretended to be asleep and through the slit of my eyes I saw a policeman in uniform. He took off his hat and rubbed his hair into a mess as Aunt Jessie began arguing with the woman whose face was still kind but whose voice was that of a harpy, one of those ugly creatures, half woman, half bird, from a book I'd been given to read at school about the ancient Greeks. And then Mrs Forsythe made us read the Aeneid and I liked that, what I could understand of it. I know this Aeneas went off with Queen Dido but he went away and left her in the end. Did men always do that?

'This is your introduction to the great Virgil, girls,' Mrs Forsythe, our teacher, had told us. 'We should read more of the classics –' her tone was reverent – 'but perhaps this book is one of the best. Remember it well.' I remembered 'the classics' now all right as the bird woman stared into my face.

I was grabbed then and pulled to my feet and the kind-faced lady, for once, had a scowl on her face. 'Your mask has slipped,' I said. She looked like she'd slap my face but too many people were watching.

'Mrs Dixon has agreed to take you back,' she said frostily. I was hustled out of the door and jammed into a black car and then we were bumping away down the lane and I looked back and saw Aunt Jessie with her hands over her face and Michael with his arm around her shoulder and it was as if I'd lost my only true friends in the whole world.

When I arrived at the Dixons' house I was thrust unceremoniously from the car. And then I was inside with the Dixons, the front door locked and bolted. I was given bread and milk for supper and we ate in silence. Then Mrs Dixon nodded to Georgie and went outside.

George pushed me into the cold scullery and shut the door. 'I'll call your mother,' I said fiercely, knowing what was coming.

'Don't bother, she's out feeding the chickens.'

'What? Arsenic? Or the acid from her tongue?'

He punched me suddenly and I fell back on the floor knocking my head against the wall. I was shocked more than hurt.

'You big bully!' I kicked out and caught him on the ankle. He immediately kicked me back and caught my knee cap. It hurt. Bad. I scrambled to my knees and bit his arm, his fist came down on the top of my head, again and again. I looked up at him and his fist smashed my nose, breaking it. In any case, I heard a crack and then it started to bleed. I sat back on the floor and wondered what to do. I rubbed my face all over his mother's clean washed sheets folded nicely in a basket – that would at least give her a good day's washing to do. I had no doubt she'd put George up to this, he hadn't the brains or the guts to do it all by himself.

'What's the story?' I said sliding against the wall to support myself.

'Huh?' He never was very quick.

'How you going to explain all these cuts and bruises when I go to school?

His eyes glazed as he thought about it and for a moment it looked like my beating was over. Then he brightened. 'We'll tell people you fell, when you ran away.' He started laying into me then, punching me wherever he could find a soft spot. And then he hit me on the head and I saw the earth and the skies explode around me in a load of coloured stars. I wished I could 'blackout', a word I'd heard a lot since the war started but I just lay there pressing my lips together to stop myself from crying.

He was breathless and fell back against the door gasping, sweat running down his face, his thick legs apart as though to support him to start another attack on me.

I saw it then, under the mangle, the iron bar kept for defence in case the Germans might come. I stealthily reached out and got it and with a mighty effort lunged forward, brought up the bar with as much force as I could muster right between his open legs.

He went down, screeching like a pig with its belly being opened. I pushed him aside and flung open the door and then I was out into the night gasping in the cold air.

In the distance I could see the tiny glimmer of a lamp down by the chicken coup, a sign that Mrs Dixon was still keeping out of the way. If she'd been in the town she'd have had the Home Guard yelling at her to put the light out; she didn't even think that to German bombers a detour over the fields of Wales was nothing but a few minutes' flight where they could unload bombs before heading home. I wished they would come and drop all they had on Mrs Dixon and her darling George.

I looked round and tried to get my bearings. Once I found the gate and was out on to the road I could be on my way. Not to Aunt Jessie, not this time, it was the first place they would look for me. I thought of Michael and willed him to come and find me again but he was probably in bed thinking me safe if unhappy at Mrs Dixon's house.

Hunger bit a hole in my stomach, I'd no proper food for a few hours now and I was a girl who liked my food. To my friend Sally Bevan it was a mystery and a source of irritation that however much I ate, I stayed small and slim. Poor Sally was plump but nicely so with nicely shaped bosoms, not huge cushions like Aunt Jessie's but round and soft and sticking through her blouse to taunt the boys. I noticed they all looked at Sally's bosoms, even John Adams.

My legs were tired and my knee ached where George had kicked me. I sat down and picked at a glossy leaf of some plant or other and in the dark scratched John's initials on it by memory and put it in my shoe. The idea was that if it turned black by morning, he loved you.

My sensible mind told me that stick any plant in a sweaty school shoe and it would go black but I put that out of my mind. I tried to think of John but instead saw Michael's face. Hastily, I took the leaf out of my shoe and threw it away. John Adams was in the past after all. Michael was here and now.

Eight

Kate dressed carefully. The skirt of her dress was soft grey wool, made from a blanket; her blouse was an old one but was mock velvet and clung flatteringly to her slim figure. She regretted it looked shiny in parts as it was much washed but at least the colour suited her.

She was meeting Eddie again tonight and her heart fluttered, a tiny colourful butterfly caught in gossamer threads inside her. She felt happy in spite of the threat of air raids, in spite of the constant play of searchlights overhead on the lookout for enemy planes. Her foot brushed against a sandbag and a shower of sand scattered over her lovely red shoes. She brushed it aside impatiently. A stone dug into the hole in her shoe but she ignored it; nothing was going to spoil her happiness. Tonight she would be with Eddie and soon, she was sure, he would propose.

She loved him, 'loved the bones of him' as her mammy would say. Eddie wasn't handsome, he had a sweet mouth underneath a golden moustache, his eyes were blue and they looked at her with love and respect. Very important that, respect.

For a moment she felt uneasy, wishing she hadn't given herself
to any other man. But then they were in need, frightened, wanting
the warmth and comfort of a woman's arms. Any woman's arms.
She was uneasy again.

Eddie was waiting for her outside the Empire and he smiled
and moved towards her the instant he saw her. He took her
hands and leaned down to kiss her cheek. She felt a flare of
happiness and cuddled his arm close to her side.

'Easy there!' he said, 'you'll give a boy unworthy thoughts.'

She wished sometimes he would have 'unworthy thoughts'. She
should be happy – but now, she was used to a man, the scent, the
touch, the thrusting passion that swamped every sensible thought.

He'd managed to get her some chocolate and he gave it to her
in the perfumed intimacy of the theatre, his fingers gently squeezing
hers. She took his hand and kissed it. 'I love you, Eddie Carter,'
she whispered in the soft darkness.

Behind her there was a shuffling sound and she glanced over her
shoulder and froze as she met the mocking gaze of Stephen, her first
pilot. He winked slowly, suggestively – and abruptly she turned away.

The audience fell silent as the curtain swished open and then
the stage was filled with light and music and dancing girls in gaudy
dresses, but under the lights they looked ethereal, beautiful.

The thought of Stephen plagued her all evening. She thought
of him as he'd been that long ago cold night, soft, clinging and
needy in her arms and yet now he looked at her so differently as
though . . . as though she was nothing more than a good-time girl.

She was glad to join the crowds singing the national anthem
and then they were in the carpeted aisle, making for the door.

'Wait up there.' It was Stephen. 'I'm going to a party back stage,
want to come, you chaps?'

Kate was about to decline but Eddie was smiling politely. 'Very
kind, old man, love to wouldn't we, Kate?' He drew her hand
through his arm in a proprietary way and Stephen looked amused.

'I might be in the skies over German territory later on, you
never know, tonight could be a matter of life or death so I've got
to make the most of it haven't I, Kate?'

He had changed so much. Stephen was hard, the baby softness
of his jaw gone, a cynical light in his eyes. 'The dancing girls here
are always so, so *amenable*, know what I mean?'

Eddie didn't. He stuck out his hand. 'Edward Carter.'

Stephen looked surprised. 'No names, no pack drill, eh, old chap?'

Eddie dropped his hand. 'No, I suppose not.'

The room in the back of the theatre was hot with smoke and ripe with heavy perfume. To Kate's disappointment, the dresses of the dancers, so lovely on stage, were no more than bits of straggly net revealing a great deal of flesh. Drinks were handed round, mock champagne but with a real kick to it.

Stephen had wandered away and was leaning over a girl with dyed blonde hair and Kate grimaced. The girl should work in the munitions, she'd have yellow hair courtesy of the Ministry of Defence.

The girl looked Kate's way and she was laughing. 'Looks like butter wouldn't melt.' The words drifted to where Kate stood. She felt the colour suffuse her cheeks and shame crawled over her like the legs of a centipede.

'Let's go,' she said to Eddie, 'I don't want to be here.'

'OK.' Eddie smiled. 'I'll just pop to the WC and then we'll be away, this isn't really our kind of thing is it?'

While Eddie was away from her, Kate fumed with impatience. The girl Stephen had been talking to looked her over and strolled to where she stood. 'So you know Stephen, do you?'

'Well . . .' Kate spread her hands not knowing what to say. To her horror she saw Stephen and Eddie return to the room together. Stephen had his arm around Eddie's shoulder and Eddie was looking pale and stunned.

He came to her side without looking at her.

'Hello,' the blonde said, smiling her lipstick smile at him. 'I'm Marybell.' It was a name as false as the quality of her dress. The dancer held out her hand to Eddie in a languid, affected pose and after a moment he took it but didn't look up.

'So you're keeping company with little Irish Kate.' She looked down from her great height at Kate. 'Little Joan of Arc, saving everyone except herself.'

'We'd better go.' Eddie nodded curtly and turned towards the door and, with a baleful look at Stephen, Kate hurried to catch up with him.

He strode away in the darkness and she struggled to keep up with him. 'Wait Eddie, tell me what's wrong!'

'What's wrong?' He spun round to face her and all she could see were the dark edges of his jaw and the tautness of cheeks. 'I've just heard you're the best blanket the forces have got, lay down for anyone.'

'Eddie! And you believe that drunken Stephen's every word do you?'

He became still. 'Are you telling me it's a lie? If you are I believe you, Kate, God, I want to believe you.'

She hung her head. 'It's true I let Stephen . . . he was frightened, flying into danger, he might not come back, ever. I felt sorry for him.'

'So was he the only one you felt sorry for?'

She was silent a long moment. 'No.'

'Oh Kate, I worshipped you, I might have known it wouldn't be true that you loved me, plain gormless Eddie.' His voice was anguished.

'I do love you!' Kate pressed herself against him wound her arms around his neck, her hand on his hair. She felt the edge of his army cap. Soon Eddie would be off to war and he would go hating her.

'You'd better go home.' His voice was breathless. She could feel him hard against her. Experienced now, she slipped open his buttons and touched him; he was so taut his skin was like silk. He groaned. 'Kate, please don't, I've tried so hard to be respectful. I've worshipped you like a goddess.'

She drew him down on the ground and took control of him. He had no will to resist though when he entered her, he was crying bitter tears. It was over in minutes and he fell away from her still crying. She held him then for a long while and they lay like wounded animals together.

Overhead, the planes began to drone, German planes. The bombs exploded round them, the incendiary bombs lit up the world. It was like a party, but in Kate's heart, it was more like a wake.

Nine

I was cold, my feet were wet, my stomach 'felt as if my throat had been cut' as Kate's mum used to say. Anyway, my poor belly was empty and grumbling, I felt angry and miserable and all I wanted to do was lie down and go to sleep.

I found a barn at last and stumbled inside and pulled bits of straw over me for warmth. Straw was supposed to be warm, according to war hints you could even cook food in straw. I could hear the sound of some animal in the darkness but I didn't care, I couldn't go another step further not even if a cow sat down at my side and fell asleep with me.

I was dozing when I heard Michael's voice, and I thought I was dreaming. I sat up when my name was called and I crawled to the door and peered out. I could see the dimness of a lantern quite near.

'Michael!' My voice quavered with weariness but he heard me. He came towards me at a run and I took his hand and pulled him into the barn.

He sat down and hugged me and then, as I winced, he began to examine my cuts and bruises. 'The bastards!' he said. 'The Dixons did this to you I suppose.'

'Well it was Georgie, Mrs Dixon was out feeding the chickens.'

He sighed. 'Aye, well, she would be. Come on, let me get you home.'

'Got the cart?' I asked hopefully.

'No, I've been searching on foot, *thought* you might be hiding somewhere after fat George came and told us you'd run away again.'

'He could manage to walk then?' I didn't explain but Michael got the message and started to laugh.

'Caught him where it hurt then? Good for you girl.' He put his arm around me. 'Let's go.'

'I can't.' I shook my head. 'I just can't go anywhere now, Michael, I'm tired and I hurt. Just cuddle me and let me sleep.'

'I really should take you home.'

'Put some straw over me, Michael, I can't walk another step.' I closed my eyes and leaned against the warmth of his chest. Now that was a chest: flat, hard, lovely to lie against. My eyes began to close and soon I could hear by Michael's easy breathing that he was asleep. I cuddled closer and his arm closed around me and a bubble of happiness erupted inside me and I slept beside him like a baby till morning.

Aunt Jessie's face was troubled when she saw us. 'Where have you been all night?' she asked, gesturing with her head that there were other people present. The 'authorities' I guessed.

'We've been walking home,' I said quickly before Michael

could open his mouth. I knew instinctively that to tell the truth that we slept in a barn would be misunderstood by the man and Miss hag-faced Preston. 'I'd run a long way from the Dixons' house and I was lucky Michael found me when the dawn was just rising.' I hoped that was the right thing to say, folk in the country set great store by the sunrise and sunset. Apparently it was.

Aunt Jessie turned my face up to hers and then held me at arm's length and examined my arms and legs. Obligingly I lifted my liberty bodice and the bruises on my skinny ribs were purple and angry.

'*Duw Anwyl! Dear God,* who has beat you so bad child?' At that cry Miss Preston came tearing out into the hall. She looked at my bruises and to my shame pulled down my drawers.

'Her lower abdomen seems unhurt, I don't think there's been a sexual assault,' she said crisply, but for once there was a glimmer of compassion in her eyes.

'No child should be beaten like this however difficult and disobedient they are,' she said. 'I shall have Mrs Dixon struck off the list of helpers and might even have her charged with assault.'

I knew she'd be wasting her time. Mrs Dixon was not in the house when George hit me – she'd claim I was as bad as him. Still, I tried a smile but by the lady's stiff look it was more shark about to bite than grateful child.

Seeing I might be listened to for once I opened my mouth. 'Can my sister Hari come to see me, I feel very sick.' If my voice was tremulous it wasn't all put on. I shivered – that wasn't an act at all – and fell into a chair. My head was spinning and all I wanted to do was go to bed and sleep for ever.

I had my wish. The man and woman vanished abruptly. Aunt Jessie washed me, very gently wrapped me into one of her voluminous flannel nighties and tucked me up in bed. 'Can Michael sit with me till I fall asleep?' I asked humbly. 'He's like a big brother to me.' That was an inspired touch.

'Of course, darling girl. Michael, the cows can wait a few minutes for the milking, sit with our Meryl for a while.'

He sighed but came to sit with me and I took his hand. 'My dear, dear Michael, you always come to my rescue, I love you.'

He ruffled my hair. 'And I love you, you little imp. Now go to sleep, there's a good girl.'

I pressed his hand against my cheek and I didn't let myself drop off to sleep until Michael had released his hand and crept away.

By the time Hari came to see me I was feeling much better but still in bed on Aunt Jessie's orders. They came into the room together, chatting like old friends, Aunt Jessie, all grey hair and pins and my lovely red-haired sister looking like she just stepped out of the pages of a model magazine.

'Oh, Meryl, you look awful, you're black and blue!' She examined my face for a good spot to kiss me and then planted a kiss on my chin, which George had somehow missed. 'That boy Dixon must be a real beast! If I got my hands on him I'd kill him myself.'

'Don't worry, the Germans might drop a bomb on him,' I said encouragingly, 'mind they don't come here often.' And then Michael came into the room.

I glanced quickly at Hari willing her not to put her foot in it. 'Michael's dad was sort of, well foreign,' I said and, being intelligent, she got the message. 'Michael's my guardian angel.' I wanted Hari to have the right impression of him. 'Twice he's been the one to find me when I ran away from the Dixons.'

Hari's face was flushed; it must have been the heat of the fire Aunt Jessie had kept blazing in the black grate in my room.

'I don't know why they sent you back to that woman, they want a good talking to and I'm the one to give it.' Hari sounded annoyed and as I thought of Miss Preston I felt sorry for her.

'I did my best,' Aunt Jessie said, 'but that awful woman would send Meryl back to the Dixons. I think it was out of spite. Well, wait until her boss hears of this palaver, her head will roll believe me.'

I imagined a bird-faced head rolling and smiled even though it hurt. Michael came forward and held out his hand to my sister. Hari took it at once and smiled, showing her perfect teeth.

'Thank you for being so kind to my little sister,' Hari said.

'Hey!' I protested, 'not so much of the "little". I'm growing up. Haven't you noticed, Hari?'

Obviously not, her bright blue eyes were fixed on Michael and his on her. I could see they were mesmerized with each other. Hari was fascinated with my Michael just as I used to be about John Adams but in a more grown-up way. They held hands for a long time and Aunt Jessie looked at me with a sympathetic smile. In that moment, for the first time in my life, I looked at my sister Hari and I hated her.

Ten

'You're putting on weight Kate and you've stopped greasing your face, you're going bright yellow like the rest of us. What's the matter chick, lost your man?'

Kate nodded dumbly. She'd lost Eddie as surely as if he were dead. After the night he'd found out the truth and they'd coupled, desperately, in an act of goodbye; she had not seen him again. That was six weeks ago.

'Didn't come back from ops, eh?' Doreen came to put her arm around Kate's shoulder. 'Look love, it happens to us all, they're there one minute and then gone, there's nothing we can do about it – see, love, it's called war.'

Kate began to cry. She didn't tell Doreen that Eddie had dropped her like a hot coal once he knew the truth about her past, but leaned against Doreen's thin shoulder and sobbed.

'He was the one,' she stammered, I loved Eddie, I would have married him like a shot if he'd asked –' she looked up at Doreen pleadingly – 'he even took me to meet his mammy so he did and his sister, he must have cared for me, mustn't he?'

'Course he cared for you, I never met my Geoff's mam and now he's gone she came to see me, asked if I had any pictures of him. Took them to be copied at the photographers, said he looked very happy with me and she was grateful.'

Doreen sighed. 'I let him, you know, but he was careful, he used one of those thingies from the chemist.'

She looked over Kate's thickening figure. 'Yours not careful, eh?'

'We only did it once.' Kate looked down shame-faced as though studying her plain black working shoes coated in yellow dust.

'Poor dab, caught first time, well it happens and it's a damned nuisance. How far gone are you?'

'Must be six weeks.'

'Well, you can't have it.' Doreen squeezed her shoulder. 'You can't have a baby, not now, there's a war on.'

'Get rid of it you mean, how?' Kate couldn't believe those words had come out of her mouth.

'I know a woman, she's a good woman, knows what it's like to be unwed and in the way. She's clean and kind and usually it works without trouble. She'll do it for a few shillings. I mean it for the best, love, but it's up to you, mind.'

'If I do it will you come with me?'

'I'll do more than that: you can stay at my place overnight then no one need know anything.'

'Why are you doing this for me?' Kate asked, 'you hardly know me.'

'You're a workmate, risking your life like me with this damn powder and all those shells stacked up in the sheds.' She looked a little sheepish. 'And Moira, the midwife, gives me a couple of bob at the end of the year for helping, savings I call it though God knows we might not be here to enjoy our savings with the Luftwaffe over Swansea like a swarm of bees round honey. They'll hit Bridgend one fine day, they'll find out we're here and all these shells and things will blow us to kingdom come.'

Kate heard the heavy thud of boots. 'The old man is coming, better get back to work. Thanks Doreen, can I talk it all over with you later?'

Bob came into the shed, his face grim. 'Disasters all over the country. London got a good pasting from those blasted Hun – the bastards flattened some of those nice London buildings. King and Queen won't leave though, bless 'em.'

Kate looked at him and he caught her gaze. 'No slacking then, girl, if the Queen can get about in the blitz and cheer folk up you can do your job right? Now get on with it.'

Kate felt like crying. There was no need for Bob to be so sharp.

'Go easy, Mr Bob, sir,' Doreen said gently, 'she just lost her man, Germans got him, didn't come back from the front see.'

'Bad luck.' He said it as if she'd lost a penny farthing but Kate nodded and lifted her empty buckets and began to trudge wearily across the rickety boards outside in the chill of the evening to the shed where the powder was kept.

It was dark by the time Kate climbed on the bus and sank into the seat she usually shared with Hari. The seat was empty as Hari was down country seeing to her kid sister. Meryl was always trouble but it seems this time she'd been given a bad beating by some horrible spoiled-rotten boy.

Would Hari bring her home? Kate hoped not, Meryl was far too sharp a kid for her own good, she saw things most grown-ups didn't even notice. One day she'd be a newspaper reporter or suchlike if she lived that long.

Kate stared out of the window and saw her distorted reflection, eyes heavily ringed with shadows, nose looking angular and over-long. She closed her eyes and thought of Eddie with pity now as well as longing. He'd been called up, been sent to what they called 'the front', near enemy lines. He'd gone willingly, a broken-hearted, disillusioned man because of her.

She must have dozed because when the bus jolted to a stop she opened her eyes to see she was back in Swansea. The sea stretched like a band of steel across the bay, no hiding that from the German planes.

The hills of Townhill and Kilvey were blacker than the surrounding skies, hidden, crouched in shadow but once the flares were dropped – those chandelier flares that hung so prettily in the sky – the town would be at the mercy of the enemy bombers.

'You're early today, Kathleen.' Her mother was lifting the heavy pot of thick broth from the hook over the fire. The smell of bacon and lentils filled the little kitchen and Kate felt like heaving. She sank into a chair and put her bag, holding the remains of her sand-wich and her canteen of tea, on the floor at her feet and sighed heavily.

'My arms ache from carrying those buckets of powder all day.'

'Well, a lot of girls are doing the same thing, my girl, it's war work, it's that or the forces, or farm work, at least this way you sleep at home safe and sound.'

Her mother poured her a cup of tea from the cherry-coloured teapot; it was strong and hot and Kate drank it, grateful for the kind gesture rather than the tea itself, somehow tea didn't taste the same these days.

'One of your friends called for you, that Jenny, the one you used to work with at RTB, she wants you to meet her at the ice cream parlour but sure, if I were you, I'd go straight to my bed after supper, you look all in.'

'I'll see how I feel later.' Kate wondered if she could summon the energy to go out tonight and yet anything was better than sitting in all evening listening to her mammy go on about the war and how in her day it was all different, in the first war the men were men and they showed the Hun that the British were not to be ruled by anyone.

As her mother filled the bowls with soup and cut great doorsteps of bread Kate heard the door bang open. 'Paul's home.' The warning was unnecessary as her growing brother barged into the kitchen. Mammy had brought him home as soon as the blitz on Swansea had eased a bit. Mammy needed her brood around her she said.

'Jesus, Mary and Joseph, take your time Paulie!' Kate shook her head. 'You're like a homing pigeon – you know fine enough when the food is on the table.'

He scrambled on to a chair and frowned under his thick fringe of hair when his mother told him to go and wash his hands.

'That girl wants to see you, the one you used to work with, said you're going out with her, she's coming for you about eight o clock.' Mrs Houlihan pushed a bowl of soup Paul's way and over her shoulder spoke to Kate.

'You look tired but perhaps it would do you good to get out a bit, you been stuck in here for days and I'm tired of you under my feet.'

So that was decided then, she would go out. In a way Kate was glad to have the decision taken out of her hands.

'Soup's lovely, Mammy.' She spoke between mouthfuls, preventing her mother from making any further comments. She'd wear her grey dress and her red shoes and that lovely red scarf Eddie had given her. Tears came to her eyes at the thought of sweet, darling Eddie but she ate doggedly and willed the tears away.

Later, arm in arm with Jenny, Kate tottered through the town towards Mario's Ice Cream Parlour. Inside the huge blackout curtains, the room was bright, heavy with smoke. A couple of lads leaned over a table in the corner looking the girls over, much to Jenny's delight. She preened and slid one leg over the other revealing a shapely knee.

Kate sat head down, not wanting to be seen. Stephen was among the gang of young men. She'd 'been' with him, let him into her drawers, he was probably telling the others about it now just like he told Eddie; they were leering and laughing raucously punching each other's arms in the way that men did when they were excited.

Kate tried to talk to Jenny but they'd never had much in common and all Jenny seemed to want her for was company while she found herself some man to keep her happy.

To Kate's horror Jenny invited the men to join them and they came hotfoot across the floor, pushing chairs into place between the girls. Stephen was beside Kate and put his hand in a proprietary way on her knee. She quietly removed it.

'Don't go all innocent on me now, Kate, you were willing enough that night outside the church, practically on a poor fool's grave. Right juicy you were, too, a bit of all right, what boys? He pinched one of her full breasts, it hurt and instinctively she slapped his hand away.

'You brazen bitch! Hot one minute and then all saintly, eh? What did I have then I don't have now?'

'You had fear,' she said gently, 'you were terrified, you begged for me to love you, you told me you were afraid of going to war.'

'Huh! As if I would be so unmanly.' He was scarlet.

Kate picked up her coat. 'And most of all you had tears, you cried in my arms like a baby. I did what I could to help you. Good night, Stephen, and good luck.'

She walked out into the dark night and made her way towards home, glad of the evening breeze on her cheeks. She'd only gone as far as the middle of town when the air-raid siren scorched her ears. She stood still for a moment, frozen with fear.

Bombers droned overhead, searchlights raked the sky. She saw them descend, the beautiful deathly candles of light, and then she began to run to the cover of the nearest shelter and cowered inside, huddled against other frightened people drawn close by the twin feelings of anger and fear for what was happening to them and to their beloved Swansea.

Eleven

Hari looked up as Colonel Edwards stopped at her desk. He smiled down at her, a lined man big and bluff who had served valorously in the war of 1914–18. He walked with a stick now but she'd found that his brain was strong and active, and his eyes gleamed with intelligence.

He sat opposite her, his injured leg jutting out awkwardly before him. 'You like your work Miss Jones, you have no desire to join the armed forces?'

She looked at him in surprise. I think I'm happy to serve my country in any way I'm needed, sir.' She wondered if it was a rebuke.

'So you are happy to do your war work here in Bridgend?'

'Yes, very.'

'Good, that's what I wanted to hear. 'You are quick to learn, articulate and clever. You are a well-educated young lady I understand?'

'I did well at my school.'

'No need of false humility,' he said almost abruptly. 'As you already know, the work you do is secret, I don't want to be mysterious but signals are passed all over the country, bomber pilot to bomber pilot, among other things. Most reach Bletchley Park but it's also my job to pick them up and decipher them, yours too if you have an aptitude for it.'

He handed her a page of writing. 'It's given to some intelligent civilians like you to do this work. Now this is the fairly easy code I use, it's a peculiar shorthand of my own. I make notes of what comes my way, it's all above board, government work, you understand? In the event of systems failing somewhere along the line, at least we here have some of the, possibly vital, pieces of information.'

Hari wondered what he was getting at. He read her mind. 'As I said, I want to teach you to share my job. Anything could happen to me; I'm getting older and slower. Two heads, I feel, are better than one and your head is a young eager one.'

Hari was doubtful. 'I'm honoured at your confidence, sir, but am I up to this sort of work?'

'Well, before we go on to the difficult work,' he said, smiling, 'I want you to do a spot of work on this machine here. It's a new listening radio I bought, or rather the government bought it. It's almost like a regular wireless but you listen out for Morse messages. You understand Morse, don't you? Learned it in girl guides like most other kiddies I expect.'

Hari nodded doubtfully. 'Only the basics, sir.'

'Well, you'll soon get the hang of it. We've found that some of the German operators get careless and make it easier for us to work out the message.'

'You think I'll be any good at this sir?'

He stood up, ignoring her question. 'The messages will be in

Morse but they will be coded, as I said. Just play with the damn thing, I'll come back and see you later.'

Oh, there's a kettle over there on the stove and tea stuff. You can't get up and go for lunch if there's an important message coming through, you understand?'

'Yes sir.'

He left her then and Hari began to panic. However much she tried to concentrate, she could make little sense of the machine. Life had been easier handling simple calls in the bigger office. She couldn't do this, she just didn't have the ability. She rubbed her eyes and then stared at the piece of paper the colonel had given her. She would just have to try her best, but first she would make herself a much-needed cup of tea.

Hari persevered throughout the day not even stopping to eat the sandwiches she'd brought with her. She drank a lot of tea and stared at the strange codes until at last they began to make something resembling sense.

The radio buzzed into life and Hari panicked. She listened to the tapping sounds that rose and fell as if coming from a distance. She hastily scribbled the letters represented by the long and short signals; she would try to work out their pattern later.

'How are you doing, Miss Jones?' Colonel Edwards' voice startled her. She looked up and put her arms over the papers she was attempting to work on and then realized how foolish she must seem. This man, this intelligent man, was well used to deciphering messages from the wireless.

He smiled. 'Well done, I see you'll be discretion itself. Now, how are you getting along?'

'I don't think I'm getting very far, sir,' she said, 'though some of the words are beginning to make sense.'

'Anything important come through?'

She was taken aback. 'I don't know, sir. I'm sorry, I wasn't taking notes I was so busy trying to understand how it works.'

He held up his hand. 'No problem, just keep trying. I'll give you a few lessons tomorrow. Go home now, I don't want you to miss your bus to the station.'

Hari felt weariness drape over her like a fog; going home on the bus, then on to the train, darkness pressed against the windows, drowning her. She closed her eyes for a moment. Kate sitting beside her, touched her arm. 'You all right?'

'Just tired. You?' Kate nodded.

'Right as I'll ever be.' She took Hari's arm and leaned against her. 'Last night, I went out, only for an ice cream and the men there, they were horrible, taunting me, telling anyone who'd listen what I'd been up to with them. I was shamed so I was and furious at their cheek. I put them in their place so I did, telling on them crying, begging me to cuddle them before they went out to face the Hun. The cat got their tongues then and I left the ice cream parlour head in the air.'

Hari felt pity tug at her. Poor, misguided Kate, she thought she was helping the young men who were about to die and gave them everything but some of them lived to tell a spiteful tale. As the train shuddered to a halt at Swansea station, she pressed her cheek against Kate's. 'See you in the morning and try not to let them get you down.'

The busyness of the station gave way to silent streets and Hari breathed a sigh of relief as she turned into her road where their old, big family house was little more than a hole in the ground. A few doors down was her house.

A few weeks ago, Mr Paster, one of the neighbours, had approached her to buy the house; it was small, terraced, but it was a home of her own.

She had grown tired of the public house, the noise, the smell of beer. She had been saving for months now and she had raised enough for the small deposit and so now she was a property owner – well, she and the local bank.

As she approached the house she looked at it with pride; small it might be but it was hers, hers and Meryl's and Father's if he came home from the war safely.

It was dark in the house, so dark with the blackout curtains and the fire unlit in the grate. Hari sighed and sat on one of the chairs in the parlour feeling too tired to do anything but go to bed. Still, she had chores, some washing and cleaning up.

She made sure the blackout curtains were in place and switched on the lights. She was lucky the house had been modernized; she had electric while some of the houses in the area still had gas lighting.

She turned on the gas stove. She would heat a tin of soup, have some of the stale sandwich from morning and as soon as she washed out her stockings and underwear she could go up to bed.

She ate the soup with little interest but it was hot and warmed her stomach. The heat from the stove had taken the chill from the air and she began to doze. Suddenly, before her eyes were the long and short symbols of the Morse code. They untangled, became clear as the normal written word and she sat up with a start as her memories from childhood came back, the days she'd struggled to send messages by tapping on an old tin to the other girl guides. Quickly, she took the paper out of her bag and unfolded it. She was beginning to see the pattern; letters were transposed in compli-cated forms but, slowly, she would make sense of it all.

She did her chores mechanically and stumbled upstairs. Once in bed she tucked the blankets up to her chin as the bedroom was freezing. She was so excited she wanted to go back to work at once, turn on her machine and really understand what it was all about. That would take some time but she was prepared for that.

She would never sleep. She closed her eyes and didn't open them again until an air-raid warning wailed into the night. She stumbled out of bed, pulled on a coat and shoes and followed all the other sleepy people on the road into the nearest shelter.

Twelve

So I was settled with Aunt Jessie and my dear Michael. I thought of him cuddling me in the barn and sometimes I felt shy of him. He had no such feelings, he seemed to have forgotten all about that night, but he talked and talked about Hari until I was sick of the sound of her name. One night at supper, over the pristine white cloth on the table in the dining room, the one place that was tidy in the whole house, he handed me a sheet of lined paper.

'What's this for?'

'I want you to write your full name and your address,' Michael said.

'Hang on, Hari only gave it to me when she came down to see me. She's bought a house, it's a new address to me,' I said hesi-tantly, 'but I'll fetch it later if you really want it.'

I knew what he was up to; he was going to write to my sister. It felt like ice was rubbing against my belly and my heart.

'OK,' he said carelessly and I held my breath.

'Anyway –' I knew I sounded aggressive – 'what do you want it for, do you think they're going to shove me out of here any time soon and you want to know where I'll be?' If only.

Michael looked confused and then he lied to me. 'Ah, something like that.' He smiled his lovely smile and I didn't know how to deal with what was happening. My Michael was falling for my sister and the pain was gut-wrenching. Jealousy was a fire inside my belly, worse than seeing John Adams with my friend Sally, much, much worse.

Later when Michael was gone to work in the fields milking the cows, planting things or whatever he did on the farm, I sat in the kitchen hunched over the fire. Aunt Jessie made me a cup of tea and sat opposite me. There was some kind of lecture coming.

'About your sister—'

'Hari? What about her, Aunt Jessie?' For a minute I felt a pang of fear. 'She's all right, is she?'

'Aye, she's all right. She's a lovely girl, a town girl, she'd never be happy in the country.'

'Well, she doesn't live in the country and never will.' Then I saw what Aunt Jessie was getting at and thought it over for a few minutes.

'At a certain age young folk get fancies but that's all they are, fancies. Oppose them and they get stubborn, pretend to go with these silly, passing fancies and that's it, they'll pass and be forgotten.'

I ran to her and flung my arms around her neck. 'Do you think I'd make a good country girl, Auntie?'

'Maybe, maybe not, but you'll probably have a lot of fancies yourself before you need to decide.'

I knew I wouldn't have any fancies. Michael was my man for good and ever but Aunt Jessie talked a lot of, well, sort of hidden sense; she spoke like the Sunday School teacher, in sort of parables, but I knew what she meant all right.

'Now, to something rather unpleasant – I want you to go to school this afternoon. Your teacher agreed to you having the morning off but this afternoon she wants you there to read the part of Titania in the school play; you're the only one to learn the lines properly, so she says. It's a good way for you to settle back in, Meryl.' She smiled. 'It's the best offer you're going to get, so my advice is take it.'

I adjusted my thought to school, to getting ready, putting on my skirt and my long socks, polishing my shoes, going back to meet up with George Dixon.

'I don't know why Miss Grist picked me, Titania was supposed to have lovely red hair, wasn't she?' We were back to Hari again.

'Don't ask me, I haven't got time to read that stuff.'

I tried not to laugh. 'Well, I suppose it's better than going back to double sums or English.' I loved both those subjects but I felt I had to give in with good grace, at least taking part in a play might be fun. I gave in. 'It's a long walk though and my leg still hurts a bit where George kicked me.'

'I thought it might,' Aunt Jessie said dryly, 'I'll take you in the pony and trap.'

School wasn't as bad as I thought. Some of the kids crowded round me and asked what George had done to me. They all seemed to have garbled ideas about the attack.

'Will you have a baby?' Mattie Beynon whispered in my ear. I stared at her in astonishment.

'How would I manage that?'

'Well,' she faltered, 'when George attacked you did he put his thing inside you?'

'No he did not!' I pushed her away. 'Look, that rat George Dixon didn't get anywhere near my knickers so don't go making up silly stories any of you.'

'That's enough of that.' Miss Grist's voice held a touch of laughter but her face was stern. 'There's no need of that sort of low talk, Meryl. Now, into the hall, all of you, and we'll get on with the play.'

So I was Titania, Queen of the Fairies. I was to meet Oberon in a fairy glade or wood or something. Oberon was Roy Clark; he was thin and had glasses but then he had a lovely smile, and his voice was good and clear.

'Ill met by moonlight, proud Titania.' His voice carried across the hall. Challenged, I put heart into my response.

'What, jealous Oberon! Fairies, skip hence.' I knew about jealousy now. I waved my hand commandingly to my invisible fairies and then, thank goodness, it was time for a break.

'Hey –' Roy caught my arm as I was about to run to the yard for the lavatory – 'you're not half bad, you'd make a good actress.'

'Not interested.' I pulled my arm away and hurried out into

the warm air. Roy wasn't bad-looking, better than John Adams really but the only man I was interested in was Michael, he had held me in his arms, cuddled me close until I could feel his heart beat and I would never want another man in place of him.

That night, at supper, I meekly handed over the address Hari had given me and as I met Aunt Jessie's eyes, she winked at me. I smiled; we were conspirators and, Michael, being a man, had no idea.

Thirteen

Hari drove to the farm in the jeep Colonel Edwards had lent her. She was a good driver even though she'd been shown only the most fundamentals of handling the gears and steering. By the time she reached Carmarthen, she was well used to the vehicle.

She saw Michael's large shape standing in the sunlight at the gate. He swung it open for her as she neared the farm. She pulled on the handbrake and stared at him for a moment and an unaccountable flutter stirred her heart.

'Meryl's still in school.' He took her hand and helped her down. 'Jessie is having a doze though she always denies it, says she's "just resting her eyes".' He was still holding her hand.

'Let's walk,' she said, and he nodded, slipping her hand through his arm. He felt solid, masculine, he smelt of grass and sunshine and an unfamiliar sensation tingled inside her.

'Tell me about yourself.' She looked up at him; it was a long way to look as he must have been at least six foot four she decided.

He smiled, his teeth were clean, straight and even – all in all he was too good to be true.

'Meryl said you are half German.'

'I was born in Germany,' he said, 'lived there until I was ten.' He paused. 'Then I came here to live with Jessie to help on the farm.' He didn't seem inclined to divulge anything more and Hari was too polite to push any more personal questions at him.

'How's Meryl?'

'She's all right. I took hold of George Dixon one day after

school and shook him till his teeth rattled. I don't think he'll touch her again.' He glanced at her. 'Mrs Dixon is another matter, she's a bad enemy to have.'

Hari wondered if the authorities knew of his German ancestry, if not Mrs Dixon could be a *really* bad enemy.

They stopped on the top of a hill, breathless and still linked together. The sky was large above them, the soft clouds floating across the horizon like a granddad puffing on his pipe. Hari turned to look up at Michael; at the same time he bent his head and his lips were on hers. Hari drew away startled.

'Sorry,' Michael said, holding up his hands, 'you look so beautiful with your face all shiny from the walk and your lovely hair like golden, red-touched clouds drifting around your perfect neck.'

Hari felt foolish yet touched, and suddenly very happy. They stared at each other for a long time and then Hari boldly held out her arms. 'No harm in a hug, is there?'

When he was close, she could feel his arousal and suddenly her lower stomach was full of heat. She'd never felt like this before; she wanted Michael, she wanted his body but she wanted his soul as well. She drew away abruptly, this was all too sudden, too dangerous.

Aunt Jessie was awake, very much so when Hari followed Michael into the heat of the farmhouse kitchen. The tantalizing smell of roasting meat made her realize she was hungry. All her senses were alert, on guard so to speak, she thought wryly. Aunt Jessie looked at them suspiciously.

'When did you arrive, Hari?' She was almost stern.

'Not long ago.' Hari didn't understand why she lied. Yes she did – Aunt Jessie wouldn't approve of a dalliance between her and Michael. Only it wouldn't be a dalliance, it would be much, much more than that. It was impossible.

Michael went out to do his work and Hari sat uncomfortably in the kitchen watching Jessie peel vegetables. 'Can I help?' she asked hesitantly. Jessie shook her head.

'No. Thanks. I'm used to doing things my own way.' She glanced at Hari's white hands and, unaccountably, Hari felt ashamed they were not calloused or stained yellow as Kate's were.

'I'm working on communications,' she said and it sounded like an excuse though why she needed to excuse herself to anyone, least of all Jessie, defeated her. It was a relief when Meryl came bounding into the house, her shoes clattering on the wooden floor of the hall heralding her arrival as she pushed open the door and flung herself into Hari's arms.

'You've got a car!' she said, hugging Hari frantically. 'I didn't know you learned to drive.'

'I'm a quick learner.' Hari kissed her sister's soft cheek. 'How's that horrible Georgie Porgie treating you now Michael's had a word?'

'You've seen Michael?' Meryl's tone was guarded.

'Briefly. When I arrived he opened the gate for me then he went off to do some work on the farm.'

Meryl relaxed. 'Mending fences and such I suppose.' Meryl sounded knowing though she had no idea what he was doing.

'Go find him, Meryl love,' Jessie said. 'Tell him dinner will be in half an hour, make sure he washes his hands – look out for him as you always do.' She glanced at Hari. 'Your sister is so good with Michael, keeps him in his place she does.' Her tone implied that Hari might be well advised to do the same.

The silence lengthened in the kitchen and then Jessie took a cloth out of a drawer and spread it like a billowing sail over the table.

'She thinks he's the sun, the moon and the stars.' She looked Hari in the eye. 'We must try not to upset her, the poor child's had enough upset in her life to last for a very long time.'

Hari was being warned off Michael and she knew it.

'But Meryl is only fourteen,' she said, 'she'll have crushes many times before she finds the real one.'

Jessie sniffed. 'She's nearer fifteen now – keep up girl. And "crushes", is that what they call it now? Well, let me tell you, Meryl is growing up fast, anyone would in this awful war. And remember, Michael is not yet eighteen, about the same age as you are but not that much older than your sister.'

Hari was silent, digesting what Jessie was saying to her. Jessie was implying that love between Meryl and Michael was not as impossible as it seemed. And yet Hari had been in Michael's arms, felt the heat of his body heat her own. It wasn't just lust, she knew it wasn't.

'What's really wrong, Jessie?' Directness was important.

'I don't want silly girls disturbing my Michael. He's safe here on the farm with me. And with Meryl,' she added.

'How could I be a danger to him?'

'I don't want him leaving the farm, going into Swansea. He'd be noticed there, some busybody would pick up on his accent.' She stopped abruptly.

'Jessie, the authorities don't know Michael is German — is that it?'

'Just mind your own business Miss Jones, go home and leave us in peace. You know Meryl is safe down here with me, just go away, forget Michael. He's not for you — do you understand?' Jessie's tone was fierce. Hari faced her.

'That's not for you to decide, is it?'

'So you do have a fancy for him then?' It was a direct challenge.

'I don't know what I feel, I hardly know Michael. You're making a fuss about nothing.'

'Am I?' Jessie didn't look at her. 'Well, that's all right then, isn't it?'

Later, dusk was closing in over the fields when Hari walked with Meryl at her side towards the jeep. Hari hugged her, realizing Jessie was right, Meryl was filling out, growing up.

'Bye, little sis. Be good, be careful . . . be safe.' She climbed in the jeep and drove away. In the mirror she could see Meryl's face was just a pale unfamiliar blur in the growing darkness. Suddenly she was painfully, very painfully sad.

Fourteen

The house was plain, set back from the road, away from the other small cottages. Kate took a deep breath and glanced at Doreen. 'This is it then?'

Doreen nodded. 'Moira knows we're coming, she'll be ready — it won't take long.'

Moira was friendly. She had a cup of tea ready and a few dry-looking biscuits on a plate, spaced out to look more plentiful and resting on a neat doily. A good try considering it was wartime.

Kate's mouth was dry and her stomach was bunched up into a tight ball as if to protect the barely formed child within her. Doreen spoke.

'This is a serious thing, mind; slipping out a baby isn't a picnic. I just want you to know that.' She sighed. 'But a lot of girls are coming to me now so you're not alone. I'm a good midwife, I'm clean as I can be and I'll look after you when it's over. Your chap dead is he?'

Kate nodded. 'I think so, he's been reported missing, that's all I really know.'

'Do you care about him?'

Kate nodded miserably. She just wanted to get on with it before she screamed out her fear and revulsion at what she was about to do. She was from good Irish stock and her mammy would be horrified if she knew what Kate was doing. But then she would be equally horrified to learn Kate was having a baby in the first place.

Moira took her cup away and led the way into a little lean-to at the back of the house. There was what looked like a doctor's examination table, long and narrow and spread with a white sheet that was spotlessly clean. A metal bowl stood at the side and a wicked-looking scalpel that glinted in the overhead gas light.

Kate got on to the table and lay back. Moira lifted her skirt and pressed her knees apart. 'You'll have to take your underwear off, you silly girl.'

Kate sat bolt upright. 'I can't go on with it.' She scrambled down from the table, pulling her skirt into place. 'I'm sorry to waste your time. I'll pay you, of course.'

Moira sighed and shook her head. 'No need, I was half expecting this. You're just not the sort. The Good Lord only knows how you'll manage but manage you will I'm sure.'

Moira rested her hand on Kate's shoulder. 'Look, let me make you a cup of tea and we can talk, perhaps that will help.'

Kate sat on the shabby, comfortable sofa in the parlour of Moira's house and looked at the faded wallpaper. It was once grand in Regency stripes, now the stripes had faded to indistinct beige. She felt numb.

'Want to tell me about it?' Moira handed her a cup of tea and Kate was glad of the hot liquid pouring down her dry throat.

'Same old thing – fell in love, let him have his way – when I fell for the baby it was all too late.' Suddenly she felt the urge to confess.

'He wasn't the first. I thought I was helping the boys face the thought of war and death but all I was doing was getting myself a bad reputation. When Eddie, my boyfriend, found out, he lost all his faith in me and do you wonder?'

'It will never change. I expect when women got the vote they thought the world would be theirs, that they would be equal to men in all ways, but though a man will take a woman with very little thought for her reputation, when he marries, the hypocrite wants a virgin.'

Kate knew Eddie wasn't like that. He had loved her, he had respected her, what would he think of what she was doing now? At last, beaten, she left the midwife's house.

When she met Doreen outside, she shook her head. 'I didn't have it done, I couldn't.'

'Oh, Kate –' Doreen sounded exasperated – 'you've done me out of a few bob now!'

Kate looked at her hard. 'So to be sure it wasn't concern and friendship that you offered me then, just a way to make an extra bit of money. I knew Moira gave you a few bob but I didn't realize that's the only reason you helped me. Thanks a million.' She forced back the tears. 'I thought you were quick off the mark realizing I was expecting a baby, trained to it now I expect.'

She walked away from Doreen, her eyes running with tears, could she trust no one to be a real friend? There was Hari of course but could she tell even Hari what she nearly did to her baby?

She didn't sleep that night and she got up for work on Monday heavy-eyed and with a pounding headache. Mammy didn't notice. She pushed a breakfast of bacon and eggs under Kate's nose and got on with the business of making a pot of tea.

Even the tea tasted off. Kate hated being pregnant, she would never do it again so long as she lived. How she was going to cope in the coming months when it was all showing and she grew fatter and fatter she had no idea. No doubt Mammy would throw her out for the shame of it.

'I'm late.' She pushed her food away. 'I'm going to have to run for the bus, Mammy. See you later.'

'Not eating, all right are you?'

For a moment Kate thought of telling her the truth and getting it all over and done with but her courage failed her. 'Just a bit too much to drink last night, Mammy, I'll be all right. I'll get something in work.'

She met Hari on the bus and sank beside her with a sigh of relief. The feeling of nausea was still with her but at least it was better now that the smell of greasy food was out from under her nose.

Hari was leafing through some papers. 'What's that – another letter from your dear little sister?'

'It's a love letter.' Hari spoke in a tone that was so matter-of-fact that Kate almost thought it was a joke. Then she saw the sprawled signature.

'Who is Michael?' she asked, bewildered. She'd never heard of any Michael, not among their crowd.

'He's the son of the woman who owns the farm where Meryl is staying. Meryl hints he's got German blood but his mother's as British as we are so I suppose he's allowed to stay. In any case, Jessie needs Michael on the farm. It's war work, isn't it?'

'You're keen on him?'

'I don't really know.'

'Is he gorgeous?'

'He's very gorgeous.' Hari's cheeks were pinker than usual behind her fall of long red hair.

'You *do* like him.'

'I suppose I do.'

'Well, don't let him anywhere near you.' Kate's voice was rueful and she knew it and knew what Hari would read from it. She did.

'What are you going to do about it, Kate?'

Kate shrugged. 'I just don't know Hari, live with it I expect.'

At the gates to the sheds Hari hugged Kate and then held her at arm's length. 'You look too small and frail for all this and you shouldn't be carrying buckets of powder or anything else in your condition. I'm going to see if I can get you a transfer to the canteen or something.'

'They'd want to know why,' Kate said softly. 'Don't feel you have to interfere, Hari. I know it's well meant but I'll handle everything myself.'

After a moment Hari nodded. 'OK then, I'd best get off – I've got loads of work to do.'

Kate watched her go and she suddenly had an empty feeling deep in her gut. What if something dreadful happened and she never saw her friend again? She shrugged the feeling away, she was depressed that's all.

She went into her designated shed and as soon as she crossed the threshold Doreen sniffed and turned her back and some of the other girls eyed Kate curiously. It was obvious they all had been told of her condition.

Some of them were kind and did a lot of the carrying instead of her but then, in the afternoon, Doreen put her foot down. 'Let her fetch her own buckets. She's got to pull her weight, we can't carry her for evermore! If she'd been seen to by my friend we'd all help for a couple of days but as far as I'm concerned I did my best, gave up my time and went with her to the midwife and then she chucks it back in my face, wasting everyone's time.'

'I'll do it for you, Kate.' Little Janey Smith smiled at her and Kate shook her head.

'It's all right, as Doreen says, I must pull my weight.'

'Come on then, I'll come with you. At least I can help you.'

The two girls set out across the misty ground. The fog was heavy, obscuring the buildings, and appeared like a diaphanous blanket draped across the chimneys of the main buildings, before seeping wetly between walls. She could hear Bob coughing and the grate of the shells across the floor as he stacked them. She heard soft masculine voices, the mumble of conversation. Everything was eerie, unreal.

Kate suddenly felt the hair on her neck rise, something awful was going to happen. She just knew it; her fears were coming true. She hesitated, her footsteps faltered. She felt a sudden blast, hot and searing, lifting her off her feet. She twirled through the air and then she hit the boards of the walkway with a heavy thump.

A roaring noise and sudden, leaping flames filled the air. She felt the heat as suddenly Bob's shed was a mass of fire and rolling smoke leaping upwards, tearing aside the mist. She rolled off the boards and lay in the earth, smelling it, feeling the dampness beneath her cheek; bits like black snow were falling on her.

She turned her head with an effort and saw Janey. She looked odd: her legs were several yards away from her body, her stocking rumpled around thin ankles. Janey's dress and overall had gone, her washed-out knickers were on full view and Kate had an insane desire to cover her friend and make her decent. There was a sudden flash as another explosion rent the air. For a moment she blacked out.

And then she felt the ooze of blood between her own legs. She knew that the life of her baby, as well as her own, was slipping away. She rested her head and closed her eyes. Perhaps it was all for the best.

'See you soon, if God wills it, Eddie,' she said, as a deep dark blackness clouded her eyes.

Fifteen

When Kate opened her eyes, it was dark. She was surprised that she was still alive; last thing she remembered was noise, flames, lying in the earth with Janey's mutilated body beside her. Now, she could tell, she was on a soft bed with iron sides. She listened to the sounds around her and realized she must be in hospital. The clink of tea cups, the swish of water in a bowl, the smell of carbolic soap disinfectant being mopped around her bed – all the sounds of morning. Soft sunlight bathed her face but she could see nothing but darkness. She sat up.

'I'm blind.'

There came the slip-slap of shoes against the floor; gentle hands easing her back on to the pillow; the creak of the bed; a depression in the mattress; and the rustle of starched apron as a nurse sat beside her.

'You've been in a bad accident.' A hand brushed the hair from her brow. 'You've been in hospital for more than two weeks but you're on the mend, don't worry. Rest now, you need to recover your strength.'

Kate felt her stomach; it was bandaged. She knew there were scars underneath the rough wrappings. Her baby must have been torn out of her by the explosion, leaving God knows what damage to her body?

'Bob? Janey?'

'No one in the vicinity of the sheds survived except you.' The soft voice was sympathetic but with a note of reproach as if she should be happy she was spared. 'As I said, you must try and rest now.' The bed creaked and lightened, the footsteps went away and Kate was alone again in the darkness.

She felt her body, curled her legs to touch her feet, everything seemed to be intact. She thought again of Janey, lying there without her legs, her knickers exposed for anyone to see and tears burned her sightless eyes. She tried to turn on her side but something was in her arm, pulling her, and she realized she must be on a drip of some kind. Blood? Fluid? She fell back against the pillow and a merciful oblivion claimed her as she sank into the bed as if into the softness of a cloud and slept.

'Kate, my poor lovely girl.' A hand was holding hers, a masculine hand. The voice was familiar, from the distant past, someone gone from her life, gone from this world.

'Kate, talk to me, tell me you're all right.'

It sounded like Eddie, smelled like Eddie. She raised her hand and made contact with a shoulder, a shoulder dressed in rough cloth, the cloth of an army tunic.

'Eddie, is that you?' She heard the incredulity in her own voice and then his lips were against hers. Her heart filled with gladness. 'Eddie, you've come back from the war, you didn't die in some foreign, muddy place after all.'

His arms were around her and she winced. She was released and eased back against the pillows.

'Sorry, sorry my darling. I know it hurts like hell just now but they tell me you're going to be all right.'

'What about my eyes, Eddie, will I see again?'

He didn't answer directly. 'Give it time, my lovely girl, you're alive and for now nothing else matters. I'm going to look after you.'

So he meant to stay with her, to forgive her. She felt warm and suddenly safe and very happy.

'Where's my mammy, why isn't she here Eddie?' The silence lengthened and she knew. 'She's hurt, dead?'

'There was an air raid a few nights ago, the house was bombed. I'm sorry, Kate, so sorry.'

'All of them?'

'Yes.'

'Hold me, Eddie, hold me, please.'

He held her gently while she cried. Mammy, the children, her home, all gone to a German bomber and she, lying in hospital, hurt by shell meant for the enemy.

'Why are there wars, Eddie?'

He kissed her brow. 'If I could answer that I'd be the world's greatest philosopher.'

'Will you have to go away again, back to the war, I mean?'

'Yes, I'll have to go back and fight, my love, but we'll be married once you're better. In the meantime you can stay with my mother while I'm away, she's promised to look after you for me. Do you want me, Kate?'

A rush of love washed over her; pain, blackness – it was all as nothing because Eddie was here and he loved her. 'Of course I want you, Eddie, my love.'

'Another visitor.' The nurse's voice, growing familiar now, was hearty. A cool hand touched Kate's cheek, the soft touch of a friend, the unmistakable perfume of Hari.

'What have you gone and done to yourself?' The creak of a chair as Hari sat down, the crack of the material of her coat as she reached to shake Eddie's hand – sounds were what Kate identified with now, sounds told her what was happening around her.

'We all heard the explosion.' Hari's soft voice revealed the horror of the moment. 'We rushed outside, saw the flames, saw the . . . the carnage. Poor Janey, and then you lying there covered in blood. I thought you were dead, Kate, along with the others. We never found Bob.' There was a break in her voice and then a pause and Kate imagined Hari's beautiful face realigning itself as she pulled herself together.

'But the nurse tells me you'll be fine, in time,' Hari said. 'Just fine.'

'I'm a bit sore, can't see a damn thing.' Kate heard her voice thin as a reed but she felt hope fill her heart, her love was here with her, her Eddie. And her best friend in all the world, Hari, was here too. Mammy and the children were gone, taken by the war, and she would grieve for them forever, but she had two people who loved her and that was more than some folk ever had – many people, now the war was overwhelming them, were alone in the world.

'Mother of God keep us all safe,' she whispered under her breath.

Kate went home two weeks later. Eddie had returned to his regiment and it was Hari who drove her to Eddie's house.

'Come inside, my dear Kate,' Eddie's mother said, 'find your way around the living room first of all and then you can explore the rest of the house when you've rested and had a cup of tea with a bit of brandy in it to warm you up.'

Kate brushed away her tears. She felt the fat arms of an easy chair and gingerly eased herself into its bulk. Cushions were piled behind her back and a footstool slipped beneath her feet.

'You are going to be spoilt rotten here I can see,' Hari said with a laugh in her voice.

The chink of tea cups was followed by the sound of liquor being added and Kate's hand was directed to the handle of the cup. The saucer was sensibly dispensed with.

Kate wondered what she should call Eddie's mammy but that problem was solved by Hari. She leaned close to Kate's ear.

'We're to call Eddie's mum Hilda,' she said, 'I've had my instructions and was told to pass them on to you.' Hari paused. 'Eddie is coming home on leave in a few weeks and then you'll be married, you lucky girl.'

The tea was hot and the brandy taste strong and Kate began to relax.

'Were they good to you in hospital?' Hari touched her arm. Before Kate could answer there was a ring on the doorbell and the sound of Hilda opening the door. Kate froze as she heard an anguished cry.

'God no, not again. So soon, it can't be!' Hilda came back into the room her footsteps dragging against the lino and the sound fading as she stepped on to the jute carpeting.

'I've got a telegram, Kate, about our boy. He went back to the front line and no one can find him.' There was a rustle of paper. 'Missing believed killed in action, it says. Dear God, I can't go through it all again.'

Kate held out her arms and the two women embraced, crying soundless tears. Her life was over. Eddie had come to her in hospital, offered her love and marriage and now he was gone again. How could she bear to live for even one more day?

Sixteen

I was glad Hari was too busy to come and see me at the farm. I knew I was jealous of her and I hated the way she and Michael had looked at each other. Aunt Jessie talked to me about it and I listened; she knew Michael better than anyone in the world. She was his mother after all, even if she wouldn't admit it. I knew she had her reasons; Auntie Jessie always had her reasons. Part of it was to do with Michael's German father.

'People often have an attraction for each other,' she explained again, with patience. 'It won't last, believe me. Your sister Hari is clever, she will go far, she's not cut out to be a farmer's wife.'

'But again, am I?' It was a question with a deeper question behind it and we both knew it.

'You might just be.'

'*Danke*!' I'd never shown Aunt Jessie I was learning German and I saw at once I'd made a mistake.

'Don't you dare use that language here girl!' She was fierce. 'Don't you realize Michael could be deported and what would we do then, eh?'

'Sorry – sorry, I won't do it again Aunt Jessie. It's just a word I heard. I think it means thank you and I was just being clever. I see now it's silly of me, "twp" as you would say.'

Aunt Jessie calmed down. 'I know you're a bright girl, you probably have a head for languages; I know you speak Welsh better than you ever did in Swansea and there's no harm in that, no harm at all – but German? No!'

'I understand.' I hung my head. We both knew I wouldn't put Michael in danger any more than she would. 'I would be lost without Michael.' It was unnecessary to say it but it pleased Aunt Jessie and she smiled.

'You'd best get ready for school, miss. You're getting older, you need your education more than ever now. The world is changing, Meryl, lots of doors are going to open to women, you see, because the war is claiming our young men, older ones too now the age of call-up is raised. See, even my farm is smaller now, just a few cattle, enough to keep us going; it's all Michael can cope with anyway but one day Michael will want to make his own life, perhaps far away from our shores.'

I knew what she meant, he might want to go to Germany, see if he could find his father again. At the thought, my heart plummeted. But that wouldn't happen, not unless he took me with him. I was decided on it.

I saw him across the fields. He was turning the big horse round. I had no idea what task he was doing, I only had the vaguest idea of farm life and didn't really want to know any more. Michael and I wouldn't be spending our life on a farm.

As I neared the red-brick school I saw George in the distance. I noticed he was bigger now, thinner but with broad shoulders. His ginger hair had darkened to a nice brown; he wasn't bad-looking now, nearly as nice as John Adams. I smiled wryly as I hadn't thought about John in a long time. I hadn't seen him – not since we were taken off the bus at Carmarthen and sent to our 'new homes'.

'*Bore dda,* Meryl,' George said. I knew he meant, 'Good morning' but I gave him a fierce look.

'What's good about it now I've seen you?'

'Nice to see you still got a sense of humour, girl.'

'Sense of humour? You wouldn't know one if it bit you on the bum.'

'I don't know anything about a bite on the bum,' he said, 'but I know well enough what a clout between the legs feels like.'

I had to laugh then. 'All right, George, you're growing up but don't think this makes us friends. I had a lot more bruises than you when you gave me a hiding.'

He went red in the face and looked ashamed. 'I wouldn't hit you now, Meryl.' His eyes roved over me and I knew my breasts were poking out through my coat. I had hair on the lower part of my belly now. I suppose I'd become a woman without really noticing. I hoped Michael had noticed.

Feeling happy at the thought, I actually smiled at George for pointing out I'd changed from a spoiled kid into a nearly grown-up woman.

George looked dazzled. 'Could we be sort of friends?' he asked. I put my head on one side and considered.

'As long as you don't try kissing me or anything daft like that.'

He clutched his cap in his hand, screwing it up into a ball. The wicked witch Dixon wouldn't like that at all. I decided to be friends with George if only to irritate his mother.

'Aye, we can be friends, George.'

He smiled. He wasn't half bad-looking these days I thought again. Funny I hadn't noticed before.

The teacher rang the bell and we filed into our classes. I was in the 'A' block for maths, so was George. He took the liberty of sitting beside me and I froze him with a look. He didn't seem to notice and soon I was immersed in the magic of numbers.

When the bell sounded for the end of the lesson I became aware of the smell of newly sharpened pencils and saw that George had put down the little blade he kept in a leather pouch. It was a shaving thing with two arms like pictures you see of Sweeney Todd, the barber. My pencils were laid in a row each with fine points on them. I glanced at George.

'Thanks,' I said ungraciously.

I was pretty good at the next lesson, English, too but I made sure I sat far away from George who didn't know how to spell and said his words all wrong. The teacher even came up with a word I couldn't say, it was picturesque and I thought it was pronounced 'picturescue' so I was brought down a peg or two but no one laughed. None of the class knew what it meant and the teacher had to explain it to us. After she finished I wasn't any the wiser. I wasn't as good at English as I thought.

We were learning some French. I didn't like the language much, which made me try harder. The words were never finished but ended in a tailing off of the letters as though the one speaking was puffing out a heavy breath. Nevertheless I learned enough to convince my teacher I was a good linguist.

I tucked my knowledge of German away inside me knowing it was dangerous but after the French class the others started calling me teacher's pet. I was glad when it was time to go home.

I wandered along the road at a dawdle and then my stomach turned over as I heard the sound of enemy aircraft. By now I could tell the difference between a Spitfire and a German plane. I crouched near the hedge as the planes swept by overhead. I thought I saw a pilot looking down at me but I suppose all he saw were fields and trees and a few heads of cattle.

I wondered how it was I could love one German and yet fear

all the others. But then Michael was half Welsh, I suppose that made all the difference.

The next day was Saturday and Hari came in her jeep with Kate at her side. I could see at once Kate wasn't herself. She blinked her eyes rapidly as Hari helped her out of the jeep and then she clung to my sister's arm for dear life.

'Michael!' Hari had spotted him near the barn and was waving her arm to him. He ran towards her while my stomach did a jig and a rush of fear and pain rooted me to the spot. Michael took Kate's arm and together the three of them went into the house without any of them even noticing me. Following them, I realized with a sharp feeling of horror that Kate couldn't see. Her feet felt for the step hesitantly and she shuffled into the hallway of the farmhouse.

The house looked better these days mainly due to the fact that I made Michael clear up after himself. The place was free of clutter, the towels and sheets were put away in proper cupboards or waited in the outhouse for wash day.

Kate was taken into the parlour and she sat gingerly on the chair near the fire. She'd been crying, her face was whiter now, the yellow colour fading. I knew she wasn't working the munitions any more – how could she go back when she'd been in a terrible explosion?

I touched her hand. 'Kate, it's me, Meryl the pest.'

Kate looked at me – at least her eyes were turned in my direction. They looked the same as ever, Irish pure blue with dark lashes that looked like they were made up with dark pencil.

Kate clutched my fingers. 'Meryl, your voice is different, you sound so grown-up.'

'You're like Hari, she always seemed to forget I'm getting old.'

Kate laughed, a proper laugh. 'Sure you're very old.'

I sat beside her, still holding her hand. 'I remember when I was sixteen,' she said, 'Mammy made a cake, a plum cake it was and she cut a candle up to make little ones, she was so clever.' Her voice halted and I remembered her mother had died in one of the raids. I was glad Kate couldn't see my face because I was remembering being under the table when our house was bombed, the way the lights went out, Mrs Evans's big toe through a hole in her slipper. And Kate's red shoes. I wondered if she still had them. Now she was wearing plain flat shoes, sensible shoes that no doubt helped her to walk without stumbling too much. No more red shoes for Kate.

I looked up suddenly. Michael and Hari were looking at each other like moonstruck kids. I wished Hari would go back home to Swansea and leave us alone.

'Michael!' – I sounded like his mother – 'come and talk to Kate.' He came at once and draped his arm around my shoulder as he bent over Kate to speak to her. I preened and there was a warm glow inside me. Michael was mine and no one was going to take him away from me. No one, not even my lovely sister Hari, however much she turned on her charms. I met her eyes and she looked away first, and then I knew there was a different feeling between my sister and me. It was probably called jealousy.

Seventeen

As Hari drove away from the farmhouse she knew she had felt the attraction again as she'd talked to Michael. He'd bent over her, his big shoulder touching hers, the magnetism between them almost palpable. Aunt Jessie didn't like it, she made that abundantly clear.

And there was Meryl, she clearly thought herself in love with Michael but perhaps it did no harm. Meryl was still a child and Michael an honourable man. In any case Jessie would keep a strict eye on things.

Kate stirred at her side. 'This is a bumpy road so it is.' She shifted in her seat and Hari slowed down.

'Sorry, I was going too fast. Habit I suppose.' Last time she'd driven the jeep it was to take some messages to Bletchley Park in England. She had no idea what the messages contained as they were shut away in a leather bag with a lock on it and she was happy she'd been kept in the dark. She was in enough danger as it was without having secrets to hide. Any German would soon get the truth out of her. With a sharp pain she remembered that Michael was half German but then he was different from the 'Huns' and the cruelty they inflicted on civilians with their bombing raids.

Hari forced her thoughts away from the war. 'How's your

tummy?' She glanced down at Kate's thin figure. Her belly bulged, still swollen, probably still swathed in bandages. Hari was only too aware that Kate was lucky not to have died in the explosion.

'Still sore.' Kate was listless and no wonder, she'd lost her sight, her baby and the man she loved. To add to her misery, her family had been bombed into oblivion in one of the raids. The only friends she had were Hari and Hilda.

'Do you get on with Eddie's mother?' she asked.

'Hilda's kind,' Katie said with a sigh. 'I'm all she's got left of her son. We share memories of him and it comforts us. She wishes we'd had the baby, a real bit of him but the Holy Mother didn't will it so.'

Hari felt tears mist her eyes. 'You'll have other children, a new life after the war, you'll see.'

Kate tried to be realistic. 'I only wanted a baby by my Eddie and he's gone, lost in some bloody field in a foreign land fighting to keep us free.' She was silent for a moment. 'Changing the subject so I am but do you think Michael is half German?'

Hari felt a chill run down her spine. 'No! I'm sure not,' she said firmly. 'He would have been deported, sent to the Isle of Wight or where ever they put the Germans. No, I think he's probably Norwegian.'

'I expect you're right,' Kate said softly. 'In any case you can't hate a whole race for what one mad leader is doing.'

Hari drove in silence for a time as it was getting dark and it took all her concentration to negotiate the winding lanes towards Swansea. And then at last she came off the common with its vast pony-ridden land and saw a glint of the sea and a big white house on the horizon that she knew led to the coast road. She was home and she was glad.

The next day Hari was back at work; the factory had been quickly cleared up after the explosion but the gaping teeth of blackened wood showed where the shed containing shells had once stood and, as Hari passed it and made her way quickly to the warmth of her office, she shivered with an icy fear.

It was a wet day with sullen clouds lying low over the buildings of Bridgend and Hari was glad to be working indoors. Colonel Edwards nodded absently and continued to write in his neat, precise handwriting.

She sat at her desk, took off her gloves and watched him. He wrote something down in swift, precise handwriting.

'How did you enjoy your trip to the country?'

'Not bad, sir, I took my friend Kate with me, the girl who was in the explosion.'

'All right is she?'

'Kate is blind, sir.'

'I'm sorry, fates of war.' He pushed a piece of paper under her nose. 'Do your best with this, there's a good girl.'

Hari gritted her teeth; he could be so unfeeling at times. Still, he was efficient, and kind sometimes, hadn't he arranged driving tuition for her? She'd gone through it very quickly, supervised by an army instructor. She could now drive the jeep and any other vehicle she chose.

Hari bent her head over the paper and began to work out the strange code, one she'd never seen before. She glanced over it. It wasn't her job to interpret it, it was still in some form of more complicated code, but it was ready now for the colonel.

Later he came into her office with the familiar pouch of leather.

'An important missive,' he said, looking at her from under bushy eyebrows. 'You must take this to the prime minister at once.'

'Winston Churchill, sir?' Hari had never had such a request before; it was an honour and she knew it. She looked at the colonel; he was pale; this was an important matter of war and she wished she knew what it was but that was not her business.

In her jeep she secured the chain of the leather pouch to her wrist and struggled for a moment with the intransient gears of the jeep. And then she was on her way home to gather a few belongings: precious soap, a towel and some fresh underclothes.

Mr Evans was standing outside her door looking up and down the street as if waiting for someone. Hari stepped out of the jeep and touched his arm. 'What's wrong, Mr Evans?'

'My dog, I got a dog to keep me company and now I can't find him. He's black and white, small, not very strong. Vet said he wouldn't last very long but I'll keep him going, it's love he wants, see, that's all we all want, isn't it?'

Hari thought briefly of Michael, the way he leaned into her when he talked, the way he smelt of grass and the outdoors. Her heart lifted. 'Don't worry, Mr Evans, your dog will come back when he's hungry. What's his name?'

Mr Evans smiled. 'It's a her, I've called her after my wife Maud, I know she wouldn't mind.'

Hari had the hysterical desire to laugh and ask who wouldn't mind, Mrs Evans or the dog. 'I must go inside, Mr Evans, I've got work to do. See you later.'

As she was putting her things into her bag the air-raid warning sounded wailing through the air like the knell of doom. Hari hesitated, should she wait for the all-clear or should she head out of Swansea and away from the bombers?

The crash and scream of tangled masonry convinced her she should wait. She went downstairs and made a cup of tea and sat at the kitchen table drinking it. Her house shook and she prayed it wouldn't get bombed, she'd hardly begun paying for it yet. It was her place and Meryl's, their home when all the madness of war was over.

Dust rose from under the door, there must have been a direct hit in the street. Hari waited until the all-clear rang out and the sounds of crashing buildings stilled. She opened the door gingerly and gave a gasp of horror. Her jeep was a burned-out wreck, she wouldn't be going anywhere in that.

For a moment she felt rage against the foreign bombers. The jeep was like her friend, she'd grown used to it, it gave her freedom of movement. But now it smouldered and the stink of petrol was all-pervading.

And then she noticed the figure on the floor outside her house. He was crouched up against her wall. His old face was blackened by smoke, the creases outlined as though with a black pencil, but she recognized him: it was Mr Evans. In his arms was clutched the tiny black and white dog. Both of them were dead.

Eighteen

Kate woke suddenly, the inside of her belly seemed to be moving as if something lived in there, but that was absurd, impossible, her baby, hers and Eddie's, had gone in the blast from the shells that had devastated her life and killed her friends. And, she thought bitterly, as darkness met her unseeing eyes, stolen her sight.

When she went down to breakfast, feeling her way along the banister and down the stairs to the kitchen, she heard Hilda moving about, heard the flow of tea into a cup, the chink of china. She felt for her chair and sat down.

'I'd swear I felt life inside me this morning when I woke up.' The words sounded foolish and Kate felt Hilda's hand on her arm.

'Just your innards settling back into place I expect. Don't worry about it, have your cup of tea.' Hilda took her hand and placed it so that it touched the china saucer. 'Be careful, it's just freshly brewed.'

The tea was hot and fragrant and yet it tasted strange. Anyone would think she was pregnant. If only. But she had been once, she must hang on to that thought; if it wasn't for the war . . . well, that line of thought would get her nowhere.

'I expect I picked up some sort of chill,' she said. Probably caught on her visit to the farm out in the wilds of Wales where the wind seemed continually cold.

Kate had sensed the tension between her friend Hari and Michael, the farmhand. She'd also sensed resentment coming from Meryl in waves. The girl, young, fanciful, thought herself in love with this Michael; he must be very handsome.

Kate felt tears come to her eyes. Her Eddie hadn't been handsome; he had a kind but ordinary face, but oh how she loved him. And the magic of it all was that he loved her in spite of her bad reputation. Why, she wondered now, hadn't she kept herself pure for a man she really cared for? And yet she thought of the men, going to war, some of them, like her Eddie, never to return, and she knew she had done her best for them, given them comfort in the only way she could.

The sirens shrieked out, shattering the peace of the morning. Hilda helped Kate into her coat and hustled her towards the door. 'Come on, we'll be better off in the shelter.'

Hilda didn't have an Anderson shelter in her garden as most folks did; the pieces of steel, curled like snow sleds lay uselessly on the garden with no one to put them together. Kate felt Hilda's arm around her, taking her along the street to the communal shelter.

'*Duw*, it's dark in by here,' Hilda gasped, and Kate almost smiled, to her it was dark everywhere. They huddled on a bench against a knobbly stone wall and Kate was glad of her coat. Someone had brought a canteen of tea and Kate was given a tin cup, which was warm and comforting between her fingers.

She shared the tea with Hilda and she was reminded of Mass when the chalice was held to her lips by the priest and his blessing said over her head. She could hear her Irish mammy saying her 'Hail Mary's' and she wondered why the Holy Mother saw fit to take everything from her. Kate had nothing, no mammy or brothers and sisters, no Eddie, no sight, no baby. What had she done that was so wrong – was it all a punishment for her being so free with her body when she lay with men about to die?

There was a crunch and then a great blast sweeping through the shelter. A child cried out, 'Mammy my ears, they hurt so bad.'

There was a shuffle, Kate heard the creak of a stretcher, she heard a masculine voice say, 'poor little bugger' and she wondered if the little child was dead.

The cruelty of war was nothing to do with punishment, or the Virgin Mary, it was war, randomly affecting innocent and guilty alike. Wearily, Kate closed her sightless eyes, lay back against the wall and began to cry soundlessly.

In the evening, Hari came to see her and Kate held out her arms. 'Give me a warm cuddle, Hari, it's been a hell of a day.'

'I know, I heard there was a raid, a few killed, one of them a little girl in the same shelter as you. Oh, Kate, when will it end?' Hari sounded downhearted and Kate hugged her harder.

'What's happened?'

'Such a lot, Kate. First of all I was supposed to go to London, take a message to the prime minister himself but my jeep got burned and then –' she caught back a sob – 'I found poor Mr Evans dead, his little dog in his arms.'

'That's terrible, but then war is terrible. What else is bothering you, is it Meryl?'

'No, Meryl's all right. It's Father, he's been injured and he's in hospital – wounded – but not too badly.' She hesitated. 'Lost a foot but he'll be home once he's recovered.'

'What do you feel about that, having him home I mean?'

'Mixed feelings to be honest; I don't really know my father all that well. He was in the army remember? Before the war started, it was his career. What he'll be like as an invalid I don't know. To be really honest, I'm dreading having him home again.'

'You'll still have to work,' Kate said. 'Chin up, your life won't change very much at all. Your daddy will have to learn to fend for himself. I know he's posh, an officer and all that but he'll have to learn to cook, to handle coupons like the rest of us.' Kate smiled into her darkness.

'Good thing your Meryl is out of the way, she's a tough one, speaks her mind without thinking. Sparks would fly if she was in the house with your dad, so be thankful for small mercies.'

'Anyway, never mind all that,' Hari said, 'I've come to ask, do you want to come on a trip with me to the hospital to see Father? I'll have a few days' compassionate leave, I can borrow a car and just enough petrol to get us there and back and we can stay in a little boarding house down the coast.'

For a moment Kate was frightened, how would she be away from her familiar surroundings? She was safe in Hilda's house, she knew the layout of the furniture, knew the feel of her little bedroom. Loved the comfort of her bed, the bed that had once been her Eddie's. She almost said she couldn't go.

She hesitated, she was young, she couldn't spend her life like a hermit, she needed to get out and about and to live as normal a life as she could.

Hari sensed her hesitation. 'Please come, Kate, I need you.' Hari's usually self-composed voice trembled. 'Please, Kate, I can't face it all alone.'

'I'll come! What an adventure, a ride to the South Coast! You bet I'll come.' Kate was shaking inside but her voice gave no sign of it. 'When?'

'Tomorrow afternoon – is that all right?'

'In that case –' Kate forced some enthusiasm into her voice – 'you'd better help me to pack some undies and things.'

Hari laughed happily and Kate felt her friend's arm around her waist. She stiffened, fearing pain, and Hari released her at once.

'Don't worry, Kate, I'll look after you, always.' It was a vow said with conviction and Kate, all at once, was comforted.

Nineteen

I clung to Michael's hands. 'I don't want to go back to Swansea, I'm happy here with you. And with Aunt Jessie as well.'

'It's only a visit, you're going to see your father that's all. In any case it's not until a few weeks' time. Why worry about it now?'

He didn't understand, he was my life, I loved him and not any longer as a child hero-worships an older man. I loved his cow's lick of hair, his broadness, his big hands, his clever, ice-blue eyes. I loved his easy affection for me even as I wanted more.

I wanted him to see me as a woman. Couldn't he tell the changes in me, my blossoming breasts, my tallness, the womanly curves of my hips?

'Your Hari's gone down to the coast to see your father in the military hospital, when she comes back she'll tell you all the news, it will be all right, you'll see.'

'I don't want to go back to live in Swansea and look after him.' I knew I sounded like a sulky little girl then.

'Don't be silly, you won't have to, you're still at school. In any case Swansea's still being heavily bombed, the dreaded "authorities" won't want children going back to all that danger, where's your common sense, Meryl?'

I was comforted, his words had the ring of truth. Of course I still had to go to school and I loved the little school outside the village; our history teacher was a grumpy old man but he knew how to inspire, how to make even dull history exciting.

Mr Funnel drew pictures on the board, showed us maps of where the Germans were. He had been in the other war, the big bad first World War against Germany and he hated the enemy savagely. I sometimes wished he could know Michael, who had a German father but who was good and kind and wouldn't hurt any living creature, but that was a secret I would carry with me to the grave if I had to.

Michael was taking me for an evening walk just as the sun was dying over the fields of ripe corn. The cows, milked and content, stood patiently in the grass, bending now and then to graze, not hungry but wanting the cud in soft mouths to chew and ruminate and be at peace with themselves. The bovine life was all gentleness and if I was gifted with words I would have written poems to the animals, poems about stoicism and yielding sweet milk for the needs of others.

'Come on, little monster, let's head back.' Michael spun me around and held me facing him. I leaned forward and planted a kiss on his mouth and lingered. And then he pushed me away and laughed.

'Hey, miss! Don't act like that in Swansea or you're likely to be taken advantage of.'

If only he would take advantage of me, hug me close, kiss me deeply, caress my shoulders, touch my hair with loving hands, look at me with loving eyes. But Michael was striding away.

'Come on, keep up, your legs are nearly as long as mine.' So Michael had noticed my legs. All at once I was warm. There was hope for us yet.

Aunt Jessie looked us over carefully when we went into the kitchen. 'You two are like hobos,' she said, 'go and get washed up the pair of you, you stink of animals and the fields.'

'Come on, squirt.' Michael caught me around the neck with his big hand. I'll get the hot water for you.'

He prepared the big tin bath, laid towels out for me, presented me with a new bar of soap as if it was a wonderful gift. Of course, these days, it was. I could hear Aunt Jessie calling him.

'Don't stay in too long,' was his parting shot, 'I've got to get in there after you.' Then with a mischievous look on his face, 'And no doing, you know what, in the water.'

I blushed furiously. As if I would. I could hear the rumble of voices from the kitchen but couldn't distinguish the words. But then Aunt Jessie raised her voice.

'She's not a child any more, open your eyes Michael, she's a very beautiful young lady and I've seen that George Dixon hanging about, carrying her books, all that sort of thing.'

I stifled a laugh. Georgie Porgy had no chance of going out with me. I wanted to hear what Michael would reply but his voice was low.

Aunt Jessie again. 'Sometimes you men won't see what's under your nose.' I think she meant me. Did Michael want to find other girlfriends then? Did he already have someone in the village? He didn't go out of an evening much it was true but then there were farmers' markets, meetings to talk about boring things like cattle fodder and, even worse, manure for the land, or lime, or the latest milking machine. How did I really know what Michael's life was all about? And then of course there was my sister Hari.

I felt uncertain and got up from the bath and stood there blindly thinking about Michael in another woman's arms. It was awful. The door opened abruptly and Michael stared at me. I stood there naked, seeing a sudden light in his eyes and I felt nothing but joy that he was really seeing me for the first time in his life as the growing woman I was.

He shut the door as abruptly as he'd opened it but I smiled a womanly, somehow triumphant, smile before I reached for the towel and began to dry myself.

I would like to think that everything changed from that moment, but it didn't. Michael was the same to me as he'd ever been, casually affectionate, and in my heart I knew he'd seen not me but an older woman, a real woman, not the child he'd rescued from the cold fields. He was seeing my sister Hari.

Twenty

Hari knew Kate was nervous. She clung to the door handle of the car, her knees were tense, and when the car swayed around a bend Kate winced as though something pained her.

'All right, Kate, if you want to stop for a bit there's a little café up ahead. Shall we have a cup of tea?'

'Please, Hari,' Kate said softly.

Hari was worried about Kate; it was as if all the life had gone out of her. She was cowed and frightened and the fun, the spirit, had left her. Kate was diminished, shrunk into a dark world of pain, changed forever by the tragic events of her life.

They drank their tea, which was stewed and the café was cold. Soon, Kate pushed back her chair. 'Let's get on,' she said, 'it's freezin' here so it is.'

The hospital smelled of disinfectant and the walls were a dowdy brown and cream; along the corridors the nurses bustled with wings of pristine hats flying.

'Hari, my dear girl.' Her father looked well, his cheeks a little flushed as it was warm in the hospital with the heating going full blast. He was sitting outside the bedclothes, his brightly coloured paisley dressing gown tied around his waist so that his thinness was betrayed by the drape of the cloth.

Hari kissed his cheek. 'Father, here's Kate who's come with me to see you.' She gestured to him that Kate couldn't see him and he nodded and took Kate's hand.

'Hello, Kate, how are your folks keeping?'

'All dead,' she said flatly. Hari saw her father frown. 'I'm sorry, Kate, really sorry.'

Hari shook her head. 'Anyway, Father, tell us what happened to you?'

He was eager to talk. 'Well, Hari, we were ordered to advance. There was a nest of Germans in a hut and, as the officer, I naturally had to go ahead and throw a grenade into the viper's bed. I got shot.' He looked sheepish and Hari suppressed a smile.

'What injuries, Father?'

'A leg wound, not bad really, but my foot got infected. In the end it had to be amputated, same as some of these other boys here.' He gestured round at the young men in the beds near him.

One of the men looked up and Hari recognized him. She had met him once at a dance; he'd given Kate stockings and Kate, well, Kate had given him comfort. All his limbs seemed to be intact but his face was badly scarred.

'Hari!' Stephen had spotted her. 'And Kate! It's me, Stephen. Come and give me a little bit of your time, there's a love. I haven't had a visitor since I've been here.'

'Who is it?' Kate held out her hand and Hari, with an apologetic smile at her father, led Kate to the other bed.

Stephen took Kate's hand. 'It's me, the brash airman who once was so young and arrogant. What's happened to you then, Kate?' He pulled her until she was sitting on the bed beside him.

'The war happened, Stephen,' she said, 'I got blown up in the munitions factory, lucky to be alive, so they tell me. I can't see any more, you'll have to tell me what happened to you.'

'Shot down, what else?' he said. 'I'm scarred, my face . . . Not too bad though compared to my friends who were burned to toast where they sat in the pilot seat. I still hear their screams. Sometimes I'm afraid to go to sleep.'

Kate touched his face with her fingertips. 'As you say, not too bad, Stephen.' She smiled for the first time that day, Hari noticed.

'Anyway, weren't you always too good-looking for your own good?'

'Kate, I'm sorry –' his voice was soft – 'not for loving you but for taking advantage. I did care about you, you know, and then I went away and when I came back I heard about the other pilots and I didn't feel special any more.'

He kissed her fingertips. 'Mind, you put me in my place very well that night in the ice cream parlour. I never felt so small in all my life.' He turned her hand over and kissed her palm. 'I've learned a lot about life and death since then.'

Hari stood undecided between the two beds, she couldn't leave Kate, she would want to come back and talk to Father and yet, their conversation was so private.

'Stephen, I fell in love – really in love – with Eddie, remember my darling Eddie? You almost ruined that for me, you and that spiteful girl you were with. But he came back, he loved me in spite of everything.' Her voice broke and Hari wondered if she should intervene but Kate's next words stopped her.

'I was having Eddie's baby when the . . . the explosion happened. Now Eddie's missing in action, I've got no mammy or family, I can't see anything at all and I feel my life is over so I do.'

'Of course your life's not over!' Stephen protested, 'you are still a very beautiful woman with your dark Irish curls and your eyes are still the cornflower blue they always were.' He stroked her hands. 'Look, will you help me when I get out of here? I'll need someone to help me – a housekeeper – I can't cook, I can't make beds, I'm a useless sort of a man it seems.'

'I'm all right as I am, living with Eddie's mammy,' Kate said. 'In any case I can only cook the simplest of meals. I'm sorry.'

'I'll write down my address in case you ever need me,' Stephen said. 'If you do I'm sure Hari will help you find me, won't you, Hari?'

'I suppose so,' Hari said reluctantly, not at all sure this meeting was what Kate wanted. Kate moved away from the bed and Hari took her arm. 'My father's getting a bit rattled, he thinks we're neglecting him.'

'We are,' Kate said. 'Come on let's go and cheer the old boy up.' Her demeanour was different as if talking to Stephen had regenerated something of her old spirit.

'Fancy he wanted me with him, Hari,' she said, 'sure I'm not entirely helpless, even if I'm blind. I suppose I could still look after a man, at least Stephen thinks so. Sure I might find the cooking a bit of a challenge but I could always open a tin of spam.'

'Thinking of accepting then?'

'No, I couldn't leave Eddie's mammy, not for the world.'

'You know that boy?' Hari's father's voice was truculent.

'Yes, Father, he's a friend of Kate's.' She paused. 'Now, when you come home I've got the perfect room for you.'

'I won't be able to get up stairs very well, Hari, have you thought of that?'

'I've got a nice little house with a parlour t the front, I'll put a bed in there for you Father, you'll be as cosy as anything. I've even got a half decent wireless for you.'

'What about that rascal, Meryl, she'll be there after school to make me a cuppa now and again, won't she?'

Hari frowned. 'Now you can't stay an invalid all your life. You will have to learn to get to the kitchen yourself – and Meryl is in the country, an evacuee, you know that.'

'I thought Meryl was at home now.'

'She will be, but only for a few days. She's happy and safe in the country, doing well at school. I wouldn't want to bring her home just to wait on you, Father.'

He grimaced. 'I see how it's going to be, poor old Father brow-beaten by his children, pushed in the corner now he's injured defending his country.' He was smiling.

Matron bristled into the ward and fixed the visitors with commanding eyes. Without being told, people stood up, pulled on coats and prepared to leave.

'When you're discharged, I'll come for you, Father. Until then you'll have to be patient, I haven't got another day off for ages.'

'All right.' He hugged her unexpectedly. 'I've been a distant father mainly due to work and all that but we can grow closer, Hari. I promise you that I won't be too much of a burden.'

'Don't be silly Daddy –' she was unaware she'd used her old pet name for him – 'you won't be a burden at all, I'll see to that!'

Kate waved goodbye in the vague direction of Stephen's bed. 'See you, Kate,' he called, and then Hari was leading the way through the front doors out into the mellow brightness of the day.

Kate was beside her and she had changed: her face had lightened and Hari understood that from feeling like a victim, Kate now felt herself a real live, wanted woman again. Her next words confirmed what Hari was thinking.

'It's nice to be wanted by a man again,' she said softly, 'even if it is only as a sort of housekeeper.'

'Don't be a fool, Kate,' Hari said mockingly, 'that's not all he wants, didn't you hear Stephen say you were beautiful?'

Kate blushed and all at once she looked like a lovely young girl again.

Twenty-One

I said my farewells to Michael and Aunt Jessie with a feeling of foreboding as if I might never see them again. I was only going home to Swansea to visit with my father for a week or two but the time would drag, I just knew it.

Hari came to fetch me and as usual she chatted to Michael, standing a touch too close to him, looking up into his face, her long shimmering eyelashes ready to bat at him whenever the moment required it which, it seemed to me, was too often for comfort.

'Come *on* Hari!' I shifted impatiently from one foot to the other and Hari at last turned her attention to me. 'If we're to get back to Swansea before dark we'd better get a move on.' I knew I sounded sulky but I couldn't help it.

Michael hugged me close. 'Sharp-tongued as ever!' he said, kissing the top of my head in an awful, brotherly fashion. I longed to wind my arms around his neck, to press my lips to his, show Hari he was mine, but I didn't dare.

When we were in the car I glanced at Hari. She had on a neat white shirt and a navy skirt, a tie and a nice fitted jacket; it was almost a uniform. 'Have you had promotion or something?'

'In a way,' she said. 'I'm attached to a signal corps but as a civilian. It makes no difference to my working life, I'm doing the same job and coming home at nights so don't worry, I'll be there to care for Father.'

'Does he need much? Caring for I mean?' I was apprehensive, I didn't fancy being a ministering angel or Hari having an excuse to bring me home from the country. 'I'm no nurse, mind.' I shuddered, exaggerating a little.

'I see to his leg before I go to work, don't worry,' Hari said, laughing.

'His leg? Good grief! What's happened to him then?'

'Father has had his foot amputated but his wounds are more or less healed now.' She glanced at me, a wicked light in her eyes. 'It will take him a bit of time to adjust to his false foot though.'

'*False* foot!' I made a face. 'I won't have to see it, will I?'

Hari grimaced. 'Not much of a heroine, are you? Grow up for heaven's sake and remember Father is a very private man.'

'How can I remember?' I was exasperated. 'I hardly know Father, he was always away, wasn't he?'

You're right, sorry.' Hari was such a nice person she sometimes made me sick. 'Don't worry, you'll soon be back in the country with Michael and Aunt Jessie.'

I sighed again with relief and thankfulness. 'I do like it there,' I admitted, 'more than I thought I would. I even quite like Georgie Porgy though I'll never like that mother of his.'

'Are you and George going out together then?'

God she could be so obtuse. Or was that a gleam of mischief I could see as she glanced my way again.

I didn't bother to answer, I just snorted inelegantly and humped into my seat and watched the countryside fly past. I must have slept because at last we came to the edge of Swansea. I could see the smoke from across the bay and I could see the twin rise of Kilvey and Townhill like a mother's breasts protectively leaning over the untidy rows of houses in the town itself.

Father was hearty in the way most older folk are when they're not used to young people but I saw at once he didn't even think of me as a *young* person. 'Come to kiss me, child,' he said.

I wanted to protest and then I paused. It would suit me to be a child I decided, that way I'd have no responsibilities. I realized I was a selfish bitch but I needed to look out for myself, I'd learned that in my fight with George all those months ago.

I dutifully kissed his cheek, which was sharp with bristles. 'You haven't shaved.' It came out like an accusation. My father apologized.

'I'm sorry, I was waiting for the kettle to boil. I need hot water, you see.'

I did feel awful then and hastily I pushed the kettle on the gas stove. 'I'll do what little I can to help you, Father.' I was repentant and looked at his pale face and shadowed eyes, wondering what horrors he'd seen at the place they called 'the front'.

'Does it hurt much?' I pointed to his bandaged stump without really looking. He replied with the bravery of the officer and gentleman.

'Hardly at all, er . . .'

'Meryl,' I supplied helpfully.

'Yes . . . Meryl.' He leaned back in his chair and stared at me and I sort of slumped, not wanting him to see I was budding under my jumper, growing up.

'It's a pity your mother isn't here to, well, to tell you things about, well . . . life.'

'Hari's here,' I said at once, 'she's a good sister, she sees I'm safe down in Carmarthen away from the bombs.' It didn't hurt to emphasize the point that it wasn't safe for me in Swansea, not when the bombers came.

In the afternoon, Hari called at the house briefly. 'I've got to work tonight,' she said casually, 'but it's a one-off, don't worry, and Meryl is here if you need anything.'

I was alarmed and must have looked it. Hari frowned at me and her look told me to pull myself together. 'It's only this once.' Her tone was brisk. 'It won't hurt you to help for one night, Meryl. You've got it easy the rest of the time.'

I'd never seen her so cross and I hugged her tight. 'We'll manage, don't worry, we'll be all right, won't we, Father?'

'Of course we will. You go, Angharad.' I was to find that Father always called my sister by her full name. 'You have your war work to do like the rest of us.'

I found myself making my father's supper for him. I wasn't a cook by any stretch of the imagination but I'd watched Aunt Jessie countless times whisk an egg with a little milk and scramble it in a pan. So I did that for my father and made a pile of toast with the bread and butter I'd brought from the farm.

He ate hungrily and for the first time I felt the satisfaction of feeding someone and watching their enjoyment of the food I'd prepared. I could hear Aunt Jessie's voice in my head.

'You'll make someone a good wife yet, my girl.' I thought lovingly of Michael and as always hugged to me the thought of us together that night, it seemed long ago now, that we'd huddled together for warmth and I'd slept with my cheek against his chest.

'You're dreaming, Meryl. Some boy is it?'

I looked sharply at my father – he was a clever man, I'd do well to remember that.

'More tea?' I lifted the pot and he smiled without saying any more.

That night there was an air raid. I hurried downstairs and Father was sitting on the edge of his bed looking for his stick. Then I saw his face go grey as he tried to stand.

'We'll need to get to the shelter, Meryl,' he said, trying to sound as if he wasn't in agony.

'Let's stay here,' I suggested. 'I'll make us tea and we'll take our chances. Folk in shelters get hurt too.' I told him what Kate had said about the girl in the shelter who had cried out about her ears and how the ambulance man had called her a 'poor bugger'.

So we sat and listened to the bombs fall. We drank tea and we talked and I began to learn a little about my father. And then a bomb fell near, very near, perhaps next door. Father covered me with his body to protect me, his big hands shielding my head. I hugged his body and felt the bond between father and daughter for the first time in my life and I knew I didn't want my father to die.

I drew him from the bed, felt him wince as his bad leg touched the floor and then I was drawing him underneath the table and we clung there together while the walls shuddered, plaster fell from the ceiling and the air raid railed around us like a thunderstorm. I looked up and touched his now-shaven face. 'I love you, Daddy,' I said softly, and we both knew I meant it.

Twenty-Two

Kate sat with Stephen in the garden of Victoria Park. He held her hand and she didn't mind. Now he treated her like a lady, he made no crude remarks, he was gentle and kind and he made her feel good again.

'Tell me what it looks like, Steve,' she said, 'Are the leaves turning red and fluttering to the ground? Is it pretty?'

'Not half as pretty as you.' Stephen kissed her hand. 'You look lovely, Kate, the sun brings red lights out in your dark hair and your skin is so white, so delicate. You're a true Irish beauty.'

'And you've kissed the Blarney stone,' Kate said with a smile. She knew she'd put on weight, she could feel with her finger tips that her waist was thicker. She could feel the scar along her jaw line and despaired. What she couldn't see was the bloom she had, a softness that appealed so much to the protective instinct in Stephen as he sat looking at her.

'Kate,' he said softly, 'I wanted to ask you, will you marry me?'

She felt a stab of pain. The only man she wanted as a husband was her dear Eddie but he was lost to her for ever.

'You were my first . . . woman,' he said.

'You can't say 'love' can you, Stephen?'

'Yes I can, Kate, now I can. Back when we first met I was too young and foolish to think of love, I knew nothing about life or love or death or pain. I do now, Kate. And, Kate, I've fallen in love with you, your gentle ways, your beautiful face.' He laughed. 'I can't deny I find you attractive – I want to lay you down and make love to you, my darling.'

She was flattered, of course she was, but then weren't they two wounded people reaching for comfort just as Stephen had reached for comfort when he'd taken her virginity?

'Can I think about it, Stephen?' she asked. 'Will you have to go back to the war? That is an important question, Stephen.'

'I will sit at a desk for the duration of the hostilities,' he said, 'I'm no longer up to the very high standard required of a pilot so you see you wouldn't be getting a hero.'

Kate knew he'd been decorated for bravery, he was modest, gentle, kind and he would look after her. 'It's only just eight months ago that Eddie went missing,' she said, 'what if he came back?'

'I'd let you go to him if that's what you wanted but I hope you would've fallen in love with me and want to stay with me, of course I do.'

She got up from the bench wondering how so much had happened to her since the first raids on Swansea in 1941. She had been with many pilots and, as the months of the war went on into years, she'd lost her reputation, her 'good name'. Men laughed about her, talked about her and she was an object of pity and scorn.

And then she'd met Eddie, who'd loved her, against all the odds, against the taunts of his friends, who told him in graphic detail how they'd 'had her'. She'd lost her family, found Eddie's mother, shared her grief when Eddie was lost. She'd been blown up by her country's own weapons of defence, lost her sight. She had settled down now to a civilian life, queuing for food, accepted now by the women for the only men around were old or war wounded and she was no threat to anyone with her blind eyes.

'I'll think about it, Stephen,' she said gently but she knew she wouldn't. Her poor stomach was scarred, her belly hung around her like a huge grotesque belt, she could feel it hard and shiny and criss-crossed with wheals and lines. She was fat, hideous, though in her loose clothing Stephen couldn't see any of that, he saw only her face, remembered the young taut-muscled girl she'd once been.

'Take me back home, Stephen, there's a love.' She slipped her arm through his, at least she could treat him as a friend, he was humbled now by his experiences, he'd become a man, more sensitive than the callow boy he'd been. The war had changed them all.

Several weeks passed and Kate still hadn't given Stephen an answer. To his credit he didn't press her and for that she was grateful. As she drank her cocoa with Hilda one night, she began to feel an ache in her stomach. She winced and Hilda was at her side in a moment. 'What is it, girl?'

'Just a twinge in my belly – as you said, things settling down inside me after the explosion.'

Kate went to bed, perhaps she would feel better if she lay down. It was chilly in the bedroom and she wished there was enough coal to light the fire. She shivered as the pain squeezed her belly. It became worse as the night hours wore on and Kate thought she was going to die.

Hilda heard her moans and came into the bedroom and put on the gas light.

'It hurts so much, Hilda, I think I'm going to die.' She clutched her belly and writhed as the pain curled around her; the bones in her back felt as if they were being torn apart. 'I feel as if my insides were going to fall out so I do.'

'Here, let me take a look for God's sake.' Without worrying about dignity Hilda pushed up Kate's nightgown and felt her taut belly.

'God almighty!' she said, 'you're about to give birth, your waters have just broke.'

Kate felt sick and then happy and then – terrified. 'A baby, how can that be? The explosion, my scars, could a baby survive all that? It can't be a baby, Hilda.'

'Listen, girl, I've had four myself and lost all of them. It will be an hour, perhaps two, but by morning there will be another addition to my family.' She sighed. 'Our Eddie's baby.'

Kate was grateful to Hilda for not questioning the paternity but then Hilda knew more than most what a hermit Kate had been since Eddie had gone missing.

'Shame poor mite will be called a bastard,' she almost whispered, 'and you a good Catholic girl.'

'No!' Kate said, 'it will not be a bastard! Fetch Stephen, fetch the priest, we will have a father for my child even though it won't be the man I truly love. The baby will be made legitimate even if it only be minutes before it's born.'

Kate hardly knew what was happening after that. In a swirl of pain she told Stephen the truth. 'Are you willing to have me now?'

He took off his signet ring. 'This will do for now, darling,' he said.

The priest was old and wise and swept through the ceremony with as much dignity and speed as he could muster.

'Another push now, good girl.' The midwife had miraculously appeared. 'The head is coming, bear down, Kate, like the good Irish girl you are.'

Feeling as if she was going to explode, Kate put all her strength into pushing the child out of her straining body.

The midwife looked anxiously at the deep scars on Kate's belly. 'Pray to God they hold,' she said, 'it's a miracle a babe survived all that but then I've learned by now mother nature will do anything to preserve humankind. Now one strong push, Kate, one more strong push and it will all be over.'

Kate pushed her chin into her chest, there was a burning sensation between her legs and then she felt the head emerge and the slide of the little body and her belly relaxed.

'It's a big healthy boy!' Hilda said joyfully, 'my Eddie's got a son.'

The baby was put against Kate's chest. He wriggled and cried, and a great wash of tenderness swept over her. She managed to grasp a flailing arm, felt for the fingers and they curled around hers as though her son recognized her as his mother. And it was then that Kate began to cry. Great tears rolled down her face as she held her squirming baby close to her and prayed to God that he would never have to go to war.

Stephen took her hand and she clutched at him gratefully, realizing she had become a wife just an hour before she became a mother.

Twenty-Three

Hari looked at Michael across the tea-stained tablecloth in the cheap café across the road from Swansea beach. The bay was rimed in frost on this early February day. He'd come for Meryl.

Meryl had been home for yet another visit to Father; it was good to see him and his daughter growing close, but now it was time for Meryl to go back to the farm and her schooling. Hari forced herself to break the silence that had come between her and Michael.

'Why did you want to see me alone, Michael?'

He shrugged, 'I borrowed a little car and managed to get some petrol. This visit I thought I'd save you the bother of driving to Carmarthen.'

'But you asked to meet me first, why?' She took a deep breath, she knew they were attracted to each other, she felt drawn to Michael more and more each time she saw him. Now that Meryl came regularly to see Father Hari had spent a great deal of time with Michael. She knew she cared for him and knew it would never work.

'I could never live in the country. I love my job in Bridgend so much I couldn't leave it.' Today she had learned that Germany had suffered its first defeat of the war, Stalingrad having at last fallen after months of fighting; the Germans were in retreat. It was good news but news she felt unable to share with Michael.

'My little sister has enjoyed her visit to Swansea,' she said awkwardly. It was true: Meryl visited the munitions as often as she was in Swansea; she loved the business of the office, the radio signals, the codes, loved it all.

She had picked up the codes with remarkable swiftness, her young mind making mincemeat of what Hari had struggled so hard to learn.

'And yet Meryl thinks of the farm as her home. I'm a town girl to the soles of my feet,' Hari said casually, hoping to deflect what he was about to say but realizing he was going to speak his mind anyway.

'I'm falling in love with you, Hari.' He rested his hand on hers across the table and she looked down into her cold cup of tea without seeing it.

'It's no good,' she said, 'there's so much wrong, the timing is all wrong. There's the war, my father, my job and, not the least, Meryl.'

'She's only a child.'

'Wake up Michael, she's sixteen, she's grown into a woman. Haven't you noticed?'

'Physically she might have changed but she's still a girl, she'll fall in love many times before she settles down.'

'You don't know her like I do.'

'Hari, this isn't about Meryl, it's about you and me.'

She felt his hand press on hers and she turned her fingers to clasp his. 'Just leave it for now, Michael, please, I've enough to worry about with my father and work and Kate and . . . well, I can't handle any more.' She stood up. 'I'm going home to get Meryl ready for the trip, give us an hour and then come for her and for heaven's sake don't mention –' she waved her arm – 'any of this.'

She walked away quickly before she gave in to his pleading eyes. Her heart was pounding, she felt more than attracted to Michael and she was enchanted by his hardly discernible lisp on certain words. She knew he shouldn't draw attention to himself, he was half German and shouldn't be in this country at all. He had risked a great deal to come to talk to her in Swansea.

Meryl had already packed her small case. Hari smiled as she saw them sitting together, father and daughter, Meryl's head bent over the newspaper as she read out the daily news.

'Father! Some more American soldiers and airmen are to be stationed just outside Swansea.'

'Aren't there enough of them here already?' Father's voice was laconic. He glanced at Hari in the doorway and winked. 'You know what they say, girl, don't you? The Americans are overpaid over here and over . . .'

'Father!' Hari tried not to laugh, her father was used to the soldier's life but rough talk that was normal in the trenches wouldn't do in a respectable house of girls. She glanced at her watch.

'Do you mind if I go to see Kate and the baby, Meryl?'

Her sister looked up at her with a bright face. 'Go on you, Michael is coming for me soon.'

Hari forced a smile. 'I might not be back so say hello for me.'

'I will.' Meryl's smile widened.

Hari kissed them both and left the house because she didn't think she could bear to see Michael and not throw herself into his arms and promise to go anywhere on earth with him. She felt tears in her eyes and it had started to rain, cold sleety rain that stung her face, and the rain mingled with her tears and ran coldly down her cheeks.

Twenty-Four

I couldn't take my eyes from Michael as he drove us away from town and headed out towards the country roads. His jaw, thin and lean and weathered, was tinged with a bright growth of beard. He looked different, older, there were furrows on his forehead I hadn't noticed before.

'Everything all right at home, Aunt Jessie well is she?' I was anxious but he nodded and flashed me a grin.

'Jessie's fit as ever, ruling the roost with a hand of iron as usual.' He frowned again, 'Your father is looking well.' He paused. 'How is Hari?'

My heart sank – so this was about Hari. Suspicion flared in me so I took a chance. 'You ought to know, you've seen her, haven't you?'

'She told you?'

My suspicion was confirmed; men could be such fools, so gullible. I'd noticed that with my father, who took everything I said on face value – come to that so did Georgie Porgy. I thought Michael had more sense.

'Of course she told me, I'm her sister aren't I?'

'Well, she . . .' He hesitated. 'It was only a cup of tea and a chat, Meryl, nothing improper took place – we were in public all the time.'

'I should think so too!' How I kept my voice steady I didn't know. So they were meeting secretly behind my back. The betrayal was too much to bear. I stared out of the car window looking at the green fields and the animals browsing, but the sense of peace the countryside had given me of late was gone. Jealousy, hot and hateful, poured like bile into my mouth, my heart felt as if it would break.

'How long has *this* been going on, you two meeting secretly?'

He gave a short laugh. 'You sound like a nagging wife. It's nothing to worry about.' His voice hardened. 'In any case, Meryl, it's none of your business.'

I felt fury rise up and drench me with bitterness and pain. 'You, you *German!*'

His mouth set in a straight line and for the rest of the journey he ignored me. I sagged in my seat, all the spirit drained from me. I thought Michael would be mine one day when he realized I was a grown-up but no, he'd fallen for my beautiful sister. How could he after holding me against his heart all night in the barn, after being my hero, finding me twice when I ran away from the Dixons? I loved him, why couldn't he love me back?

Aunt Jessie saw at once there was something wrong between us. 'Been quarrelling?' Blunt as ever.

'Not really.' Michael answered for me. 'Just a funny mood of Meryl's. She's trying to tell me how to run my life and I'm not having it.'

Aunt Jessie stared at him. 'You can be very blunt at times, Michael.'

If I hadn't felt so low I would have laughed, talk about the pot calling the kettle black. 'It really doesn't matter, Aunt Jessie,' I said, 'I just think Michael is silly meeting Hari in Swansea like he does.'

She put down the tea towel she was holding and shook her head. 'You foolish boy! Do you want to be transported out of the country, perhaps arrested as a spy? Think, boy, how would I manage on the farm if you were taken away from me?'

'I'm only half German remember.' Michael glanced at me, the reproach in his eyes intended for me.

I wanted to speak but then Aunt Jessie was fighting the battle for me very well on her own.

'You fool! Do you think that will matter? Those poor Jewish people were turned out of their shop in the town just because they were foreign. They are not even the enemy. The Germans are bombing our towns into dust. I know you can't help it all happening but at least promise me you won't visit Swansea again until all this war thing is over.'

'Sorry, I can't and won't promise that. Face it, Jessie, I'm a man. If it wasn't for you and the farm I'd be fighting the war out there on the front line.'

'Good thing for the farm then.' Aunt Jessie's voice was acid. 'Because I'm not too sure at all on which side you would be fighting.' She threw down the tea cloth. 'Cook your own damn food.'

As she went out I knew she was crying. I looked at Michael and made a move to go after her but he shook his head.

'No,' he said flatly, 'I think you've caused enough damage for one day, don't you?'

After that everything was different, Michael went off some days and I knew he was going to Swansea to see Hari. Aunt Jessie was tired and dispirited and sometimes when Michael was out we'd sit close together, listen to the wireless and try not to think too much about the man we both loved facing danger in Swansea's busy streets.

On the way to school one day George stopped me as I was struggling with my books. 'Can I carry some for you, Meryl?' His tone was humble and the books were heavy so I nodded. He looked happy and took my bag.

'I wanted to ask you a favour,' he said hesitantly. I glared at him.

'If it's to go out with you, forget it.'

'No, I wondered if you'd help me with my English, I can't seem to grasp the book we're reading – the one about the stupid couple who fall in love and then kill themselves.'

I tried not to laugh. I knew he meant Romeo and Juliet but I teased him. 'Was that the one where the daft girl stood on the balcony calling this lovesick twerp's name.'

George had the sense to look uneasy, he sensed a snub coming a mile off. I changed my mind. 'All right,' I said, 'I'll help.'

He looked startled, half afraid to trust me but I smiled encouragingly and sat down on one of the grassy banks at the side of the winding road – there were plenty of them, winding roads and banks, this was the country. 'Get the book out then.'

So I sat with George, explained the story to him. 'Their families hated each other,' I said. 'The Montagues and the Capulets were enemies, they didn't want their children ending the feud so they opposed the relationship.'

George sighed. 'My mum hates you,' he said. I stared at him with narrowed eyes.

'The feeling is mutual.'

'I know we're like the families in the book so no one would want us to get together.'

'George –' my voice was acid – 'there is no chance of you and me getting together ever.'

'Aw, come on, you don't know.' He made a sudden grab for me and pushed me over backwards. His mouth was soft and wet on mine and I gagged.

'Get off me you fool!' I pushed him but he was heavy and he weighed me down against the grass. 'I just want to kiss you that's all,' he said, but his hand was pushing my school skirt above my knees. I knew my knees were prettier now, not so bony as they used to be, but I didn't want George seeing them and I slapped him hard. He didn't waver.

'Get off!' My scream was shrill, shattering the still air. Then George was being pulled away from me and I saw Michael, his face grim, spinning George around and then Michael drew back his arm, bunched his big fist and aimed it straight at George's chin. George fell like a log and lay prostrate on the grass looking ridiculous in his check suit and a lump swelling on his mouth.

Mrs Dixon must have been watching us, for she screamed like a banshee as she came pelting along the path waving her arms, her hair coming out of its roll, her apron flapping around her bony knees. Again I was reminded of the harpies from mythology, half cruel bird, half skeletal woman. She fell on the ground beside her son and keened over him until he sat up and begged her to be quiet. She got to her feet and her voice was venomous.

'There's something strange about you lot up at that farm and when I find out what it is you'll pay dearly for what you've done today.'

Suddenly, I was afraid for Michael. I clutched his arm and, as we began to make our way back home, I prayed for the first time since the bombs had come and asked God humbly if he would take care of my dear, sweet Michael who had once again come to my rescue.

Twenty-Five

Hari was engrossed in her work. The Colonel was off sick, his old war wounds playing him up, and Hari took on his work as well as her own. She was tuned now to both his codes and the noises on the radio; the crackling, almost intelligible sounds making sense to her. She could cope on her own but she was concerned about the old man and decided she would go to see him after work.

She listened, the tip of her tongue touching one soft lip. She wore bright lipstick, the strong creamy red cheering her up and making her feel more confident. She was more alive these days but she was reluctant to own it was her feelings for Michael that had changed her; not her new lipstick nor even her new job, but knowing Michael loved her.

She loved him in return, but what future was there in a romance born under bomber-filled skies with destruction all around. And then there was Meryl, those baleful eyes, those knowing eyes looking accusingly at her.

Meryl was now full-grown. Her once bony body had evolved into the magic time when the skin of childhood fell away and the glow of womanhood broke through like the bud bursting into colourful life from the green, spiky thorns of the rose tree.

She was young enough still to betray her feelings in every soft look, every admiring glance that she gave Michael. And yet it was more than hero worship, there were deep feelings in Meryl and that made it all the more difficult for Hari.

She couldn't fool herself that Meryl's love for Michael was a passing fancy; she knew that when Meryl gave her love it was for life.

A buzz of urgency came through the phone lines and Hari gave her work all her attention. She quickly deciphered the message and her heart chilled: tonight there would be a heavy bombing raid on Swansea.

A little while later, she spent time with the colonel in his big, elegant house. He handed her a sherry and nodded sagely when she told him of the latest news.

'It had to be any time now, a big push forward; the Huns think they've caught us unprepared but thanks to our intelligence we are forewarned.'

He waved her away and picked up the telephone, and Hari, knowing he had urgent work, let herself out of his house and stood in the quiet garden for a moment wondering at the peace of the day, knowing it would be shattered once darkness fell and the bombers came.

On the way home, Hari stopped at Kate's house.

'Well, Hari, I'd know that scent anywhere. Come on, give old Kate a kiss, it's about time you came to see me again, my darlin'.

As Hari hugged her friend she could hear the snuffles of the young child sleeping in the wicker washing basket curled up like a cat.

There was the clink of china from the kitchen and Hari knew Hilda was putting the kettle on the gas stove. 'Hilda's always in the kitchen making tea,' she said, smiling. 'A cup of tea, lovely, just what I need!' she called to Hilda.

Hari turned back to Kate and her smile widened. 'You're looking extremely well, Kate, especially with one of your baby's feeding bottles hanging shamelessly out of your blouse for all to see.'

Kate stuffed her breast carelessly away and fumbled with the buttons. 'It's not funny, Hari as you'll find out one of these days. That brute of a boy pulls and sucks me with such an appetite I think he'll drink me dry one day.'

She tidied her collar. 'I've had a letter. Stephen's working in Cardiff for a while in some air force place but he'll be home at the weekend. I don't know how Hilda will take to him being around the baby.' Her voice trailed away as the door was pushed open and Hilda came into the room with a tray.

'Evening, Hari,' she said gently. 'Any news?'

Hari struggled with her conscience for a moment. 'Probably be a raid tonight, a heavy one, get to the shelter early.' She said it quickly as if that would make it less of a leak of privileged information. 'How's your arthritis, Hilda?'

'Still there.' Hilda shrugged. 'What can't be altered got to be borne. I hear your dad's gone back to work then, desk job is it?'

Hari sighed and nodded. 'He misses the active service. Still Father's glad to have any job. Staying in the house all day was driving him mad. To tell the truth it's a relief for me too, I was so sorry for him, lost like he was, alone all the time feeling useless. When the letter came offering him the position in the London office he shed ten years.'

Hari glanced at the clock with a lifting of her heart – soon now, soon she would see him. Michael.

Kate felt her mood and turned sightless eyes towards Hari. They were still as blue as ever, with no sign they could see nothing but darkness.

'Got a date?' Kate said with uncanny perception.

'Mind your own business, nosy parker,' Hari said with a tone of mock indignation.

'It's love this time isn't it, Hari?'

'Afraid so.'

'God! You're as bad as Meryl!'

'What do you mean?' For a minute Hari thought Kate had guessed it all, the whole tangled mess about Michael, a triangle from a love story but with a huge difference, her rival was a vital, intelligent, impressionable young girl. Her sister.

'You don't give much away, that's what I mean. What else should I mean? Is there a secret then?'

'No secret.' Hari laughed uncomfortably. 'It's just the war. Should I tell him there will be an enemy attack tonight? Oh, all sorts of things. It's not the ideal time to fall in love is it, Kate?'

'You're lucky if love comes your way at all, any time,' Kate said. 'Make the most of the feeling, Hari, it will never be repeated.' Her voice was wistful; even though she had Stephen now, she clearly still pined for her Eddie.

'Drink your tea, girls.' Hilda's voice was gruff with emotion. She missed Eddie too, her only son, *his* son lying asleep in the huge washing basket her greatest consolation.

Hari glanced at her watch and pushed back her chair. 'I'll be off then – don't forget, go to the shelter early, mind.'

Kate hugged her. 'We'll be all right. Don't you stay out too late, it's you taking the risks so it is.'

Hari wondered if her words had a double meaning but Kate's

face was devoid of any guile. 'Come and see me again soon.' Kate kissed her nose, missing her cheek by a mile. She smiled. 'You smell good. Your chap is a lucky man and if I'm any judge you're looking more beautiful than ever what with being in love an' all.'

'Go on with you.' Hari mimicked her friend's Irish accent and was rewarded with a flip of Kate's hand that just managed to brush her shoulder. The baby started to wail and Kate disappeared at once. 'Men,' Hari murmured, 'they've got you on a string from the moment they're born.'

Michael was waiting for her near the beach. The sand was blown like sparkles of diamonds in the wind. He looked taller, bigger in his coat and muffler. He smiled as she drew nearer and, with a tug at her heart, she saw his nose was red with cold and his face was white and pinched. She guessed that the farm would be barren, the earth hard, frosty and unyielding, the animals keeping to their stalls away from the winter weather.

He took her hand and though he wore gloves she could feel the cold of his fingers as they twined in hers. She knew this moment would be brief, she must send him home to his beloved countryside before the raids began. But for the moment he was hers.

They embraced and she knew the scent of him, the strength of his arms, the way his body responded to hers, and she knew that this moment might never come again. Tomorrow might never come.

She took his hand and led him towards the town, towards her house. The streets were bright with icy clear air. No one was about, all probably huddled around the coal fires, toes toasting, backs freezing from the draughts blowing through the cracks in the buildings ravaged by bombs.

In the bedroom he looked at her doubtfully. 'Are you sure, Hari?'

She was scarlet. 'Are you prepared, you know?'

He shook his head. 'I never presumed.'

Hari went to the drawer and without looking at him took out a small packet. 'Here.'

There was an embarrassed silence as they both undressed, but once they were in the bed, the sheets like ice beneath them, they were close, skin touching silky skin. He kissed her gently, nuzzling her neck. And then a fierce fire blazed between them, wanting, needing each other with a desperation that transcended all doubts.

And then Hari cradled him, holding on to Michael's broad shoulders, bonding him to her, knowing whatever happened now they were mates for life. In that moment she knew happiness, pure and invincible, and she held him close and tender and it was as if they would never be parted again.

Twenty-Six

When Michael came home from Swansea that night there was a glow about him and my heart sank, I knew the truth, he and Hari were lovers and he was lost to me for ever.

That night Swansea took a pounding from the enemy and Michael sat, head in his hands, in a dark corner of the farm living room close to the radio, while Jessie and I looked at each other helplessly.

When I couldn't stand it any more, I went to him and put my arms around him like the friend he'd always thought me. 'Hari will be all right,' I said reassuringly, 'she'll be up at Bridgend, away from the worst of it.' He looked up at me with such heart-breaking hope in his eyes that I needed to swallow hard to keep back the tears.

'Where is Bridgend then?'

'It's a few miles from Swansea.' I only had the vaguest idea myself. 'Hari said they never get bombed because the buildings are on low land and the mists cover them. The German bombers don't even know they are there.' I didn't add that there were enough shells and things in the factory to wipe the whole place out of existence.

He seemed more cheerful then. 'I'll make you pair a cup of tea,' he said, 'I know you women like your cuppa.'

I smiled. 'That seems to have helped, Aunt Jessie,' I said.

'I think you can drop the "Aunt", Meryl, you're a woman now, you actually put the feelings of Michael and me before your own. Well done. Come and give Jessie a hug.'

We clung together in silence. I could hear Michael in the kitchen;

he was even whistling now unaware my heart was breaking. Jessie and I untangled ourselves as we heard his footsteps coming towards the door. I even managed a smile as he put the tray of tea down on the table. He grinned at me.

'This Bridgend, Hari's safe there you think?'

'She's in an office, Michael, she's working on a machine, a radio thingie.' I knew I shouldn't say too much as what Hari chose to tell him about her job was up to her, but it wasn't very much judging by his attitude of complete attention.

I needed the tea, my throat was thick and I felt as if I'd swallowed a rubber ball whole. My chest hurt and I was constantly fighting tears. It was a work of art to stop my mouth from trembling. My Michael belonged to me, and Hari, with her lovely hair, her Madonna face, had taken him from me.

Only Jessie sensed my feelings; she leaned over and squeezed my hand but the sympathy made the tears brim into my eyes. I gulped my tea and the hot liquid eased my throat a bit.

'I'll go up early tonight,' I said. I kissed Jessie's cheek, which was damp, and her eyes meeting mine swam like blue fish in a pool. She was almost as anguished as I was at the turn of events.

'Don't go up yet, let's go for a walk,' Michael said easily, taking my arm. We often went for a walk but now everything had changed. I took a deep breath.

'All right, but please don't talk about my sister all night, it's so boring.' I winked at Jessie and she winked back, encouraging me to act naturally.

It was a lovely moonlit night; now and then a flash of light crossed the sky as a bomb exploded somewhere. Seconds later there was a tiny *crump* and another flare lit up the earth, just a tiny pinprick of light that was so far away but real and frightening for all that.

'We're having some land girls arrive tomorrow,' Michael said, 'they are going to help me on the farm.'

'Lovely for you –' my tone was sarcastic – 'they'll probably faint at the sight of a mouse.'

I wondered what Hari would make of that, young ladies on the farm with Michael. I . . . well, I was jealous as hell and that was daft of me as he was taken already: he loved my sister; he'd fallen all the way for her and no amount of eager women would tempt him away from Hari. I knew Michael well enough to understand he was the faithful sort.

I shivered and Michael put his arm around me. 'Remember the night we cuddled up in the barn?' he said, his lips against my hair. To him I would always be that small needy girl he'd humoured and comforted.

'Oh, yes, when I ran away from the Dixons, I remember,' I said as though it had been the furthest thing from my mind. I thought of it constantly, the way he'd held me against him, protective, loving almost. Almost but not quite.

A plane droned heavily overhead, one of the enemy had obviously lost the way to the town. I remarked on it and Michael took my hand.

'Run!' he said fiercely, 'he's going to unload the rest of his bombs here before he hits the Channel.'

My legs worked like a lamb in the spring as I leaped over hillocks and rocks and went wherever Michael was taking me. I heard the screech of a bomb and then I was flat on the ground with Michael lying on top of me. The bomb exploded in a gulley and I suppose that's what saved our lives. But the sound of it crashed into my ears, my head, and shook through my whole body in waves of shock.

Michael had raised his head and took my face in his hands. 'Are you all right, Meryl?'

I became aware then of him and of my own body. My nipples tingled, I felt all moist and strange. I had the urge to raise myself up against his pelvis but I restrained myself. Michael would be horrified. I knew that within the core of my being, just as I knew I had been aroused to desire by the man I loved, the man I would always love.

Twenty-Seven

Hari was very aware of Meryl standing behind her staring at the radio and her eyes narrowed. She could feel the animosity coming from her sister in waves. Meryl was clearly hurt and angry. Any moment now she would speak and, with a feeling of dread, Hari knew exactly what was on her sister's mind. Meryl knew in that strangely intuitive way of hers that Michael and she were lovers.

For a moment Hari gloried in the thought, she felt his body taking charge of hers, felt his hands caressing, delighting her, his body bringing hers to thunderous paroxysms of pleasure.

'You've . . .' Meryl hesitated. 'You and Michael have . . .' She was unable to speak the words.

'"Made love" is the phrase you're looking for.' Hari felt compassion but also anger that her private joy had been dragged out of her in an atmosphere of resentment. She thought Meryl might cry but she didn't.

'I had him first –' Meryl's voice held a defensive note – 'Michael was supposed to be mine.'

'You've never "had" him,' Hari said softly. 'Not in any way.'

'That's all you know!' Meryl's tone was harsh. 'Did he tell you that we spent one whole night together in a barn?'

'He did, as it happens,' Hari said, 'he was kind, he held you, comforted you, and to suggest anything else isn't worthy of you or him.'

Meryl was quiet for a long time. 'You're right,' she said at last. 'He thought I was a child. He still thinks of me as a child. I'm sorry, Hari, I shouldn't have implied there was anything else.'

Hari got up from her chair and faced her sister. Meryl was as tall now as she was; she was lovely with her silky chestnut hair tied away from her face and her eyes bright with unshed tears. She closed her arms around Meryl.

'I love you, sis,' she said, kissing Meryl's cheek, 'and I'm so sorry I've been the one to hurt you but I love Michael so much I just can't help myself.'

Meryl kissed her cheek and disengaged herself. 'You needn't talk to me about being hurt, I know all about it.' She said the words softly. 'So does Jessie, she worries herself sick every time Michael comes into Swansea.'

She sat in Hari's chair and abruptly changed the subject. 'Right, show me how to work this machine. Let's take our minds off Michael, shall we?'

Hari hesitated, her work was secret, the codes carefully guarded and yet, when she married Michael and had a family, perhaps Meryl could take over her job here. It would be a challenge for her and would keep her away from the war for as long as it lasted, which could be for some years yet, so Colonel Edwards predicted.

For several hours Hari tutored her sister on the working of her machine. Meryl was quick to learn, so quick deciphering the new daily codes that Hari felt slow and dull by comparison.

'How do you learn things so quickly?'

'I don't know,' Meryl said, 'I'm just good at languages and things. I speak German almost as well as Michael does and, although my French doesn't come so easily, I'm not bad at that either.'

'And I know your Welsh is excellent, you should aim high Meryl, be a teacher, a linguist, aim for the top.' She paused.

'Maybe it will all come in useful one day.' Meryl suddenly lost interest and, taking the hint, Hari picked up her bag and gloves.

'Come on, let's go home. Daddy will be arriving for the weekend later today and we'll have to get his bed ready.' She hesitated. 'I've asked Michael to come to tea, I hope you won't be upset.'

Meryl's face brightened for an instant. 'It might he dangerous but I suppose you both know what you re doing.' She abruptly changed the subject. 'It will be fabulous to see Daddy again but I'll be going back to the farm on Monday, remember.'

'I know –' Hari held up her hand – 'I've got a few days off, don't you worry, you can return to your precious farm, no one is going to stop you.' She heard the tone of sarcasm in her voice and took a deep breath.

'Don't worry,' Meryl shot back, 'your Michael is all yours, there's nothing I can do to take him away from you.' She paused. 'I just feel at home in Carmarthen now, I like being with Jessie and, I admit it, I like being around Michael although he will never be mine.'

Silently, the girls walked out of the office along the board path that led to the sheds, past the ruined shell store that stood – a blackened ruin – alongside the other sheds, and finally out on to the road where the buses waited. Soon they would get the train home, they would make preparations for father's weekend visit and perhaps, just perhaps, Hari's burden of guilt would be lifted for a while.

When they arrived home their father was already there and Hari saw at once that Meryl had become her father's favourite daughter. The way his face lit up when he saw her, the warm hug, the way he smoothed her hair and the shine in his eyes told a graphic story. She understood it: Meryl was the image of their mother; Hari's colouring, her pale complexion, her red-gold hair, had all come from Father's side.

Meryl had bright, impish looks and her hair, almost brown, her cheeks warmed by the country air, her smile of delight, gave her a vivaciousness Hari knew she would never have.

They were about to have tea, consisting of bread, salt butter, strawberry jam and cake all laid out on a pristine cloth. Hari had planned this for days, pulling strings, receiving favours, just to give her father a good homecoming. And of course, warm within her was the knowledge that Michael would be here any minute now.

The knock on the door brought a smile to her face and Meryl turned her head sharply, her eyes wide and accusing. 'Michael, I presume?'

Hari forced herself to open the door slowly. There on the step were two tall military policemen. Then without her permission they were inside and had closed the door.

'Michael Euler?'

'Who?' Hari said, bewildered. Suddenly, Meryl was at her side. 'There's no one here of that name, sir,' she said. 'Come in, we're just about to have tea, you can see for yourself there's only family here.'

The men followed into the warm kitchen and stood near the door as if on guard. 'We understand the German is on his way here,' the older policeman said in a harsh voice. 'It's a criminal offence to harbour the enemy.'

The room was silent, then a coal shifted in the grate and the kettle on the stove began to boil. Absently, Hari made the tea. She looked desperately at her father; his eyes were narrowed, his brow furrowed. He had no idea what was going on.

Meryl smiled at the police. 'Why don't you come back later?' she asked innocently. Hari watched her. Her sister was cunning, bright, but even she couldn't find a way out of this trap.

The men ignored her. Meryl sank into a chair, defeated. Hari took in a ragged breath. 'What information do you have that there is a German coming here to my house?'

The two men remained tight-lipped. Hari saw Meryl's eyes snap with temper; she opened her mouth and then closed it again. If she said the name of Michael's betrayer she would confirm what the military already knew. Thank God she kept her mouth shut.

And then Hari heard them, footsteps coming towards the door, her darling Michael was walking into a trap and she could do nothing to save him.

Twenty-Eight

I could not let it happen. 'I have to go to the lavatory,' I said briskly, and before the men could move I was out the back making my way around the side of the house. I couldn't let Michael be hunted like a wild animal. I stood against the door like a fly stuck to paper as the two men came round the side of the house. I saw Michael in the distance and began to shout and hit at the two men and act as if I was generally gone mad. Michael caught on and disappeared into a side street.

'You wicked child, what have you done?' One of the men pushed me roughly aside and ran after Michael. Slowly I went back inside.

'I warned you not to make Michael come to Swansea!' I was aware of the accusation in my voice and my sister just stood there, white-faced, silent, in stunned disbelief. And then Hari crumpled, she sank into a chair and began to cry.

I picked up my coat.

'Where are you going?' Hari pulled herself together and I took a deep breath.

'I'm going back to the farm, see if I can do anything to help.'

'I'll drive you,' Hari said desperately.

'No, we might be followed. I'll get there on my own. I'll take the bike.'

'It will take you all night to get there.'

'So?'

I had no patience with Hari at that moment. I tied a scarf around my head and kissed my bewildered father. In the street, there was no car, no lurking men. I took the bicycle from the side path. The tyres were good – no punctures – it would get me to the farm if I had to push it by sheer force of will. I swung on to the road and began to pedal my way out of town and on to the road leading to Carmarthen.

The dawn was streaking the sky with light, trees were turning from lavender and grey into green by the time I reached the farm. I'd done a lot of thinking on the way down and had worked out some sort of plan in my head, a plan to get Michael out of the country, perhaps to France or neutral Ireland. Aunt Jessie was in bed but wide awake, worrying.

'There's a message from him.' She handed the crumpled pencilled note to me and my heart was beating fast as I read it. He wanted me to meet him at the barn, the barn we'd slept in like lovers. I felt warm. He knew I would come to his aid, he trusted me, relied on me, not Hari.

'He wants food and money, all the money we can get together,' I said. Jessie nodded. 'You have one of those perm things here?'

Jessie frowned, 'yes, but . . .'

'Cut my hair and perm it, Jessie. I'll wear lipstick, no one will recognize me.'

'Who's to recognize you anyway? I don't understand.'

'Those men who came to the house, they saw me as a kid with plaits, they might be outside, watching. Come on, Jessie, the sooner we start the sooner I'll be ready.'

Some time later, I made my way from the farmhouse and mounted the bike. My backside was raw from the cut of the saddle but nothing would stop me getting to Michael. I could feel that my funny short curls were still damp, my hair had lightened by some chemical reaction to the perm and, with a coating of lipstick and the stolen clothes of a land girl, I knew I looked entirely different to the girl who had left Swansea hours ago.

Over my shoulder was a bag, in it a canteen of tea and some bread and ham; wrapped around my waist, snug and secure was a purse of money, all I and Jessie could find in the house.

There was a soldier guarding the gateway to the road and he waved me down. I stopped cycling and put my booted foot on the dew-wet ground. 'Lo there, soldier.' I did my best to imitate the London accent of one of the land girls and smiled up at the uniformed man. He blinked.

'Any identification, miss?'

I rooted around in my pockets and shook my head. 'But then I don't need anything to identify me to the stupid cows. They don't bleedin' care who I am so long as I ease their poor udders. I got a dog tag round my neck if that's any good?'

After a moment the soldier shook his head. 'I'd be eager to fish for them but I'm a happily married man. Go on then, milk them beasts, rather you than me, lady.'

As I rode away, I was jubilant. The soldier would have been given a description of me, perhaps even a photograph to look at, and he hadn't recognized me. My disguise had worked. That was one hurdle over.

Michael was nowhere in sight. I took a deep breath and stood waiting in the silent dawn light of the barn knowing he would come. A few minutes later, a plank of wood moved at the back of the building. He was there and I ran to him and threw myself into his arms.

'I knew you wouldn't let me down,' he said thickly. I sat with him on the straw-covered floor and Michael stared at me. 'God, you look different!'

'That's the whole point.' I gave him the food and the tea and watched him eat hungrily.

He winked at me. 'The look has improved you no end.'

I hit him across the arm. 'Don't be facetious – you could have been captured, shot even. You were reported, obviously.'

'Mrs Dixon?' he said.

'Or Georgie Porgy,' I said dryly.

'Look outside.' He brushed crumbs from his mouth and I longed to kiss that very same sensitive mouth. I went to the barn door and strode outside, I was a land girl wasn't I? I looked well on the land.

'All clear,' I said, not even a cow or a sheep in sight.'

'I'd better go then.' He wrapped his arms around me and rested his chin on my head.

I stayed for a moment in his embrace then shifted myself. I shrugged out of the overalls and an old skirt of Jessie's came tumbling out. I straightened it and stuffed the haversack up inside the skirt and tied it around my waist. Then I hid the remains of the meal and lastly I took the ring Jessie had given me and pushed it on my finger.

'What on earth do you think you're doing?' Michael said.

'Don't look so gormless. Jessie and I made a plan. I'm your pregnant wife – at least as far as the coast – that way you won't stand out like a sore thumb.'

'But . . .' Michael waved his arms.

'But nothing,' I said fiercely, 'I'm coming with you and that's all there is to it.' He stared at me dumbly and then shrugged in resignation and we left the barn together.

Twenty-Nine

Hari was still in tears the next morning. She was all sorts of a fool for asking Michael to tea, showing off really to Meryl by bringing him to Swansea yet again. Her father held her while she cried and then begged her to tell him what was wrong. 'Is it Meryl?' His voice was anxious. 'She vanished so suddenly after those men came to the house.'

Hari shook her head. 'No, well . . . yes.'

'Where is she now?' His voice was fearful and Hari knew he was anxious about his youngest daughter; she was afraid for Meryl too.

'She's gone, she's probably in Carmarthen now or captured by the military police.' Hari felt the tears well up again. 'It's my fault, I wanted Michael to come to Swansea. Meryl warned me of the danger but selfishly, I just wanted to see him.'

'Don't blame yourself, Angharad –' her father put his arm around her shoulder – 'you and the boy are in love, it's only natural you wanted to be together.'

Hari hadn't credited her father with so much understanding and, impulsively, she hugged him. 'But about Meryl,' she began. He shook his head.

'We mustn't worry about her,' he said, 'our Meryl has a core of steel, she can look after herself.' And yet his voice shook even as he spoke.

Hari was working nights and before she left the house she made her father corned-beef hash and opened a tin of peas to go with it. She had some dripping in the pan from last week's pathetically small roast and she used it to mix with flour and potato water to make the gravy. She ate very little and hoped her father wouldn't notice. Of course, he did.

'Starving yourself will do no one any good.' His voice was stern. 'Come on, girl, eat up. Have some bread to dip in the gravy, it really is very tasty.'

Hari longed to be alone so that she could worry in peace about Michael. Where was he? Had he been caught? She longed to drive down to the farm but knew it would be foolish to take the risk as she might be followed.

It was with relief that she kissed her father's cheek and climbed into her car and drove away. Although she loved her father dearly, she was becoming tired of sharing her life with him. She was used to being alone, dealing with her problems on her own.

All night, Hari took messages, insignificant messages, and then, when she was almost asleep, the news came through that Italy had surrendered and for a moment hope filled her heart – was the war almost over? Listening hard, Hari heard that Germany had taken over where the Italians had left off and once again her heart was plunged into fear and despair. Would the war, the danger, never end?

Thirty

Eddie's son grew more like him every day. Kate listened to Hilda's description of the baby's dear face. Both of them doted on the child and Hilda told Kate how well he was learning to walk. Kate heard him talk in an endearing, stuttering way, his soft hands clinging to Kate's skirts.

Hilda, although getting older and more careworn by the day, loved to hold the boy in her arms, gather him against her thin breast, kissing his downy head with tears in her eyes.

On the weekend, Stephen came home from his business trip and, to Kate's relief, Hilda treated him like the man of the house he was. She generously made a large supper for Stephen and when he came into the little kitchen, dropping his bag on the floor, he took a deep appreciative smell of the roasting lamb.

'Something good is cooking.' He shrugged out of his jacket, hung it carefully on the back of the chair and sat down with a weary sigh. 'Cup of tea, darling?' he said to Kate.

'Sure you picked a good time to come home, it's all quiet here for once.'

'His lordship is asleep I take it?'

For a moment Kate was irritated, she wanted to say her son's name was Edward but she thought of Stephen's goodness to her, remembered how Hari had described his scars, and softened.

'Kettle's just boiled,' Hilda said and Kate felt for a chair and sat down close to her husband. 'How's work treating you?'

'I went up to Island Farm today, I had to take them some new typewriter equipment.'

'Oh?' Kate felt his hand touch hers. 'How did the prisoners treat you?'

'Well, seriously, some of them are nice blokes,' Stephen said. 'Some are hard bastards, begging your pardon, Hilda.'

Without turning she poured the water into the teapot. 'Don't mind me! I think Germans are *all* bastards, they killed my Eddie didn't they?'

'Hilda,' Kate said softly, 'it's wartime, we are killing Germans too. Sure as Mary was a Virgin the Germans can't all be bad.'

'Humph!' Hilda was not convinced. 'Rather him than me –' she nodded in Stephen's direction – 'rather him than me work with them sods.'

Stephen drank his tea and said nothing more. Kate felt a pang. Eddie, she still loved him, down deep inside of her. She was happy she had a bit of him in the little one and yet respect and even love was growing for Stephen, who was a good husband and a good stepfather to her son.

He worked hard and brought enough money home to keep them all in reasonable comfort. If it wasn't for Stephen they would be poor as church mice.

'Hungry, Stephen?' she asked.

'I'll be dishing up for the lad in a minute, don't worry.' Hilda had softened, she seemed to have picked up on Kate's thoughts. 'After all, Stephen is master of the household now. We are beholden to you, Stephen, and grateful.'

Kate examined Hilda's words for sign of sarcasm but found none. Hilda was truly grateful to him. Stephen was embarrassed.

'No need to be grateful, it's me should be grateful, I've got a home and a family now and me with my ugly mug all scarred and burned – I'm one lucky blighter.'

Kate felt tears well in her sightless eyes and her fingers curled in his.

'To me you will always be the handsome boy I first knew back in those days in the Glyn Hall,' she said softly.

She heard Hilda move sharply from her chair and leave the room. 'I'm sorry,' she said to her husband, 'she's still grieving over

Eddie and,' she sighed, 'so am I sure enough but you are very dear to me Stephen, never forget that.'

'And you are the most beautiful girl in the world, my Kate. I never knew I could love anyone as much as I love you.'

In the next few days Kate's suspicion became a certainty: she was expecting Stephen's child. She was excited, thrilled and fearful. There were doubts in her mind, worries more like. Would her scars hold, would Stephen be pleased even though it meant another mouth to be fed – and what would Hilda think?

She waited till nightfall and then went to see Hari. Darkness was no threat to Kate, for her it was always dark. In any case, she knew the streets of Swansea well enough. To her delight, Hari was home from work.

'Kate! My lovely girl, what are you doing out alone when there could be an air raid any time? Come in, come in. There, sit by the fire while I pour you a drink of sherry.'

Kate felt for the chair and sat down. It wasn't cold outside and yet the heat from the fire was comforting. When the drink was poured, Hari guided her hand to the glass. 'I'm so glad you came,' Hari said, 'I'm so worried.'

Kate's spirits lightened, she wasn't the only one with problems, her dear friend Hari had some too by the sound of it.

'What's wrong, Hari, is it Meryl again?'

'Partly.' Kate listened while Hari told her of the night the military police had come looking for Michael. 'Since then they've both disappeared into thin air.' Hari's voice was breaking. 'I've been to the farm and no one's there. Jessie's gone away and the farmer next door is looking after the stock.'

'Michael will get in touch with you, Hari, to be sure he will.'

'How can he when they're looking for him to arrest him for being half German. They think he's a spy or something.'

'Look,' Kate said firmly, 'if he's got Meryl with him he'll be just fine, you know what's she's like.'

'I do.' Hari's voice had lightened. 'She's a bossy little boots but she's strong and efficient, she'll work it out, you're right enough, Kate. I'm so glad you came and talked sense to me.'

As Kate put down her glass, feeling carefully for the edge of the table, the siren shattered the silence of the little kitchen. 'Well, you'll have to be bossy and efficient now,' Kate said dryly, 'come on, take me to the nearest shelter.'

Later, when the all-clear sounded, Hari walked Kate to her door and hugged her. 'I'm not coming in,' she said apologetically, 'I've got to be up early in the morning. Take care and love to Stephen. You're lucky to have him you know.'

'I do know.' Kate's words were heartfelt.

She waited until she and Stephen were in bed and then she put her arm around his broad chest and felt his hair tickle her skin. 'I've got something to tell you so I have,' she whispered.

'I know,' he whispered back.

'How can you know?'

'I've got eyes. Sorry! That was crass of me. Your eyes are so beautiful I sometimes forget you can't see.'

'I can't be showing yet,' Kate protested. She felt her belly. It wasn't as loose and fat around the scars as it used to be but it was still not flat and hard as the body of a young woman should be.

'Hilda told me,' he said.

'Hilda knows?'

'Obviously.'

'Well, I'll go to the bottom of our stairs.' Kate felt relief surge through her as she had dreaded the ordeal of telling Hilda the news and the old woman had known almost before she had.

'Are you pleased?' she whispered to Stephen.

'Pleased? I'm damn well delighted,' Stephen whispered in her ear. 'In fact so pleased I think we should make sure just in case.'

He took her in his arms, so gently, so tenderly, and as Kate clung to him, she felt tears of happiness begin to roll down her cheeks. If she couldn't have her Eddie, there was no other man she'd want to be with but Stephen.

Thirty-One

The fishing boat chugged its way slowly down the coast towards the Irish Channel and I stared at the water fearing the depth of the sea beneath the ship even though one of the fishing crew assured me it was as calm a day as I could ever wish to see.

We were travelling in a weather-beaten fishing boat and had been blown off course in a storm. It had pulled into shore at

Milford Haven on the coast of Wales to be repaired, which was a stroke of luck for me and Michael. It was an Irish ship flying the Irish flag to show its neutrality, so there was little chance of it being attacked by a submarine or so the sailor assured me.

I looked at Michael. He was staring into the distance, no doubt hoping, as I was, to reach land. The sea journey to Cork would take many hours but at least I was with Michael. I had got him away, me, Meryl Jones, not my beautiful sister Hari. The thought gave me a warm feeling of triumph even as a pang of guilt shot through my chest. Though 'my chest' was no longer flat but was a fully grown 'bosom' now.

My Irish accent, and I was always a good mimic, copied from Kate had been good enough to convince the captain that I just wanted to get home from a war-torn Britain. Still it had taken most of our money to persuade the man to take us on his boat.

'You could be spies,' he'd said. I'd patted my fake belly. 'Do I look like a spy to you?' And at last convinced, he decided to take us.

It grew dark after a few hours and the sea was black and more intimidating than ever. I thought of the German submarines that lay off the coast of Ireland ready to pounce on our British ships returning from abroad, and trembled.

Michael sensed my fear and took my hand. 'Be calm,' he said, 'we'll soon reach dry land and you can have the baby in peace.'

If only he was my husband, if only there was his baby safe inside me, how happy I would be. One of the merchantmen smiled at me.

'When's it due? I've got two little ones of my own so I have.'

I thought quickly. I looked quite big but I didn't know quite how many months I would be to look this size. I played it safe. 'Not long now.' I lowered my eyes bashfully. 'It's a honeymoon baby.'

He winked at Michael. 'You're not a Jaffa then?'

I looked at Michael, frowning. 'Seedless,' he said, briefly looking embarrassed. I tried not to laugh. Suddenly I felt happy, every moment the ship was taking us away from danger, from the men who wanted to arrest Michael, perhaps charge him as a spy, shoot him even. If he had nothing to hide why didn't he declare himself, that's what they would say.

A sailor came from the front of the small ship. He was dripping with sea water. 'I can see the lighthouse,' he said eagerly, 'we'll soon be ashore.' He grinned at me. 'I was worried you'd give birth before land, I'm what passes for the ship's doctor and I didn't fancy the job of midwife.'

'No danger of that,' I said, 'I'm not going to be relieved of this burden till I'm in Ireland.' I took Michael's hand and squeezed it and it was his turn to stifle a laugh.

There was a sudden clunk against the side of the ship and the sailors looked at each other in alarm. 'Mines! Holy Hell!'

The object had jagged points poking out of it and was drifting away from us but not far enough. The sound of the blast was loud in my ears. Flames seared above my head. A great jagged hole appeared in the side of the boat and water, cold and rough, swept around my legs. I clutched my belly as if it was indeed a precious child. One of the sailors thought he understood. He was bleeding profusely from his chest, the blood running between his thick fingers.

'Get your wife out of here!' He gave Michael a push and Michael responded at once, leading me as quickly as he could towards the hole in the metal. The sea was coming in fast now and I knew the boat must sink soon. I looked at the vast expanse of water and fear made me feel sick. Gently now, I was pushed towards the jagged tear in the ship's hull.

'Get clear!' the sailor instructed Michael, 'get as far away from the ship as you can or else you'll be tugged down by the wake.' The sailor pushed my arms into a life jacket, his own I think. 'The Holy Virgin go with you.' And then I was in the cold, unfriendly sea.

'Hold on to me,' Michael ordered. I was a good swimmer but the utter hugeness of the sea terrified me and I put my arms around Michael's waist and let his strong arms, bulging with muscles from his work on the farm, take us away from the doomed boat.

The bag under my skirts dragged at me and I thought of abandoning it but I could see two of the sailors bobbing around us. They were injured and floundering but there was nothing we could do to help them. Perhaps none of us would ever get out of this damn sea, we would drown and sink to the bottom to be eaten by the fishes. I began to kick against the heavy seas with all my strength.

'There's a beam of light ahead,' Michael gasped, the water slopping around his mouth and nose so that he began to cough.

'It's a sub, it's heading towards us, just hold on sweetheart, we're going to be picked up.'

I tried to help Michael by treading water but soon I got tired and sank back on to the life jacket. It was a cumbersome thing and felt like sticks of wood but it was doing a good job of keeping my head above water.

The submarine still had water running down its slug-like sides as it came to a restless, uneasy stop some way away from us. Michael began to swim towards it, towing me like a sack behind him.

A man appeared, kneeling on the side of the huge shiny sub. He shouted some words and I felt every nerve in my body tense.

'Let me do the talking,' Michael said. 'For once you keep your little mouth shut.'

Michael shouted back and waved his hand, calling out in his native German. My heart shrank with fear – we were being rescued by the enemy.

Thirty-Two

'Where are they?' Hari sat next to Kate on the sofa in her little parlour and drank the endless cups of tea Hilda insisted on making for them. When she brought in the tray yet again, she was dressed to go out.

'I'm taking Teddy for a walk. I won't be long.' She dressed the little boy and winked at Hari. 'I might get myself a little drink when I'm out, not much mind, just enough to warm my belly.'

When the door closed behind Hilda and the baby, Hari touched Kate's arm. 'I haven't heard a word from any of them. I'm so worried, Kate.'

'Have you heard anything on that machine of yours in the office, anything about escaped Germans?'

Hari shook her head. 'That's a thought. Meryl knows enough to get a radio signal through to me if she can only find the right equipment. Perhaps they're both in France looking for a resistance group. I've got to hope, Kate, I've got to have hope.'

'What's this about a resistance group?' Kate sounded bewildered.

'Some of the French are fighting the Germans, others of course have given in, collaborated.'

Hari swallowed hard. 'I suppose the worst thing is my sister and Michael could both be dead.' Her voice was flat, heavy. An unbearable pain filled her, a physical pain like she had never experienced before. 'How could I live without them?'

'You'd have no choice.' Kate's voice was suddenly filled with tears, 'you just find a way to go on, you have to.'

'I'm sorry, Kate,' Hari said at once, 'of course you do, you've lost your Eddie, I know the pain must haunt you day and night.'

Suddenly she was weary. All Hari wanted to do was lie down and sleep. 'I'd better get back,' she said, 'it's getting dark.'

Kate went to the window as if she could see outside. 'Hilda's keeping the baby out a long time, she hates the dark, especially these days when there's no street lights and windows are all blacked out.'

Hari saw the irony of her words, to Kate everything was blacked out. 'Look, shall I go and find them?'

'Stay a bit and talk to me,' Kate said. 'Talk about anything, I just don't want to be on my own. If they don't come back in, say an hour, go and look. Hilda might have taken little Teddy to Maggie, you know the good Catholic lady who lives near the Lamb and Flag?'

'That's likely.' Hari's voice was deliberately cheerful. 'Hilda loves to show the baby off.' She smiled, though Kate couldn't see her. 'She'll probably persuade Maggie to fetch them both a bottle of stout from the pub.'

'Hilda says he's the spit of Eddie. I feel the boy's face sometimes, trying to see through my fingers.' She shrugged. 'But at least I can tell he's strong and sound with good lungs that I can hear well enough when he's screaming for attention.'

'And what about Stephen — is he good with Teddy?' Hari's conversation was banal and she knew it but she was desperately trying not to talk about her own worries.

'Good enough, but he wants a child of his own so badly.' She put her hands across her belly. 'I hope to the Holy Mother I can carry this baby safely.'

'Oh Kate, you're expecting and me going on about my worries!' Hari put her arm around Kate's shoulder. 'If even an explosion couldn't shift Teddy you must be born to be a mother, of course you and the baby will be fine. Not sure I'm born to be a mother though,' she finished dryly.

Kate forced a smile. 'Go and get us a drink, Hari.' Her voice ached with tears. 'Pour some brandy for us both, give us both a lift, we need it to live through this hellish war.'

The time passed slowly. Hari tried not to think about Michael or her sister, out there running, hiding or injured in a field somewhere. She kept up a flow of chatter until there was the sound of the door opening.

Kate stood up, her blind eyes looking across the room. 'Thank God! They're home.'

It wasn't Hilda and the baby who came into the parlour but Stephen, his eyes dark-ringed, his scars standing out sharp against his pallor.

'There's been an explosion,' he said. 'I tried to help but when the firemen came, and the ARP, they sent me home, said I looked as if I'd given enough to the war effort.'

'Where was the explosion?' Kate's voice was icy calm.

'Just by the Lamb and Flag, nowhere near us. Don't worry, there's no air raid.' He sagged into a chair. 'I'm so tired I could sleep on a razor.'

'Go to bed, love.' Kate said, 'I'm going to see Hari to the door.' Hari watched with an aching heart as Kate walked into the kitchen and felt for her coat on the peg. Hari took her arm.

'Look, you don't know that Hilda was over at Maggie's. Stay with Stephen and I'll look for Hilda.'

'I have to look for myself.' Kate's answer brooked no argument.

Arm in arm, Hari walked with Kate over the devastation that Swansea had become. Her home town wasn't alone in this: London, Coventry, Manchester and many other big cities had been blasted to the ground. The German Luftwaffe seemed intent on bombing Britain into submission.

Hari saw at once that the Lamb and Flag was a dark, smouldering ruin with a few flames still shooting up intermittently from the rubble. She heard a faint, anguished cry fading to a ghostly stillness and her blood chilled.

'For God's sake Hari, the houses, Maggie's place, what in the name of all the saints has happened?'

'Some of the houses are bombed but Maggie's is still standing.'

'The Holy Mother be praised.' Kate sagged against her and Hari

swallowed her tears. 'There, the baby is fine, come on let's go look
for him.'

Maggie's door was open as it always was but the house was
empty. Mary Pryce appeared from next door. 'Maggie took Hilda
and the baby to the Lamb and Flag,' she said heavily. Wanted a bit
o' a drink she said.'

'Oh Holy Mother and all the angels no,' Kate said. Then her
head lifted. 'Hush!' She stood like a hunting stag listening, sniffing
the air. 'I hear him so I do, I hear my Teddy's voice.' She stumbled
forward into the smoking, ruined building. Hari followed her and
tried to hold her back but Kate pressed on, climbing over huge
chunks of debris until she disappeared from sight.

Hari knew that Kate's sense of hearing, the touch of her finger
tips in the darkened ruin of the Lamb and Flag, would be assets
that sighted people would not have.

Hari heard Teddy wail and her heart quickened. She moved
forward instinctively, waving her hands in front of her face, trying
to dispel the smoke and the smell of burning. She touched a soft
shoulder and dimly recognized Hilda. There was a rumble beneath
her feet, the floor to the cellar must be burnt through, any minute
they might crash downwards with the tons of twisted metal and
masonry they were stumbling over. Hari dragged Hilda into the
street.

Once safely outside, Hilda sagged to the ground. 'I'm all right –'
she began to cough – 'help Kate for God's sake.'

But Kate needed no help. She emerged from the smoke and
handed Teddy to Hari. I'm going back for Maggie,' she said and
disappeared into the smoke once more. And even though Hari
called her until her voice was hoarse there was no reply.

Thirty-Three

I sat on a bunk in the small cabin that looked as if it might belong
to the chief engineer judging by the range of strange equipment
on the desk. I had a blanket wrapped round me, which was just
as well, because my 'baby' had gone when the bag had vanished
into the sea in spite of my endeavours to keep it. All I could hope

was that if any of the sailors from the Irish merchant ship had survived they would be kept well apart from us. I imagined they would, they were crew and Michael at least had been taken for the son of the fatherland, which of course he was. How he would explain our presence in the sea I couldn't imagine.

I knew we had bypassed Ireland; when the mine struck, the ship had floundered, drifted way off course and now, hours later, we were on our way to Germany, making our way past the coast of France.

Michael came into the tiny cabin accompanied by some sort of officer.

'My wife,' Michael said in German. The officer scarcely acknowledged me. I was relieved I didn't yet know what we were supposed to be doing at sea in the first place.

The officer nodded again and left us. Michael sat down beside me and rubbed his face. 'Speak German,' he instructed me, 'and only speak when you have to, I'm not sure they trust me.'

'*Was wirst du ihen sagen?*' I huddled close to him.

'The story is you came from Ireland but from German parents,' he replied. 'We were returning to Germany when the Irish boat was accidentally sunk by the sub.'

'We would have drifted off course,' I said. 'And what about the crew, the good men we were with?'

'Poor sods,' Michael said. I gathered that none of the Irish crew had survived.

'Let's try to get some sleep.' Michael pushed me to the side of the bunk and stretched out beside me. I wanted to cry but Michael would think me even more of a child. Even now, when I had womanly curves and had got away with being an expectant mother, he treated me as if I was his kid sister.

He was lying beside me, our bodies touching out of necessity, the bunk was so narrow. It was torture for me. I wanted him, touching me, holding me, being inside me. I was a woman and human but Michael was in love with my sister, profoundly in love and he would no more betray her love than he would hand her little sister over to the enemy.

Eventually, I slept.

I was woken roughly by hands pulling me from the bunk. I opened my eyes sleepily and saw one of the sailors gesturing for me to go with him. I looked at Michael and he nodded. 'Go easy with her,' he said in German, 'she's very young and a bit slow-thinking like most of the Irish.'

I bit my lip as I realized Michael was acting in character. German people thought every other race was slow compared to them. The man holding my arm had clear blue eyes that seemed to penetrate my skull, he was someone to be reckoned with that was for sure.

An officer invited me to sit opposite him and nodded to me politely. 'Frau Euler?'

I nodded.

'Tell me what's been happening to you and your husband.'

'He was taking me to his homeland, he wanted to fight for his country.' I hoped my funny accent would be taken for the Irish part of me.

'Where had you been?'

'Been? I don't know what you mean, sir.' I know I sounded stupid, at that moment I felt stupid.

'Where have you been living?' he said slowly and loudly.

'In Ireland, sir.' I hoped that was a good enough answer. He seemed to be waiting. I dabbed my eyes. 'My mammy, she died while I was at her bedside.' I stopped then as Michael had warned me not to say too much. The officer looked at me without expression.

'Where did you live in Germany?' It was like a bullet from a gun. Where did I know of in Germany? What would I say? I decided to stay as near the truth as I could.

'On a farm. Michael was working the land for food for the troops, his mother Mrs Euler was very old, she too died. So,' I sighed heavily, 'we went to say goodbye to my family before Michael joined the . . .' I didn't know the word for 'forces' so I took refuge in wiping my tears on the edge of my skirt again. The officer averted his eyes from my dimpled knee.

'That will be all, for now.' He stood up and I quickly left the room. I don't know how much of my story he believed, he gave nothing away, but as I was marched back to the cabin, Michael was being taken out. I put my arms around him and pressed my cheek to his.

'I told them about the farm in Germany,' I whispered, 'didn't give a name to the district.' I kissed him, savouring his unresponsive lips. '*Liebling,*' I said more loudly.

'We'll be back home in Hamburg soon,' he said and kissed me softly. And then they took him away from me and I wondered if I would ever see him again.

Thirty-Four

The smoke that would have blinded most people made little impression on Kate's eyes, she could see nothing anyway. She did start to cough and, clearing her throat, she shouted as loudly as she could.

'Maggie! Where are you, you old baggage?'

She heard a sound like a cat mewling and went towards it. She stumbled over some rubble and, on her hands and knees, careless of the tearing of her stockings and the grazing of her shins, she called again.

'Maggie, keep calling me, I'm coming for you.'

There was no reply but her sharp ears caught the sound of movement and she scrambled towards it. There was the noise of stones, a shower of them falling, and then her hand reached out and touched a warm, human hand. From the sticky feel of it Kate knew Maggie was bleeding.

'Come on.' She coughed out the words. The smoke was getting thicker, heavier, and time was limited if she wanted to survive.

Maggie didn't speak but her hand clung desperately to Kate's. Following the sound of voices, Kate headed towards the open air dragging Maggie, stumbling behind her. She could breathe. She fell to the ground feeling hands on her, lifting her. She knew, by the scent of him, through the smell of smoke, she was in her husband's arms, her true but unwedded husband, her wonderful Eddie.

She touched his face. 'Is it really you, Eddie, you've come home again! You're alive and I'm not dreaming?'

'It's me, my darling, it's me, I've come back to you. Don't worry about me, worry about yourself. You have to go to the hospital, just to be checked, Maggie is going too but mum and the baby are all right.'

Kate seemed to fade then into a mist of a world, a mist inside her head. All she was conscious of was Eddie holding her close, still loving her, he was safe and well and home with her again. It was a miracle and she would bless the Virgin Mother for it every night of her life.

When she opened her eyes again, she was in her own bed. She could hear sounds from downstairs, muted voices, Hilda putting the kettle on the gas, talking baby talk to little Teddy.

Eddie; had she been dreaming she was in his arms, was it lack of air in her lungs causing her to have weird dreams? 'Please, Virgin Mother, let it be true,' she breathed.

She stirred and tried to get up but her knees hurt. She felt her legs and they were covered in bandages. Further down, her ankle was swollen and had a sort of stocking on it holding it tight. She must have been unconscious all the time she was at the hospital.

Her hands seemed all right but when she touched her hair it was frizzled and burnt and smelled heavily of smoke and burning wood. She tried to get out of bed though every part of her body ached and once her feet touched the floor, she heard steps on the stairs, the heavy tread of a man.

When he came into the room Kate knew it was true, she knew his scent so well; her dear, darling Eddie was alive, home, safe with her. He took her in his arms and held her gently.

'How?' she asked, her hands exploring his face. There was stubble on his chin, he hadn't shaved in days, but what did it matter? He was in her arms, he wasn't a dream, a figment of her imagination, he was real flesh and blood.

'I was missing for a while then I was taken prisoner. Then, one day on a forced march, I took my chance and escaped. Look, none of that matters now, I'm safe, I'm home and I love you my darling little Kate, my beautiful girl.'

She found his lips and kissed him and then, gently, he lay beside her and held her in his arms. 'I love you so much, Kate,' he whispered in her ear. Kate wondered for the first time why people whispered when it was love talk: was it for intimacy, privacy, or a desire to hide feelings from the rest of the world?

Later, he helped her downstairs. Hilda silently made tea. She had baked cakes, dry, because there was not enough marge to make the cake light and there was very little fruit, but it was a gesture, a gesture of hope and welcome for the son she thought she'd lost.

Kate was in a dream, she was back in the days when she and Eddie danced without a care in the summer fields, hugged and kissed and made love with the joy of youth.

Hilda coughed. 'The smoke,' she explained, 'it's still in my chest. You were a brave girl, Kate, to go into the ruins and fetch poor old Maggie out.'

Reality began to trickle into Kate's euphoria. 'How *is* Maggie?'

'In hospital, but she'll live,' Hilda said briskly.

'Eddie, are you home for good?' Hilda said, her voice hard-edged. 'If so there are things we have to talk about.'

Reality came closer and Kate tried to push it away even as she listened to Eddie's answer.

'I don't suppose I'll go back now,' he said. 'As of now, I'm unfit for duty.'

'Thank God for that,' Hilda said. 'So you'll be back here living with us?'

'Of course, mother,' Eddie said, 'where else would I live but with my family?' He was puzzled by his mother's attitude and Kate knew she must speak – explain – but the words stuck in her throat.

'Kate?' Hilda prompted. 'Tell him, tell Eddie the truth.'

But she didn't have to. The door opened and she heard Stephen's voice, loud and cheerful. 'I'm home! How's my wife and my unborn son then?'

The silence was long and hard and edged with fear and Kate felt her happiness dwindling into a tiny sphere that at any moment would just fade away and disappear into nothingness.

Thirty-Five

'I want you to go to Bletchley Park.' The Colonel was stooping more noticeably, now he leaned more heavily on his stick. Hari watched as he eased himself into a chair.

'Sir?'

'The place where the clever people break codes.'

'I know what Bletchley is for, sir, I just don't really want to go away just now, and sir, what use would I be even if I went to Bletchley Park?'

'I want you to have some training there, specialist stuff.' He took out a huge hankie and blew his nose severely. He seemed to be short of breath for a moment and then he spoke again. 'You must put personal issues aside, young lady, and do your duty.'

Hari felt exasperated. 'I thought I was doing my duty, Colonel Edwards. I am working at a munitions factory and one of my best friends was blinded in an accident here. We are all in danger every day, isn't that duty enough?'

'Well, in Bletchley you aren't likely to get blown up by a shell are you?' His eyebrows hid his eyes.

'My personal safety is not an issue, sir, I'm just not clever about codes and ciphers and things.'

'I'm not arguing. You have to go, at least for a few weeks or so.'

She faced him, her hands firmly on the desk. 'Have I displeased you?'

'You are an unmarried lady.' He was suddenly irate. 'We work together a great deal, alone in an office. Do you see what I'm getting at?'

Hari did. She was amazed. 'People are talking about us?'

''Fraid so.'

'But, sir.' Hari stopped. What she had been about to say was insulting.

He said it for her. 'I know I'm old enough to be your grandfather. Still, there it is.' He ran his hand round his collar; his neck was red.

'Look, Hari, It will do you good to have a break from this stuffy office, to see the innovative, creative work those brain boxes at Bletchley do. If I was twenty years younger things would be different, very different.'

Hari didn't know if he was referring to the talk about them or working at Bletchley Park.

'All right, sir.' Her voice was meek. She thought of Michael and Meryl and her heart sank; they just wouldn't know where to contact her even if they could. They might not be alive and, if they were, God knows what dangers they were facing. And there was Father. When she got home she would write to tell him she would be away for a while.

That night she went to see Kate to say her goodbyes.

Kate was alone in the house. She lifted her head when Hari walked into the kitchen and held out her arms. 'Hari, please help me.'

Kate's instincts amazed Hari. 'How the hell did you know it was me?'

'I know your scent, the sound of your footsteps, oh, it's lots of things. Pour us a drink there's a darlin', I'm flummoxed I am so.' Her voice wavered. 'I think the Virgin Mother herself must have sent you to me.'

They sat and drank brandy and soda. Stephen, it seemed, was rich enough to get drink on the black market. Hari sipped the fiery liquid and waited for Kate to unburden herself.

The house was silent, not even the radio played out: no dance music; no news of war; nothing. 'What on earth are you doing sitting here alone like this?'

'Oh Hari!' Kate began to cry, hot, bitter tears. She put her hands over her face as though she was ashamed. Hari went to her and held her while Kate sobbed like a distressed child.

'Is the baby sick? Hilda – is she all right?'

Kate's words tumbled out like a river in full flood. 'Eddie's alive and well – he came home and sat with me and kissed me and I thought I was in heaven. And then Stephen came in and said about the baby I'm carrying. Eddie was so hurt that I was with Stephen and didn't wait for him. I tried to explain that this time when he was missing I thought he must have been killed. Anyway, he took little Teddy and walked out. Hilda went after him and I haven't seen any of them since yesterday.' She cried again, her voice rising, she was on the verge of hysteria.

'And Stephen?'

'Stephen packed his things and left me, they've all left me. Oh God, Hari, what am I going to do?'

Hari rocked her as though she were a baby – how could she tell Kate that soon, she too would be leaving for Bletchley Park in England? 'I'll get us another drink,' she said, but Kate clung to her.

'Stay here, hold me Hari, tell me everything is going to be all right. I can't bear all this unhappiness. Haven't I put up with enough with my blindness?'

It was the first time Hari had ever heard Kate complain about the accident. They sat together, clinging to each other until, with a sense of relief, Hari heard the latch of the door being lifted.

Kate lifted her head. 'Hilda!' she breathed, 'what's going on, tell me or for sure I'll go mad.'

'Here.' Hilda put Teddy in Kate's arms. 'You've got your child and you've got me for as long as I last in this life. As for the menfolk, your guess is as good as mine.'

Hilda's solution to any crisis was to put the kettle on the gas stove. As she put out clean cups, her face was red from weeping and Hari felt a pang of pity for the woman who was worn and worried and heavy with the knowledge she had no power to make things right.

'How was I to know he was alive?' Kate's hands were held out imploringly. 'I needed my son, Eddie's son, to be born in marriage. I sure didn't want him being called a bastard, you know that Hilda –' her hand touched Hari's – 'and so do you my dear, dear friend.'

'No one's blaming you.' Hari's voice was soft.

'Too right no one is blaming her,' Hilda agreed.

'Eddie is and so is Stephen come to that. How in the name of God and all the angels could I have made such a mess of my life? I had two fine men to love me and now I've lost both of them.'

'Which one do you really want, that's the question,' Hilda said sharply.

'I want my Eddie,' Kate said simply.

A voice from the doorway was full of love and gladness. 'It's me, Kate, Eddie. I've come back home and what you've just said, that's exactly what I needed to know.'

They clung together, weeping, and Hari left them and walked the empty, silent streets towards her home.

Thirty-Six

I looked at the strange land of Germany and felt alien and frightened. I had to remind myself that Michael was born here, lived here until he was ten before Jessie took him home to Wales.

The German officer had managed to contact Herr Euler and eventually believed our story and let us go once we reached the coast of Saint-Nazaire. We had been dropped ashore and we needed to head through Germany, making for the farmlands North of Hamburg. There, his father would no doubt arrange for papers for us both; our excuse for not identifying ourselves was good – all our possessions had been lost at sea.

I grew up then, all at once. I looked at Michael and knew without doubt he could never love me; it was a dream of mine, a hopeless, helpless dream. He talked incessantly about my sister; he talked about Hari's amazing hair, her beauty, her warmth of spirit. The trouble was I agreed with him; Hari was all those things. I loved her and I hated her.

An army lorry drove by us filled with uniformed soldiers. They stopped with a screech of brakes and sharp words, most of which I understood, shot like bullets at Michael. He replied quickly, explained our situation, mentioned the submarine commander and his father and then, magically, we were gestured to board over the back and into the well of the truck.

Michael talked about his father and one of the officers frowned. 'Euler?' he said, and Michael nodded. After that, the men became respectful but distant. I had the impression they knew of Michael's father and feared him. I must have fallen asleep against Michael's shoulder then because when I opened my eyes we were in farmland, flat with not a hill or a mountain in sight, not at all like Jessie's place in Carmarthen.

I heard the familiar, mournful sounds of the herds and the fussy, gossipy cluck of hens as they scratched with sharp claws at the ground. If I closed my eyes again, I could be back in Carmarthen. I wished I was.

Michael helped me down on to the road and thanked the driver of the truck. 'You don't talk much,' the man said to me in English. I looked at him blankly. He wasn't going to catch me that easily.

Michael took my arm and set off across a field, straddling the rows of green weed things that showed the crop was potato, perhaps turnips. I never did learn a lot about the land.

Back home with Jessie I knew less about plucking a chicken and cooking it, so how we were to survive on the German farm was a mystery. I'd spent my nights at home learning German with Michael. Lovely times, they were, sitting at the fireside listening to the radio or to the coals shifting in the fireplace.

The farmhouse came into sight. 'Home.' Michael spoke in German and I looked at him sharply. 'This isn't home,' I said, 'are you forgetting Jessie and Carmarthen already? Are you turning into a *German!*'

He was silent. I never ever knew what Michael was really thinking.

The house was built of stone, mellow and yellow in the fading light and criss-crossed with wood, something like the old Elizabethan houses at home. The windows appeared blank like eyes that couldn't see and I found I was shivering.

Herr Euler was waiting for us. He was a tall man with a moustache, a soldier in uniform. There was a familiarity about him, and then I realized there was a strong resemblance between father and son.

'Michael?' His tone was questioning, he peered closer. 'Mein Gott! Come inside, boy.' His strong guttural German was hard to understand. He hardly looked at me, miserable old sod.

'I'm Meryl,' I said in German. He looked down at me from his great height. He didn't reply.

'Michael, what are you doing here in Germany, come to fight a just cause at last have you, boy?'

The room had no lights. Michael ushered me towards the fire and the flames from the logs threw shadows of us into corners and on to floors and walls – everything was strangely unreal.

I must have dozed while Michael told his father the story of what we'd been through but I was awake enough to know it was carefully edited.

'And who is this woman?' Herr Euler's tone was hostile as though I was a camp follower or something.

'I'm Michael's future wife,' I said quickly. I had the feeling that if Herr Euler thought any different I would be tossed out on my ear. 'We lost everything in the shipwreck, we've no papers or anything.'

'Why did you bring her?' His father's tone was abrupt.

Michael shrugged. 'It's a long story. Can you help us get papers?'

'First, food.' And then he did something that I thought must be out of character for him so awkward was he: he hugged Michael and patted his back. 'It's good to see you back in the Fatherland, my son.'

Michael's eyes were misty and I felt a pang of unease. Would he be a turncoat now he was back in Germany?

We ate chicken and potatoes and then we all went to bed. I was muddle-headed and worried but I was too tired to stay awake. I cuddled myself with my arms, used now to sleeping alongside

Michael's warmth. He had never treated me as anything other than a sister but nevertheless we'd been side by side curled together, a pair. I shivered and Michael hugged me, just for comfort. I knew that was all he had to offer me.

Herr Euler was very clever and next morning he set the wheels in motion for acquiring papers for both Michael and me. He chose a church in the small village nearby for our marriage by a proper German clergyman, and by some miracle Michael and I really were man and wife. But, only in name, I warned myself. As soon as we got back home, if ever we did, I knew the marriage would be annulled.

We had no wedding breakfast, just a drink of some German stuff and a slice of bread and cheese, but I had a ring on my finger and my papers would carry the name Frau Euler.

My short-lived euphoria disappeared when Michael's father warned us that matters were desperate and even younger boys than Michael were being called to serve their country. 'You will have to join the forces.' He spoke sternly and Michael glanced at me before nodding.

A few days later, Herr Euler had a sheet of paper in his hand when I got up for breakfast. The fire was still not lit and there was no sign of food. Michael came into the room from the back-yard, his hair was wet and glistening with diamond drops of water.

'My leave is over,' Herr Euler said. 'You were lucky that you came when you did otherwise you'd have been in deep trouble.' I didn't catch everything he said but I got the gist of it and I was suddenly frightened. He had offered us security, got us a legitimate identity, papers we could show anyone who cared to examine our presence in the country.

Now he was leaving us alone and though Michael was courageous, inventive and adaptable, he was unfamiliar with the working of Germany, of this Hitler who ruled everyone and stuck his arm up in the air and shouted like a buffoon.

'Thanks for being so kind,' I said, in German. Herr Euler nearly smiled.

'Your German's not bad, not bad at all,' he said. 'I have something for you; it was my mother's. As Michael's wife, it should be yours.' He handed me a ring. 'It's a black opal,' he said. 'Very rare.' I glanced at Michael; he looked sour but what was I to do? I took the ring and slipped it on my finger. It glimmered with colour and I was fascinated.

We heard a car outside. Herr Euler clipped his heels together, shook hands with Michael, nodded to me and left us. The engine outside revved as the truck drew away.

'What now?' I said anxiously.

'We get a message to Jessie and to Hari. Can you do it, Meryl?'

'If I can find a radio I can use.' My mouth was dry, he hadn't forgotten about home then.

'I'll find you what I can. There should be some bits and pieces around my father's house, he always did like to tweak the radio.' He smiled. 'You and he would have a lot in common.' From the little I had learned about radios the task of making one would be much more difficult than Michael realized but I kept my own counsel about that.

We settled down to a sort of routine; we would search for pieces of electrical stuff, anything I could use to make a signal. In the evenings when it was too dark to work, we sat near the fire and talked, really talked, and I knew Michael was more mine then than he had ever been. If only he would love me as a man loved a woman. But it might happen, I really hoped it might happen given time. A week later Michael was called up.

Thirty-Seven

Hari drew up at the door of the farmhouse tired and blurry-eyed; she'd driven all the way from Buckinghamshire. Jessie was waiting at the door, wiping her hands in her apron. Her face was lined and anxious. Hari felt overwhelmed with hopelessness, it was obvious Jessie had heard nothing from Michael.

'Jessie?' Hari's last shred of hope faded as Jessie shook her head.

'No news. Come in, *merchi*, sit by the fire and talk to me before I go mad with loneliness.'

'I'm no *merchi*,' Hari said softly. 'My girlhood is gone along with Michael and my sister. Where can they be, Jessie?'

Jessie ran her thick-veined hand through her grey hair. 'The good Lord is the only one who knows that.'

She led the way into the warmth of the kitchen, which still bore signs of Meryl's cleaning habits though it was gradually declining into the chaos that Jessie was accustomed to.

'I have to stay in England for a while,' Hari said. 'I'll leave you my address Jessie. If you hear anything, please, please write to me.'

Jessie nodded. 'Same goes for you.' She put her head in her hands. 'They're searching for him, the military, they think he's a German spy and my boy loving Wales like he never lived anywhere else.'

'Meryl is with him.' Hari swallowed hard not wanting to admit to the jealousy that gnawed at her whenever she thought of them together. She should be glad that her quick-thinking, intelligent sister would use all her initiative to bring the pair of them home.

'Please God they are not dead already.' Jessie's voice cracked.

A thrill of horror washed over Hari. 'Try not to think of such things.'

'I do try but at night I see them, bloody and dead in a ditch somewhere. Where can they hide?'

'Trust Meryl, she's good at inventing things,' Hari said, 'she's clever, intuitive and a damn good liar.' There was no malice in her tone. 'They will survive this, you'll see. Let's pray the war will soon be over and then they will turn up like new pennies I'm sure of it.' But she wasn't sure, not at all.

'How long will you be in England?' It was as though Jessie had just digested Hari's earlier words. Her face was lined and worried beneath her sun-dried, greying hair.

'I have to be there at least a month,' Hari said dully. 'I'd much rather be home but, as everyone says, this is wartime and you can't always do as you want.'

They were both startled as there was a sudden, loud rapping on the farmhouse door. Hari followed Jessie, ready to protect her against intruders.

'You, Georgie Dixon, how dare you show your face around here after what your mother did?'

'There's a message.' He thrust out a piece of crumpled paper.

'From where?' Jessie's tone was still hostile. 'If your mother is trying to apologize she can go to blazes.'

'It's not from my mother, it's from some man. He was funny . . . foreign, didn't understand why Mam wasn't you.'

'Oh, right then,' Jessie said flatly.

Hari looked at George. He was taller now, a man, he should be serving in the forces by now. They returned to the kitchen and Jessie opened the paper. She sank into a chair, her face white.

'It's from Michael's father.' She handed it to Hari.

The words danced before Hari's eyes. They were typed but smudged, and covered in stains. 'Mrs Dixon's had a good look at this.' Hari's voice was bleak. Jessie took the letter back and read it aloud.

'Son and new bride doing well under my wing M.H.E.' She looked up at Hari her face alight with joy. They're alive, Michael and Meryl are with my husband in Germany, they're safe!'

Hari sank into a chair. 'And married!'

She stayed with Jessie until the daylight was almost fading; neither of them spoke much as there seemed nothing to say; their loved ones were alive but at what price?

Dawn was breaking as Hari took the long drive back through Pen Caws Road on the way through Swansea and back to England.

As she neared the town she heard the bombs crashing and whining as they hit the terraced houses on the slopes of Mount Pleasant. Fires burnt on Kilvey Hill as German bombers tried to beat the docks into oblivion, missing important targets but decimating the buildings and killing many of the inhabitants who scampered, too late, towards the comparative safety of the shelters.

She drove through it all and stopped outside her home. She would sleep at her home whatever happened and then, tomorrow, she would pack more of her things and shake the dust of Swansea from her feet and make for England and Bletchley Park. She might just as well stay there for good; Michael was now a married man, he had chosen her sister and her own hopes were in ruins.

Thirty-Eight

Only a few weeks after arriving in Germany I found myself, courtesy of Michael's father, sitting behind a desk in a German signal office. I worked beside both men and women and they accepted my accented German knowing, or believing, I had lived in Ireland, and making allowances for my foreignness. If only they knew.

Michael had been taken away to be a pilot in the Luftwaffe and if it wasn't so damn well serious it would all have been laughable.

I'd cried a little when he left me, unfamiliar in huge flying jacket and big boots. He'd hugged me close and whispered caution in my ears. This show of sentiment usually abhorred by the Germans was acceptable, even deemed sweet, in a young married couple. I watched Michael climb into the aeroplane for his lesson and my heart was in my mouth as he careered down the runway and took off into the skies.

He would be expected to bomb Britain, his home, his loved ones; it was grotesque and I didn't know how he was going to get through it.

I heard footsteps behind me and glanced over my shoulder to see Frau Hoffmann standing behind me, watching; she was small and blonde and very pretty but we were all a little afraid of her.

'Aren't you doing any work today, Frau Euler?' Her German was precise, sharp. I had to drag my mind to the task in hand trying to remember what I'd learned at Hari's side in her funny little office.

I adjusted the earphones and began to take notes hoping my spelling in German was adequate to the job. As the messages were in code, I expect I could get away with it but there was no knowing with a woman like Frau Hoffmann.

When I had been helping Hari it had all been easy to me, a little experiment, a chance to show how clever I was. In the German language, it was tricky but I was quick to learn and the codes were similar patterns to those we used at home. Numbers allied to certain letters soon became translatable even with a sort of haphazard kind of accuracy and I began to earn the respect of my fellow decoders.

Simple messages came through, usually nothing of any consequence and I waited expectantly for something big to arrive, some
plot of the enemy to communicate to someone, perhaps Hari in
Wales. I would be a spy – how I didn't know – but I would help
my country win this futile war, that I was sure of.

After his training was over and before he was sent on active
service Michael was given leave and we went together to his father's
farmhouse and talked. I wanted him to talk about us, about our
marriage, sham though it was, but his first words were about Hari.
I might have known.

'Those radios you use, the signals you send, could you let Hari
know how we are and all that?'

'Tell her we're married in name only, you mean?' We knew the
contents of his father's brief message to England. 'What do you
think I am a witch? I'm struggling enough not to show myself up
as it is –' My tone was sharp – 'and you want me to take such a
risk just to let my sister know you're not unfaithful, is that it? You
would risk my life and possibly yours for such a small thing?'

'Speak German,' he said, 'it's safer.'

'Even when we're speaking treason?'

'Treason?' – he sounded wounded – 'I wouldn't ask you to do
that.'

'That's exactly what you are doing.'

'No I'm not –' he thought about it – 'well I suppose I am really.
Sorry.'

'If I signal Hari, *if* I manage to work out how, it will be about
something far more serious than you and me, Michael.'

'What do you mean?'

'Make a guess,' I said, knowing my eyes were narrowed.

'For God's sake don't take risks.'

'Oh, it's taking risks to send vital intelligence to my country
but not to contact home to give a trivial message to my sister.'

'It's not trivial to me,' he said.

I suddenly felt the anger, the fight, the hope go out of me. 'I
know.'

For the next few days we lived like a married couple except for
one important matter, at night we went to separate beds and I
would lie awake thinking of him, wanting him, most of all wanting
his love. But I cooked for him, managed the unfamiliar foods.

I washed his clothes, his intimate underwear, and all the time he treated me casually, as he always did.

Michael tutored me some more in German though by using it every day I was losing my foreign accent and speaking in the same guttural way as he and the rest of my working friends did. I thought of the word 'friends' with surprise; the Germans were our enemies and yet the very intelligent men and women I shared my days with were human just like the Welsh stock I came from.

I was glad to go back to Hamburg and to the office, glad to be free of the desire to fling myself at Michael's feet and beg him to love me. And yet, once at my desk, with my headphones flattening my permed unruly hair, the idea of communicating with home began to grow and ferment.

Frau Hoffman seemed to soften towards me and, watching her, I knew, incredibly, that she was in love with one of the brilliant men who worked in the office that housed the weird machine that appeared to be a typewriter but was much more.

I went to have a better look at it one evening when the office was almost deserted. There wasn't one but several of the machines and I couldn't think how they worked.

'A little out of your league, Frau Euler,' Frau Hoffman said with a hint of a sneer. I was startled. I hadn't heard her come up behind me.

I agreed with her at once, nodding my head as if I was in a Punch and Judy show.

She looked dreamy. 'I was widowed, you know.'

This was unexpected. 'Iron Drawers and Iron Jaw' I'd named her in my mind. I didn't know what to say but I soon realized I was not required to say anything.

'It was in the early days of the war. He was a pilot, you know, just like your husband. They don't last long, Frau Euler, so be prepared.'

She moved to another machine and touched it almost with affection. 'But love can come again even to the most unlikely of us.'

Unwisely I offered my opinion. 'I don't think I will love any other man than Michael.'

'You may never have the choice.' Her tone was hard, she was Iron Jaw again in an instant. 'Now get out of this office, you have no business to be here. Don't you realize you could be regarded as spying? We break ciphers here so that we can bomb the enemy, the arrogant British, into oblivion.'

I looked as dumb as I could and apologized, shaking my head at the machine as though it was beyond me, as indeed it was. I retreated hastily and set off for the farmhouse on my bike.

I was fuming. How dare Frau Hoffman sneer at my homeland, my people? We were all human but then she had no humanity in her. This was a side of the German people that was beyond me.

It was a long ride home, giving me a chance to think. I would try to make my radio work somehow. Now I could take discarded pieces home from work, at least I had some important pieces of equipment. I would make contact with home – now I would be a spy, though unofficial and untrained, with a glad heart and a clear conscience.

Thirty-Nine

Hari looked around the bedroom of Mrs Buckley's lodging house and knew it was her home at least for a month or two until she got a place to rent. Until now she'd stayed in a small room at the Bletchley Mansion but it had been temporary accommodation only. Her own house in Swansea was locked up though Hari was fully aware that at any time the building could be bombed and burnt to ashes, but now she was calmer she knew one day she would go back even if only for her father's sake.

The room at the lodging house was nicely furnished but very floral, floral bedspread, floral curtains, even flowers on the lamp-shade. It was clearly what Mrs Buckley thought a well-brought-up lady required.

Hari unpacked her case and put away the few more essential clothes she'd brought: plain dark skirts, white blouses and a few good sweaters in case it got cold in the nights. She put her under-clothes and stockings in the bedside drawer.

She washed at the small sink in the corner of the room and, once dressed, explored the landing, finding three single toilets and one very old bathroom with a big contraption fastened to the wall that she took to be the gas boiler.

Supper was at 'seven prompt' and Hari obediently went down the stairs and followed the sounds of voices to the dining room.

'Miss Jones, please come and sit down. I've put you alongside another lady worker at the old BP buildings.'

'I'm Babs.' The girl at her side had a cheery face, dark hair turned back in a sort of roll and Hari felt conscious of her own free-flowing mane of unruly curls.

'Hari.' She took the proffered hand and decided that tomorrow morning she would tie back her hair into a bun before she went to work at the Park.

'What do you do at the Park?' Hari asked.

'I work in hut six. You've been working on signals haven't you? – But I understand you're to come in with us. Don't worry, it's not so bad, there's a lot of us civvies and no slave-drivers to irk us. So long as we do our work we're left to our own devices.' Babs had a very cultured voice.

Mrs Buckley could obviously see that Hari was impressed. 'Babs went to Girton,' she said proudly. 'Most of my guests are from Cambridge colleges.'

'Well, I'm not,' Hari said. 'I went to an ordinary grammar school in Swansea, didn't even get to university, the war put a stop to that. In fact, I'm wondering what use I can be to anyone in hut six, it's all beyond me.'

'You must be very bright to be sent here,' Babs said. 'I'd rather someone bright and quick thinking than the somewhat stereo-typical boffins you get at BP. I'll give you a lift in tomorrow if you like.'

Hari nodded eagerly. 'Thanks, it will be nice to have moral support.'

One of the other girls stifled a laugh. 'That's not what we'd call our Babs, is it girls? Good-time Barbara is more like it.'

'Oh, shut up, Cicely,' Babs said good-naturedly.

'That will be enough of that silly gossip, young ladies'. Mrs Buckley's voice was stern but there was a twinkle in her eye as she ladled out the soup.

In the morning, Hari was up early, anxious not to be late for breakfast and certainly not wanting to miss her lift to work. The dining room was quiet: everyone seemed subdued, even Babs; early morning blues perhaps. There was no sign of Cicely.

Hari looked at Babs questioningly and the girl shook her head.

'Cicely's chap is a pilot. He didn't come back last night.' Her voice broke. 'She was out there last night counting the planes over and when there was one missing, she just knew . . . she just knew.'

Hari picked at her breakfast and thought of Michael, wondering where he was now, how had the Germans treated him, was he all right? She remembered the one night they'd had together when he'd made tender love to her, made her a woman, his woman. Now he was somewhere she couldn't reach.

With a dart of guilt she remembered that Meryl, her little sister, was in Germany too. Together they would both survive, she was sure they would, wasn't she?

The grounds of Bletchley Park were beautiful this morning and now she'd been away from it for a night she saw it with fresh eyes. It was an old country house and looked grand and solidly imposing. Small huts were built around the grounds. Hari was grateful that Babs was there to point her in the right direction for hut six.

'I'm glad you're in hut six with me,' Babs said, drawing the car to a noisy halt. 'You'll listen when all the others just want to talk about themselves.' She smiled, her teeth were very white; she was a fine, healthy-looking girl. 'The work is not too difficult, don't worry, I'll ease you into it.'

The first thing Hari noticed was how untidy the hut was. It was a long room with a series of tables to the sides and centre. At one end stood a cupboard, the doors half open. Overhead were strip lights rather high to the ceiling, one window shed some daylight.

Pieces of discarded sticky tape were spread across the floor in small strips; girls were already working, sat at machines, absorbed in whatever they were doing.

'Morning,' Babs said, and one or two of them waved a distracted hand in greeting. 'Come and sit at my machine with me –' Babs touched Hari's arm – 'and don't look so worried, this is well within your capabilities, you'll see.'

Uneasily Hari perched on a chair and stared at the unfamiliar machine. She clearly wouldn't be working on signals in here. What on earth did Colonel Edwards have in mind for her now? Since she'd told him she was probably staying in England he had changed his plans for her.

'No!' His voice had been stern. 'I will be needing you here. You must come back to help me, I'm getting too old for all this, didn't I tell you?'

'I'll explain.' Babs voice brought her attention sharply into focus. 'Don't look so puzzled.' Babs had seen her bewilderment. 'Some of our clever blokes have found the key for today,' she said cheerfully, 'now it's up to us to decrypt the words on to our machines.' She tapped the metal surface of the cipher machine with her elegant finger.

'Sounds simple then.' Hari's sarcasm made Babs smile.

'Don't worry, we just pass the stuff on to another hut and they somehow make sense of it all.' Hari doubted her ability for the job but she paid attention just the same and as the day wore on she found she was actually enjoying the challenge of it.

That night Cecily came into dinner at the guest house. Her face was blotched, her skin mottled with weeping. Babs immediately hugged her and patted her back as if she was a distressed child.

'It's confirmed then?' Babs spoke so softly Hari could scarcely hear her.

'He went down in the sea, in flames. No hope of survivors, none at all.' Cecily forced the words between her trembling lips. 'Oh God, why did I fall in love with a pilot – I must be mad?'

Hari thought of Kate and her tangled love life, her men – one in the army, one in the airforce – and both of them coming home alive. Life could be so cruel and death so arbitrary. Her heart felt as if it were beating its way out of her chest as she thought of Michael in Germany perhaps fighting on the side of the enemy.

After a while at hut six Hari felt she was beginning to get used to the work. She was playing a small, very small, part in decrypting messages from the awesome Enigma machine. She found she was enjoying the company of the other girls, the sharing of pleasures, the sharing also of grief. She told Babs that her Michael was missing but she couldn't explain further, it was all far too complicated. What would the girls think if they knew Michael was half German and married to her little sister?

Eventually, she had her own machine and she sat timidly before it staring at the strange keys that could offer permutations of messages beyond measure.

It was men like Alan Turing – a strangely private man – along with his talented colleagues, who had the impossible work of finding the key to the day's ciphers and Hari saw them only from a distance. She and Babs and all the girls in hut six were ants in comparison.

And then she had a phone call; it was from Colonel Edwards. 'You'd better come home, I've heard from your sister. Don't worry, everything is well, but come home at once.'

Was this his way of bringing her back to Swansea or did he really have intelligence about Meryl? Her trembling nerves got the better of her and she covered her face with her hands. And was there any news about Michael?

Forty

Kate sat in the doctor's waiting room hands folded in her lap. Everything was fine, the baby, Stephen's baby, was growing normally and the scars looked as if they would hold for another birth. If not, the doctor said, Kate could have the child by Caesarean section.

She heard the door open and lifted her head. Hilda had come to fetch her. She heard Teddy snuffle, he had a cold and he started snivelling when he saw Kate and bumped against her legs. She held him, took out her handkerchief and by some instinct found his nose.

They went outside. 'Everything's fine,' Kate said, afraid to voice her real thoughts that she wished the baby would slip away. It was such a betrayal carrying Stephen's baby in her womb when her real love had come home to her.

'Teddy's caught Eddie's cold,' Hilda said unnecessarily. 'Eddie's gone to bed, sent in a sick note to work, he'll be laid up for at least a week. You know what babies men are.'

Kate felt Hilda stiffen at her side.

'Hello, Kate.' It was Stephen, his voice was kind, concerned, there was pain underlying every word. Kate tried to smile. She held out her hand and Stephen took it.

'The doctor said the baby is fine.' She hoped she sounded re-assuring. 'I'm fine too. There could be trouble with my scars but if there is they'll operate, nothing to worry about.'

Stephen coughed as though to hide his feelings. 'Can I give you a lift home?'

'You've got a car, you must be doing well,' Kate said.

'Now I'm no longer able to fly I'm no great use to the force. I've set up a new business but I can tell you about that another time, let me give you a lift home, the rain is getting heavy.'

Kate was going to refuse but Teddy began to cry.

'Car,' he said, 'I want to go in car.'

'All right,' Kate said humbly and let Stephen hand her into a soft back seat. Huffing and puffing, Hilda sat beside her with Teddy on her lap.

'It's very kind of you I'm sure.' Her tone was not cordial. 'Perhaps you'd like a cup of tea or something when we get back?'

Kate knew what the invitation had cost Hilda. She liked Stephen, was grateful to him, even, for supporting them all the time Eddie was away, but now her son had returned and she had every mother's protective instincts where her own were concerned.

'I would very much like to –' Stephen must have caught Kate's tiny shake of the head – 'but I'm afraid I'm busy today.'

He drove on in silence and Kate felt like a traitor. She had married in haste, for the best reason in the world – to give her son a decent future – but now she was paying a terrible price.

Stephen left them at the door and, for a moment, Kate touched his hand. 'Thank you for your kindness,' she said softly. 'I'll keep in touch about the baby, I promise.'

She heard him sigh. 'I was so happy there, for a while, Kate . . . you, and my baby on the way – what more could a man want?'

'I'm sorry, Stephen, I do love you, in a way, but Eddie is my . . .'

'Don't say any more –' Stephen's voice was suddenly harsh – 'I don't think I can bear to hear it. Look after yourself and my child, that's all I ask of you.'

Kate felt her way into the house and the warmth of the kitchen reached out to her. She could smell tea, hear it being poured into cups. She sank down into a chair and burst into tears.

Hilda held her. 'There, there, life's been hard on you girl but remember one thing, you have a lot of people who love you, that's worth more than gold any day.'

What Hilda said was right but why then did Kate feel such a

desperate pain, finding it so hard to come to terms with the awful situation she was in? Two men, two children; such tangled lives. She sighed. Why was she worrying, tomorrow they could all be dead.

Forty-One

I was at home in the German farmhouse alone. I had a week's leave from the radio control room and I was glad to be out from under Frau Hoffman's beady eye for a few days. Her last words to me as I left were: 'When do you intend to provide some fine sons to fight for the fatherland?'

'As soon as you do.' I knew at once it was unwise of me to say that. Frau Hoffman's face darkened and she stared at me with her cold eyes that would freeze a sea over, if there had been a sea anywhere near us.

She raised her hand and slapped my face hard and I had to bite my lip and apologize. 'I am sorry, Frau Hoffman, that was rude of me.'

'Go!'

I went. Now I was alone in the farmhouse wondering why I could not stop my sharp answers even now when I was in such a precarious position.

I looked out into the yard and saw the few chickens stalking about as if they owned the world. They must be German chickens, I giggled to myself. And then I thought of Michael, my love – how could I be against the race that had reared my darling man? Michael would be home on leave in a few days and my heart did a flip of joy.

'*Duw*,' I said to myself, 'I'm turning into a silly, soft woman, what in heaven's name is wrong with me?'

I looked again at the chickens; if I wanted to eat I would have to kill one of them. I shuddered. I'd reluctantly plucked chickens, cut them into pieces, but it had been Jessie who'd actually done the killing on the farm in Carmarthen.

On the other hand I'd brought bread and cheese from one of the small shops near Hamburg; I could always make do. I stared out at the hens again and took a deep breath. I would have to do it sooner or later. Now, while I was alone, might be the best time. If I made a fool of myself I would be the only one to see it.

The hens took no notice of me as I tiptoed near them a sharp knife hidden up my sleeve. I picked out one hen, black-feathered, dainty claw raised like a dancer. 'Sorry dear,' I said in German, 'it is your turn to die for your country.'

The damn thing understood me and started to run for its life. The other hens scattered, wary of me. They must have a language of their own and the obstructive black hen had warned them what I was about.

I chased the creature into the clump of bushes at the edge of the field and fell on it. The hen wriggled and clucked and I lifted its beak and thrust the knife in deep into its throat. Now I had to hang it up to drain it of blood. That's what I'd seen Jessie do. She'd had the niceties of a shed and a bucket I had to make do with a branch of a tree and the bare earth.

The poor thing gave a strangled cough and dropped its head as though giving up. I stood back and was violently sick. I heard a soft thud from the other side of the bushes and I jumped as though the wrath of God had fallen on me. I was trembling.

After a moment, I peered through the bushes and saw a woman lying on the ground, a silk parachute tangled like a bridal dress around her.

I stood dazed, staring at her. At her side was a little brown case, her weekend undies I thought hysterically.

She started to mumble and I crept nearer. Her eyes were closed but her lips were moving. '*Iesu Grist beth sydd wedi digwydd?*'

Incredibly she was speaking Welsh. I knelt beside her and smoothed her forehead. Whatever hat she'd been wearing had been torn away, there were ties around her neck. 'What are you doing in Germany saying "Jesus Christ" and asking what's happened, in Welsh?'

She opened her eyes and stared at me and then, fearfully, looked round. She saw the dead chicken hanging from the tree dripping blood and tried to edge away from me. 'Look –' I still spoke in Welsh – 'I'm from Swansea, it's all right I'm not going to hurt you. Can you stand? I'll help you back to the farmhouse.'

'The parachute, the case . . .' She broke off uncertain how far to trust me.

'I'll hide them.' I stuffed the silk tangle of the chute into the bracken and hid the case a little way off in some soft ground. It was heavy and my heart quickened as I guessed it was just what I needed: a radio.

'*Barod?*' I asked, 'ready?'

She was unhurt and after a moment she walked steadily at my side. A tall woman, strong-shouldered but with a sweet face and curling dark hair. She was silent as I let us both into the farmhouse, looking around as though she still didn't trust me. I didn't blame her. I'd be suspicious too of a woman who lived in a German farmhouse.

We drank some brandy, we both needed it and, gradually, she began to relax.

'Do you live here alone?' It was asked casually but it was really important to her safety, we both knew that.

'At the moment.'

'Go on.' She spoke in English now and was very well spoken, cultured, well educated. Probably from a rich family, a spy, well trained and trying to interrogate me.

'Nothing to go on about.'

'Why are you here?'

'Why are you here is more to the point.'

'Sharp aren't you?'

'I have to be,' I said. 'I'm living in Germany.'

'I want to know . . .'

'What you want to know is irrelevant, I have nothing to say, I have no need to explain anything to you. Just be glad it was I who found you. We'll eat now.'

It was too late to start on the chicken and I didn't have the heart. I went out to get some eggs and the woman followed me, still suspicious.

'What's your name?'

She stared at me. 'Mind your own business.'

I shrugged and picked some eggs from under the hens. They clucked disapprovingly as though knowing what I'd done to one of their own. The woman stood by and then followed me back to the farmhouse like a doppelgänger and I almost felt afraid of her.

I made cheese omelettes and cut some fresh bread and all the time she didn't take her eyes from my hands. 'If I wanted to hurt you I could have done so when you were helpless on the ground,' I snapped at her.

She nodded. 'You're right. I'm Rhiannon,' she added reluctantly.

After that she relaxed a little and we ate in silence. I was hungry and ate three slices of bread as well as the egg and cheese. I was also very tired.

'I'm going to bed,' I said. 'You can go in the spare room if you like.'

'I'll sleep down here.' She was unfriendly again.

I shook my head and went upstairs and gladly crawled into bed. It took me a long time to sleep but eventually I drifted off. I was dreaming of Michael and of a proper wedding where I wore a flowing veil and he smiled down at me and my body grew warm with wanting.

The sound of a gunshot woke me. I ran from the bedroom, bare feet and nightgown flowing, to find Michael standing in the hallway arms raised. Rhiannon was holding a gun and by the look on her face she was not afraid to use it.

'That was a warning shot.' She spoke in impeccable German but it was slightly accented, though perhaps it was only my sharp ears that picked it up.

'Stop it!' I shouted, 'he's my husband.'

She lowered the gun and I sighed with relief. 'You should have told me he'd be home.'

'I wasn't expecting Michael for a few days,' I said defensively.

The door was barged open and Herr Euler stood there resplendent in his officer's uniform. Outside I could hear the sound of German voices and a car's engine revving.

Suddenly Rhiannon swung the gun in my direction. '*Bradwr*,' she said in Welsh.

'I'm not a traitor—' She fired just as Michael kicked her shin. Her shot whizzed over my head.

Suddenly there was mayhem. Herr Euler had Rhiannon by the scruff of her neck and was pushing her out through the door. A few minutes later I heard a shot and I winced as I realized I would never see Rhiannon again.

Forty-Two

Herr Euler went to bed as calmly as if nothing had happened. Michael came in with me as his father expected him to do, after all in Herr Euler's eyes we were a normal married couple.

I turned my back on Michael and he on me. I was shivering. I felt horrified by the events of the night and yet if I thought about it reasonably, Michael had saved my life and his father, well, his father was only doing his duty, he was shooting a spy who was trying to kill us all.

When I eventually slept, a nightmare dogged me. I could see the dead chicken bleeding and the blood was falling on Rhiannon's pretty face. I must have cried out because, when I woke, Michael was holding me, shushing me, telling me everything was going to be all right. I started to cry, something I rarely did, and he held me and kissed my forehead and my eyes and then my lips.

I kissed him back, hotly, greedily, my fears gone, my senses dazed by his warmth, his nearness, his obvious arousal.

'Love me, Michael, please love me, I need comfort so much,' I whispered against his ear.

He made love to me gently, knowing I was virginal, and I loved him so much and for so long that the joy and pleasure soon outstripped the pain.

We lay afterwards in each other's arms. Close and warm and sated. In the morning, we made love again and I felt the tumbling sensations of passionate fulfilment, cold words for such wonderful feelings of complete abandon.

We had a few days when we lived like man and wife, none of us spoke of Rhiannon. Or, more importantly, about my sister Hari.

Herr Euler sometimes looked at me with a strange intent gaze and I knew I had to make some explanation about the sudden appearance of a spy in our midst.

We were sitting in the slant of the sun in the farmhouse kitchen when I tried to explain. 'I found that woman in the top field, making for the farmhouse.' I said.

'That's half a mile from here, what were you doing wandering about like that?' he asked.

'Come and see.'

I led him to the spot where the chicken still hung dried-out and half eaten by some nocturnal creature. 'I was going to cook for Michael –' I pointed to the chicken – 'and then she appeared. She made me take her to the farmhouse and give her food.'

'Did you see anything with her, any signs of how she got here, any suitcase, anything?'

I shook my head, avoiding a direct lie. 'I think she'd been walking a long way, she seemed exhausted but she was so big and strong I was half afraid of her.' That much at least was the truth.

'What language did she speak?'

'German,' I said at once.

Michael came into the room just then and put his arm around me.

'You don't think Meryl was harbouring this woman voluntarily do you father? After all the spy nearly killed her.'

Herr Euler regarded me for a moment, taking me for being a bit slow. He shook his head, convinced by my story.

'It's a pity you didn't see which direction she came from, we might have found some useful information and some equipment. She must have been dropped by plane, that's what usually happens.'

'I was so busy trying to catch the chicken I didn't notice anything till she was there beside me.'

'Strange she should come here when you were at home,' he said.

'Who would know I'd be here?' I asked. 'In any case, I was expecting Michael to join me, remember?'

He nodded, accepting the sense of this. He clicked his heels. 'I must go, my car is outside, my driver is patiently waiting for me. Take care, daughter-in-law. Take great care.'

When Herr Euler's car drove away I looked at Michael and shrugged. 'How could I know she was coming?' I decided to confide in him. 'She was Welsh you know. Spying for our side.' I began to cry and Michael hugged me and kissed me. 'And remember if I hadn't come in when I did she would have killed you.'

He scooped me in his arms and as I pressed my lips to his, he kicked open the door and carried me upstairs to bed.

Forty-Three

'I can't believe my sister is working for the Germans.' Hari had been welcomed back warmly by the colonel. He was sick but he was staying on, at least for a few days, while he brought her up to date with what had been happening.

'She's married to a German, that says it all doesn't it?' The colonel was pale, his lines graved deeper into his face. He needed to retire; he knew it and Hari knew it.

'But Michael lived here in Wales from the time he was ten,' Hari protested. 'He wouldn't work for the Germans even though . . .' she broke off. How did she know what Michael would do now he was in the Fatherland? He had married Meryl, hadn't he, after promising himself to her?

'We've had intelligence —' the colonel looked at her shrewdly — 'that Michael Euler is flying German planes against us. What more proof do you want?'

Hari put her head in her hands. The colonel's voice was hard. 'Face up to facts, girl, they are both traitors to this country and your job is to pull in any messages you can to try and trap them.'

Hari lifted her hand. 'I know.' She took a deep breath. 'You go home now, Colonel Edwards, you look very tired.'

'I am very tired. Sure you can manage?'

'I can manage.' She looked up as he stumbled to his feet. 'And you can trust me, I give you my word.'

'If I didn't know that I wouldn't be handing over to you.'

He left the office and Hari put on the headphones. She thought of her friends in Bletchley Park and wished she was there with them. A voice came over the air; she caught just enough German to take in the message. Quickly she wrote it down. As soon as her shift was over she would have to send any important messages to the hall in case they had been missed by the radio officers there. And she would ask the girls to listen out to any unusual coding from a strange 'fist' as they called the mark of the individual radio operator. Her sister maybe.

A wave of nostalgia washed over her, she wished she was back in the Park with all her cheerful friends; at night in the boarding house they'd been like schoolgirls, eating at midnight, putting beetroot juice on their lips in the evenings when they went out dancing, rubbing cheeks to make them red; it had all been such fun. Now that she was back home she had time to think about Michael and her sister, their betrayal of trust, and she felt nothing would ever be right again.

She didn't feel like going straight home after work so she called on Kate. Little Teddy was crying, stumbling round the kitchen on plump legs. Hilda was slumped in a chair looking old and drained.

'Kate, how are things?' Hari sat close to Kate and held her hand. 'How are you feeling, baby moving yet?'

'Not yet,' Kate said softly. 'I hope it never moves. I don't want it, Eddie doesn't want it, only Stephen wants this child.' She put her hands over her sightless eyes.

'We saw Stephen, he wants to keep in touch. He's doing well, car, everything, but he sounds so sad. Oh what a horrible mess my life is. Why did I give in to the men, let them do, well . . . you know.'

'You were young, you only wanted to help and comfort the boys because that's all they were before the war got them, boys!' Hari squeezed Kate's hands.

'Don't think of the baby as a burden, it's your child remember, yours, you'll love it when it comes.'

'I hope to God and all the saints you're right, Hari, because I don't love it now, that's for sure.'

Hilda stirred herself from her half daze. 'I'll put the kettle on.' She rested her hand for a moment on Kate's shoulder. 'You can't help what the Good Lord chose for us, girl, this baby was meant to be, you can't change it and I for one will love it whatever it is.'

Hari marvelled at Hilda's forbearance: a child was coming into her world, into her home and she was accepting it with good grace. She seemed to read Hari's thoughts.

'Stephen is a good lad. He worked and kept us all while Eddie was missing; he generously kept my Eddie's son, gave him his name, fed and watered the babe; we owe him a debt for that and don't you forget it, any of you.'

'She's right,' Kate said, 'I'm a horrible pig, I must pull myself together and stop feeling sorry for myself.'

Hari hugged her and kissed her soft cheek. 'Night, dear Kate, I'd best get home, if I still have a home after the air raid this afternoon.'

Kate held on to her hand. 'Any news?'

Hari knew what she meant.

'They're both safe,' she said gently. 'That's all I know.' How could she tell Kate how her sister was betraying her country?

She walked home in the darkness, instinct leading her through the familiar streets towards her house. Good thing she hadn't let it yet or she would be homeless. She felt her way inside, into the passage and shone her torch into the darkness. She closed the door on the world and followed the beam of light towards the stairs. She paused; should she make some tea, should she light the fire and stay up and read a book or listen to the gramophone?

She shone the beam of light up the stairs and crawled fully dressed into bed too tired to light the fires. Her stomach heaved as she thought of Michael lying with Meryl, making sweet love to her.

Her heart turned over. How could she still love him now after all he'd done to her? And yet she did, she loved him with all her heart and soul. And now, now he was married, to her sister, and he was nothing more than a traitor to her beloved country. Hari didn't know what upset her most, Michael's betrayal of their country or the betrayal of her love.

Forty-Four

I didn't think I could love Michael any more than I already did but once we were lovers I realized what closeness really was. He possessed me and I possessed him. He became part of me, one flesh, and at last I knew what that meant. And if I felt a pang of guilt and pity for my sister it soon passed, it was a different life now, a different world.

When he was leaving the farmhouse to return to his squadron he held me close. I breathed him in, the smell of him, the faint scent of the grass and the flowers and the fresh air. And beneath it all the musk, the scent of love and of passion – even as he pressed me close I could feel his arousal.

'Goodbye, *Liebling*.' It was our habit now to speak only German; it would be too easy to be caught out. He held me a moment longer and then he left. I could hear the rumble of his motorbike engine and I stood quite still until it was silent again.

I would not let myself cry; this was a dangerous world, an enemy world, in spite of the friends I'd made. I had a duty to my own country, to Britain. I had a duty to myself as well. I couldn't let myself be seduced by the countryside, the fondness I was beginning to feel for my 'father-in-law' Herr Euler, who had done all he could to help me. To my colleagues at work, all of whom were human beings and had their own problems. Even Frau Hoffman, for all her hardness, was just being patriotic.

I could not understand her attitude though, to Herr Hitler; she seemed to worship him as though he was a messiah saving the world; to me he was doing his best to destroy it.

I poured a glass of wine from the bottle Michael had brought me and smoothed the glass gently, lovingly, as though it was his skin. I sat for a good hour watching as the sunlight moved in different shades and patterns, the light lower in the sky as evening drew closer. I had never been so happy and then the euphoria faded as I knew that soon I would go out to the field where I killed the chicken and try another one. I shuddered at the thought but it was something I would have to get used to if I wanted to stay strong, able to serve my country.

I lingered until it was almost dark and then I made my way to the spot where I had killed the bird and where I had met the woman who tried to kill me and my loved ones. I caught a chicken with ease this time and killed it almost cold-bloodedly, it was nothing after what had happened with Rhiannon.

Later, I found the spot in the shrubbery where I had hidden the case. I brushed away the leaves and earth and hurried back to the farmhouse. The case was locked. I broke it open with a knife and there inside was my prize: a fully functioning radio. I hadn't dared show it to Michael as I knew he would have been afraid for me.

I examined the set minutely and I realized then I'd have had little chance of building one like this. It had metal valves and when I switched it on it sprang to life. I heard a German voice gabbling,

talking quickly, excitedly. I pressed the earphones close and turned
pale with excitement and fear. Something big was going to happen
– and soon.

I listened for a while, took down the coded message and tried
to work it out. The shadows were filling the room, I had only the
light from the fire but as the words danced in my eyes and became
legible I sighed with relief; I'd made out the code. Mussolini had
been arrested – not of great import to the war but at least decoding
the message was practice for me.

I went back to work the next day and was greeted by my friends
with such warmth and companionship it was hard to remember
that these people were the enemy. But no, the enemy were soldiers
with bayonets and bombs. I thought of Michael in a plane, perhaps
over Wales, and tears burned my eyes.

That night I went to the pictures and in the middle of the
programme was a short film about how well Germany was doing
in the war against Britain. A powerful German voice emphasized
how many planes were in the sky. I saw tanks with soldiers smiling
and waving and it seemed an Oder bridgehead had been breached
but I didn't know what that meant.

I went home on my bike and the long ride wearied me. I was
missing Michael so much it was like toothache. I climbed into bed
too tired even to touch the radio and fell instantly to sleep.

When I arrived in the radio room the next day I was greeted with
silence. For a moment I thought I'd been caught out. I was so
frightened I nearly forgot to speak German, nearly but not quite.
'What's wrong?'

'We had to disarm the Italians,' Frau Hoffman said, 'we've seized
military control of Italy and our forces have rescued Mussolini. We
will punish the enemy, we will beat them into the ground, their
humiliation will be final and death will follow for those who dare
to oppose the righteous regime of Herr Hitler.'

I held my breath – this information could be of use to my
countrymen. I would have to send a message home that night.

It was easier said than done. I decided I would call Bridgend,
the only radio operation I was familiar with. Perhaps my sister
would take the message. Would she know it was from me? Perhaps
better not.

I eventually remembered the sort of code she and the colonel used and tapped out a message hesitantly over to what I imagined must be a Bletchley Park receiver, expecting loud boots at the door and a pistol to my head at any minute. There was some response, which I didn't understand, and I sent the message again more confident with the Morse this time and then closed down the machine and packed it away.

Forty-Five

Hari sat beside the hospital bed staring out of the window afraid to look at Colonel Edwards' grey face. He was sick, gravely sick. He had no relatives and he had wanted her beside him when his moment came.

Outside, the hospital blocks staggered downwards to a dip in the hillside. Old House Lodge had once been a hospital only for those unfortunate people afflicted with infectious diseases, but now it was wartime it had been turned into a hospital for the sick and wounded from the services.

The colonel opened his eyes. 'Hari,' he said softly, 'don't grieve, I've had my day and I want to say I love you, my dear. I would like to add, as a daughter, but it wouldn't be true. I love you as a man loves a woman; that's why I sent you away you know, to Bletchley.'

Hari rubbed his hand. 'I know,' she said. 'I know, David.' It was the first time she'd spoken his Christian name and he smiled beautifully.

'You're a good lady, Angharad Jones, and I want you to have all the happiness in the world.' He touched her cheek. 'You're just a young slip of a girl, you'll meet the man who loves you and you will love him and I know you are going to be very happy one day.'

'I have already met the man I love,' Hari said painfully. 'And he's just not meant for me.'

'My dear Hari.' There were tears in the colonel's eyes and, too late, Hari realized he'd misunderstood. He kissed her hand. 'You've made me the happiest man in the world dear, dear little Hari.' He closed his eyes and with her hand against his lips, he died, softly.

Hari began to cry, tears for him, but also tears that she knew were self-pity. The nurse touched her on the shoulder. 'I'm sorry about your father, dear, or is he your granddad? He had a good life and you saw him happily on his way. God bless ye and look after ye, not many are there for their loved ones at the end.'

Hari stumbled out into the night and sagged against the railings fronting the lodge. She had a sister and a father and neither of them were there for her when she needed them. Hari slid to the ground and began to cry. Around her the tang of autumn sharpened the air, the leaves, gold and bronze in the sun, looked sullen and dull in the evening light.

Overhead, the clouds cleared. Through the chill air came the faint drone of planes. The sound intensified, filling the world. Hari ran instinctively for shelter. Bullets hailed down as though searching for her. They spat on the ground at her heels. She dived for the sparse cover of the bushes on the outskirts of the lodge and threw herself flat, the smell of earth in her nostrils and the tears she was still shedding sinking into the ground.

Was that Michael up there in one of the bombers? Would he fly over Carmarthen as well as Swansea and bomb the farm and even his mother into oblivion?

And then the lodge itself took a direct hit. The walls were gone, huge chunks of masonry flew like massive missives towards her. One whole wall landed within inches of where she lay; flames shot into the darkening sky, licking at the night, illuminating the surrounding area.

Hari stayed on the ground feeling leaves crackle against her cheeks as she turned her head to look at the devastation that was occurring all around her. The bombers, their targets lit and exposed by the flames from the old hospital buildings, dropped more bombs, easily hitting the surrounding houses. The whole world seemed to be in flames. Hell had come for her before she was even dead.

Eventually, the bombers droned away, their task complete. Hari sat up and looked at the still-burning lodge, the funeral pyre for all those inside. Hari cried for Colonel Edwards but was glad that he had died before suffering the indignity of being blown to death by the Luftwaffe.

Eventually, she staggered to her feet and looked into the basin of Swansea Bay. A ship that was waiting for the incoming tide was on fire. Flares of flames like bonfires showed where houses had been hit. Tiny figures ran about the devastated streets like ants. She waved her fists to the sky in a useless gesture of anger.

Hari began to walk down the hill, making her way back to the town. If she was lucky her house would still be standing and she would lie in her own bed and sleep all the pain away.

As she rounded the corner she saw her house was there, solid and welcoming and she closed the door on the carnage outside with a sigh of resignation and relief.

The talk at Bridgend the next day revolved around Colonel Edwards. Hari was asked many times how he had died. She told them briefly. 'He passed away peacefully before the bombing.' And silently she thanked God it was true.

She went to her radio at last but there was nothing coming through. She sat with her head in her hands until, at last, she heard the tap of the machine.

The message was being passed on from Bletchley Park; she could tell it was passed on by Babs. After the official code and brief, precise message, the tapping became faltering, the sender clearly inexperienced. Hari took down the coded message with difficulty, the transmission was intermittent and then unbelievably she recognized some words not in code but in Welsh. Her own name, Angharad, the word for darling, *cariad*, and 'it's me, sis. Black Opal.' And the radio went dead.

Forty-Six

The next day I went out into the fields and tried to figure out the radio, wishing there was a book of instructions with it, but of course any official spy would have been properly trained on its use. I had finally worked out that the big dial was the frequency finder. God knows how I had managed to send a message at all I was so ignorant. All I could hope was that someone, hopefully not the Germans, would have picked it up. I didn't know how useful the information would be and, in any case, perhaps some real spy had sent the message using the transceiver properly.

I had to hide the case again so I closed it securely and wrapped it in a stiff cotton pillowcase and an old mackintosh, so big it must be Herr Euler's, and then carried the radio out further into the field and dug a pit. I went back to the farmhouse then to cook myself some lunch.

I had the usual eggs and bread and, luxury, a bit of chicken, and sat outside to eat my meal in the quiet of the countryside. I wished Jessie was here to cook with her usual efficiency and chatter at the same time. I was lonely. But tomorrow I would be back at work, among my colleagues, my friends, if I was to be truthful. Friends and enemies – how do you distinguish them?

The silence was suddenly broken by the sound of cars driving up outside the farmhouse. I got up wondering, with a beating heart, if Michael was home.

The man who stepped out of the car was a stranger; he stood there shoulders hunched to break down any resistance and stared at me suspiciously.

'I am Frau Euler,' I said, 'what are you doing here if I may ask?' It paid to be polite to big hard men in SS uniform.

'I am Von Kestle. I have to search your house. Anyone else here?'

I shook my head. 'My husband is in the skies somewhere bombing the enemy.' I hoped that he was dropping his bombs in the sea. 'And my father-in-law Herr Euler is no doubt busy working for the fatherland in his office in Hamburg.'

The man paused, taken aback, and then he clicked his heels. 'Forgive the intrusion Frau Euler,' he said quickly, 'but we have reports of enemy activity in the area, we have to search.'

'There was a spy here some time ago but Herr Euler got rid of her,' I said quickly.

'They work together these traitors,' the man said sternly. 'There is usually a nest of them – like vipers. Now, I'd like to come inside, Frau Euler.'

I stepped back hurriedly and waved my arm. 'Please come in, you are welcome to search my house if only for my own safety. Can I fetch you any refreshments?'

'*Nein! Danke.*'

I moved away and sat at the kitchen table. I didn't have to try to look afraid. I was nearly wetting my knickers as I'd done when I was a thirteen-year-old girl being evacuated to the country. What a lot had happened to me since those days when all I had to fight was the bullying of Georgie Porgy Dixon.

I knew the case was not in the house but it was not very well hidden either. I had been too careless; I would have to make better arrangements in the future – if I was allowed any future. I knew I would be arrested or even shot if I could be tied in somehow to the radio set.

Eventually the men went outside and searched the chicken coup and the broken-down barn. I heard them swish at the bushes with their guns and cringed with fear until they went away defeated with just a salute in my direction.

I would have to go further away to send any more signals as I couldn't risk being anywhere near the farmhouse again. I hadn't thought they could track the signal so easily.

I sat shivering for most of the evening trying to work out the safest way to get messages home should I need to. The difficult thing would be finding the correct frequency. I knew from the time I'd spent in Hari's office that it was changed every day.

Anyway, there was no news to send at the moment, nothing that was of any importance. When there was, then I'd tackle the problem.

I dug up the case early in the morning and fitted the parts into a large biscuit tin. Then I made a bonfire of the paperwork from inside the case, poor Rhiannon wouldn't need it now. I wrapped the case in newspaper and hid it under a pile of horse manure.

A shopping bag tied to the handles of my bike hid the tin. I'd taped paper to the lid and printed 'Sanitary Goods' on the lid. I couldn't think of anything else to do.

The next morning, I took the shopping bag into the building where I worked. The security man took a brief look inside and, embarrassed at the writing on the tin, handed the bag back to me. I hung up my coat and stuffed my scarf into my pocket. It all looked very innocent.

I put the tin in my desk drawer for now; later, I would find a cupboard where I could hide it. In the event that the radio was found, I couldn't be blamed any more than anyone else in the building.

I worked hard through the day and listened for anything out of the ordinary to come through my earphones. I sent the usual signals, giving information to airmen or the navy vessels off shore at Antwerp. Mundane tasks that made up my day.

When I arrived home at the farmhouse, there were cars every-where and men in uniform digging in the shrubbery. I caught sight of Von Kestle and he came towards me, his huge booted feet covering the ground swiftly.

'We have found evidence of the ground being tampered with,' he said. 'Somebody was there, digging.'

I put my hand to my mouth. 'Oh my God!'

'You know nothing of this?'

'How could I? I have been at work in my Hamburg office all day,' I said.

'The signal that was picked up twenty-four hours ago was from here, on this farm.'

'I told you,' I said. 'Herr Euler found a woman here, a spy, he dealt with her. Whatever she left behind has got nothing to do with the Euler family, I give you my word on it.'

After a moment the man nodded. 'I understand. But we will have to keep observing this area, just in case.'

I wasn't sure he believed me but without evidence there was nothing he could do. The soldiers went away and I drank some tea, telling myself I wasn't cut out to be a spy. I didn't like taking risks but there were certain things that had to be done for the sake of my country.

I went to bed early and lay awake thinking of the biscuit tin in my drawer at the office and I knew I would have to find some-where to hide it before the SS began looking at my life too closely.

Forty-Seven

Stephen took Kate's hand as she felt her way through the gate of the park. 'Come and sit down,' he said gently.

They had sat there together before in very different circum-stances. 'I'm well Stephen,' she said. 'There's no need to worry about me.'

'And the baby?'

Kate was a long time answering. Her baby, *their* baby, had been born two weeks ago, a small, weakly boy.

'Kate?'

'He's not very well.'

'I must come to see him.'

'But Eddie.'

'Damn Eddie!' He gripped her hand tightly. 'I'm the father, Kate, I have a right to see my little son.'

Kate hung her head. He was right of course and Eddie should understand, being a father himself. 'All right.'

'Come on, I'll take you in the car.' Stephen put a hand under her elbow and urged her to her feet.

'We'll walk,' Kate said firmly, 'the last thing I want is the neighbours talking about your big posh car stopping outside our house.'

It was a fine autumn day and Hilda had just hung sheets on the line in the back garden. Kate could hear the snap of the sheets in the wind. 'Adam has been sick again,' she said.

Kate's heart sank. The baby, born three weeks too early, had been sickly from the start. 'I hoped he was growing out of that by now.' Kate was weary, there was so much to think about, to worry about, and now Stephen was making demands, complicating matters even more for her.

'Can I pick him up?' Kate heard him move the covers from Adam's crib.

'Carefully then,' she said, 'we don't want him to be sick again, do we?' The chair creaked and Kate knew that Stephen had seated himself with the little baby in his arms. Suddenly Kate felt very ill. She leaned back against her chair and tried not to think.

The door opened and she could smell the scent of her husband. She heard the pause as Eddie took in the scene.

'Eddie.' She tried to stand but then she was falling, falling into a deep well and, thankfully, she let herself fall.

She was in bed, in hospital. She recognized the sounds from when she'd been in before. The rustle of starched aprons, the slap, slap of soft-soled shoes on the floor and the all-pervading, unmistakable smell of cleaning fluid.

'What's wrong with me?' Her voice was thin, weak.

'It's all right, dear.' A cool hand touched her forehead. 'You've had an operation, that's all. You're going to be just fine.'

'An operation – what sort of operation?'

'You've had a hysterectomy. Your abdomen had split open, scars broken down – there were complications – but you've come through it very well, you'll be fit again in a few weeks.' The hand was removed, the sound of feet dying away, and Kate struggled to come to terms with what she'd been told.

There had been a danger all along that her old scars would open when the baby was born but that hadn't happened. Why now?

She heard footsteps approaching once more. Her arm was lifted and a sharp prick of a needle pierced her arm.

'There, rest now, have a good sleep and when you wake your loved ones will be here to see you.'

'Loved ones . . . am I going to die then?'

'There was no answer, the nurse had gone away and Kate was left alone to wonder if she would live to rear her firstborn and her poor, sickly Adam.

Forty-Eight

Hari drew up outside the farmhouse and Jessie appeared in the doorway, her brow furrowed but a hopeful smile on her face.

'Any news, Hari?' Her tone was eager. 'Come in, *cariad*, come in and sit down.' Hari sat in the living room, which was a mess. Dust had built up like clouds on the furniture and Jessie was looking gaunt and old. She coughed incessantly.

'I've heard from Meryl in a roundabout sort of way,' Hari said. 'A message over air waves, a bit of Welsh, my name.' She could say nothing more; the rest of the message was secret and might not even be correct.

'And Michael?'

'I don't know.' Hari's voice was low with misery. 'I assume he's alive or Meryl would have found a way to let me know. But, and it's a big but, he's either in prison or on active service for the Germans.'

Jessie sighed heavily. 'His father would have influence. I'm sure he'll look after Michael. I'll make us a cup of tea.'

Jessie's answer to every crisis was a cup of tea. She was very affected by her son's disappearance, her footsteps faltering as she made her way to the kitchen.

Hari followed her. The kitchen was in a terrible state and Hari took off her coat and washed the accumulation of dishes. Jessie made a faint protest but there was a look of relief on her face as Hari brushed up the debris on the kitchen floor.

Hari was silent for a long time but as she put away the brush she looked at Jessie.

'I need your help,' she said.

Jessie's face brightened. 'Anything girl, you've been so good to me since . . . well, you know.'

'I want you to come and stay for a few weeks,' she said. 'Father is home for a break, he'll be all alone while I'm at work and he's not very good on his one leg.'

It wasn't true; her father was well able to look after himself. Jessie obviously wasn't, not just now.

'Leave the farm? Oh, I don't know, Hari, what about the cattle?'

'I'm sure the man on the next farm would take them in, there's so few of them now, anyway.' She touched Jessie's arm. 'It would only be for a short while, in any case, and I do need your help, really I do.'

'When?' Jessie asked.

'Father's coming home Monday, what if I come for you next Sunday, would that suit you?'

'*Duw*, I suppose so. It's only for a while though, mind.'

'I know.' Hari smiled with relief. 'I'll expect a nice cooked meal for Father and me when I come home from the factory, though.'

'So long as we put our rations together it will be all right. Could I bring a few chucks with me for eggs?'

'We could manage chickens in the garden, I suppose,' Hari said. 'Just so long as you don't bring a pig for bacon as well.'

Hari had the satisfaction of knowing the house looked tidier when she left and Jessie was busy washing clothes to bring to Swansea with her. A spell with company might just be what Jessie needed; she was all alone in that deserted farmhouse, alone and afraid.

As she drove along the farm road towards the main thorough-fare for Swansea, a figure suddenly stepped out in front of her car. She pulled up and saw George Dixon wave his arms at her frantically.

'Help me, miss – it's my mother, she's taken really bad. I don't know what to do; I don't know how long she's been sick. I've just come home on leave, see?'

George was in army uniform, he was a junior officer, commissioned no less. Mrs Dixon must be well connected. 'Get in.'

Hari drove to the Dixon Farm and hurried across the yard into the house. Mrs Dixon was in bed; it was clear she had a fever. Her face was flushed, almost cyanosed, her eyes were puffy and she had strange red marks on her skin.

'I've called the doctor,' George said. 'I ran to the post office in the village and used their phone but so far there's no sign of anyone coming.'

'She is very ill.' Hari looked at her watch. 'If the doctor doesn't come soon we'll take her to the hospital.'

As she finished speaking the doctor came plodding up the stairs. He was very old with a white moustache and a shock of white hair under his hat.

'Doctor Merriman.' He nodded briefly to Hari and went straight to the bed. After a moment he shook his head. 'I'm too late,' he said. 'Mrs Dixon is dying, she's had scarlet fever for at least a week. I'm sorry.'

'How long?' George's voice was hoarse.

'You'll be lucky, son, if she lasts the night. I'll give her something to ease her and then all you can do is sit with her, talk to her gently, help her slip away peacefully. I'm sorry.' He repeated helplessly, 'It's just too late to help her.'

'If only I'd been here,' George said angrily. 'This bastard war.' He put his head in his hands and wept.

Forty-Nine

I became accustomed to the routine of going to work on the radio section in the big, sprawling building that stood out like a landmark on the flat countryside near Hamburg. I became so used to speaking German that sometimes, even in my thoughts, I used German words.

The girls around me became my firm friends, especially the flirtatious Eva, a fluffy blonde girl with a beautiful face and a clinical, clever brain. Even Frau Hoffman had warmed enough to smile occasionally. As one of the girls remarked, 'She must be in love.'

And yet sometimes, feeling absurdly like a traitor to Germany, I would take my box of 'sanitary products' with me into the fields as far away from my home and my workplace as my bike would take me and send any potentially useful pieces of information back, I hoped, to Hari in Bridgend.

The winter of 1944 was long, spring seemed determined not to come. I spent my evenings mostly alone in the farmhouse, practising codes on pieces of paper.

One night, I was almost sleeping in my chair with the fire dying in the hearth when I heard the sound of a car outside. I sat up; it must be Herr Euler, who sometimes made a call home at odd times. I wondered if it was to check up on me but so far he'd caught me doing no more than reading or writing endless letters to Michael that he probably seldom received.

The door was opened by a lady driver. She stared at me and I stared back, wondering what the heck was going on now; Herr Euler had no time for lady drivers.

And then my mouth split from ear to ear as Michael came hopping into the room on crutches. He looked well in spite of the bandaged foot and his smile matched mine when he saw me.

'*Liebling!*' I went forward to meet him, elbowing aside the pretty lady driver jealously. 'Thank you for your help but I will take charge of my husband from now on,' I said pointedly.

'Give the lady a cup of tea,' Michael said, making an eye gesture at me, showing he'd read my feelings well. 'She's to meet her fiancé later but she surely has time for some refreshment.'

Fuming, I made the tea and then I sat as close to Michael as I could get in view of the fact his crutches were poking into my legs. 'What's happened my love?' I touched his hair with wifely concern. He grinned, well aware of my jealousy.

'I crash-landed; luckily I made it back to the airport but the Focke's undercarriage came off and a bit of twisted metal caught my ankle. It's nothing; a couple of stitches fixed it up and the plane's not too badly damaged.'

'A nasty gash though,' the driver said knowingly. I gave her a piercing glance. 'Well, thank you for driving my husband home I expect you'll want to be on your way.'

She hastily finished her tea and smiled at Michael. 'Take care sir, and good luck.' She glanced at me defiantly as she rested her hand on Michael's shoulder. I resisted the urge to kick her out of the house.

'Goodbye.' I shut the door before she got to her car. 'Lights,' I said to Michael, and he laughed.

'Green ones in your eyes?'

'Are you saying I'm jealous?'

'I am.'

'Well, what do you expect arriving home with a fluffy blonde? She was very familiar with you considering she has a fiancé.'

'War has a strange effect on people.'

'Not strange enough for you to flirt with her.'

He caught me in his arms and placed me on his knee. 'Mind my ankle,' he said and kissed me.

It was wonderful to wake in the morning and see Michael asleep beside me. He was so dear, so handsome, so mine – at least for now.

He opened his blue eyes fringed by long lashes and smiled his sweet smile. I turned into his warm body and he put his arms around me. 'I do love you,' I said softly. He said nothing though he planted a kiss on my forehead. 'At least I've got you for a little while,' I said, hoping he would say something like 'forever' but he did not speak at all and I wondered if I would ever know the truth of his feeling for me. Did he still love Hari or did he love me more now? I was too afraid to ask.

At first he did not make love to me and I was afraid it was over, that his conscience had stricken him when he thought of betraying my sister. But being together in a bed every night breaks down barriers and one night, I clung to him and deliberately pressed my full breasts against him.

I felt him respond; he groaned and then he was kissing my shoulders, my breasts, taking my hard nipple into his hot mouth. Was it just the lust of a man too long without a woman, facing death every time he took to the skies? I didn't care, he was here and for now we were together, really together and nothing else mattered.

Fifty

Hari found herself with a house full of people: Jessie took charge of the kitchen and of Hari's father – who liked the attention – and tried her best with George Dixon, who sat around like a lost soul. Hari's small house seemed to bulge at the seams and yet soon, the disparate group of people became like a family.

Hari went into the small kitchen that was filled with the warmth of the fire and steamy with pots of vegetables boiling on the gas stove. 'Jessie, how are you managing with all this work?'

'It's the breath of life to me.' Jessie was serious. 'I was dying a slow death in that farmhouse with no one to look after.'

She did look better, more alive, there was a light back in her pale blue eyes and her mouth turned up in a smile. 'I feel in my gut that Michael is safe and you know Meryl is alive. She's a fine, honest girl, whatever she's doing it will be for the good of her country, mark my words.'

'I know.' Hari touched Jessie's arm. 'But why did they marry, Jessie? Michael said he loved me, he . . .' Embarrassed, she stopped speaking.

'They are meant for each other,' Jessie said. 'From the moment I saw them together I knew that much about them. They're like two sides of the same coin. As for love –' she shrugged – 'I'm afraid you'll learn that a man says he's in love, perhaps even *believes* he's in love, when he wants to bed a woman. They don't mean it, Hari, it's just their way. I'm sorry but you might as well learn that now as later.'

It was a long speech for Jessie to make and Hari knew she meant well but Michael was not the type to be ruled by the urges of his body. He was an honourable man. And yet he'd married her sister, hadn't he?

Her mind kept running round the problem, eating away at it, trying to make sense of it. He'd meant it when he said he loved her, she was sure of it. Wasn't she? And yet she woke each morning to a sense of foreboding, as if some tragedy had occurred, and then she realized it had. Michael was lost to her forever, there was no hope for her, he was married to Meryl and even if they all survived this awful war, what future was there for them?

Spring came and turned into summer and Hari had a few small messages from 'Black Opal'. Nothing really of note but each was like a knife wound, fear tangled her entrails each time a message came because she might read that Michael was dead. Hari was never able to respond and the signal was soon lost, possibly swept away by the Bletchley Park's impressive might. Worse, she could imagine Meryl packing everything quickly away in danger of being shot. Every time she sent a message she was risking discovery by the Germans.

After the death of the colonel Hari was put in charge of the small radio section at the munitions factory. She was sometimes lonely without the gruff presence of the old man and heavy with the responsibility that had settled upon her shoulders, but all she could do was her best, or so she told herself.

'I'm in late tonight,' she said out loud. She interrupted her father, who was reading something from the paper to Jessie who, face alight, was listening to him intently.

He looked up and blew Hari a kiss. 'Try and get your head down if only for an hour or two, you're looking tired these days, darling girl.' He paused. 'I'll be off your hands Monday, I have to get back to London. I have work to do after all.'

Jessie's face stiffened, but she said nothing. Hari said it for her.

'Oh Dad, we're all going to miss you very much.' Jessie looked silently down at her hands.

That night, Hari drove to Bridgend through the darkened roads and looked up at the sky wondering what on earth was going on in the moonlight beauty of the night. Was Michael coming over to bomb Wales and England tonight? Could he possibly be a traitor to his country as well as to her? The questions raced mercilessly through her mind.

She sat in her office with hardly anything to do. The radio tapped intermittently but nothing important came through. It was about twelve midnight when she heard the sound of German planes overhead. She went outside and looked up at the sky but she could see nothing through the low cloud that always hung in the dip of Bridgend.

She saw one of the girls from the factory come out on to the roof; Hari knew it was the usual practice for one of the girls to look out for planes overhead and caution the workers to stop all activities though no one took any notice anyway.

Hari put her hand over her brows and tried to see through the darkness but it was just the hum of engines she heard. She caught a flash of light at the corner of her eye and saw that the girl on the roof was holding a torch that sent a pool of light over herself and the roof. Hari hurried upstairs to the roof.

'Doreen, put that light out, you fool!' It was the girl who'd tried to get Kate to abort her baby. 'Doreen, stop shining that light! Put it out!'

A bomber swooped low over the buildings and, with a cry, Doreen dropped the torch, teetered on the edge of the roof and slowly, like a rag doll fell into the darkness. At the sound of the screams, shadowy figures rushed from the buildings. The planes roared away as if intent on other business and Hari surmised the airmen had not seen anything of the small light from Doreen's torch.

She hurried back down the stairs; outside a crowd had gathered round the crumpled girl.

'Hari —' blood trickled from her mouth — 'I'm dying. Come closer to me.'

Hari was on her knees in an instant, regardless of the hard earth scratching her legs.

'In my house, top drawer, bedroom cabinet, money.' Doreen coughed on her own blood. 'My ill-gotten gains.' She drew a ragged breath and a gush of blood poured down her chin.

'Use it, Hari, to bury me, decent, mind, and may God forgive me for my sins.' Doreen fell back against the ground, her eyes staring unseeing up at the skies.

'Bloody war!' one of the girls cried, 'and bloody, bloody Germans.' Violet waved her fists at the cloudy sky but there was no sound except for the crying of Doreen's friends.

Fifty-One

It was sunny when I woke, the spring breeze wafting gently into the bedroom. I sighed and snuggled down under the blankets again. It was the weekend – no work – and I had two whole days free to myself. I indulged in sweet memories of Michael holding me close, loving me, possessing me, and the moment's dreaming was delicious.

After breakfast I went out to the barn and drove out the old jeep I'd found there with a screech of the brakes. The chickens scattered like so many fussy hens, which of course they were.

With the help of one of Herr Euler's men I'd worked on the jeep and made it presentable. The engine was good and once the mud and mulch were wiped away and all the relevant parts oiled and cosseted the thing was quite presentable.

Herr Euler approved and even presented me with some petrol. He was glad I had something to do in my spare time.

I took my jeep for a run into the country. I had the radio tucked away in a battered old picnic basket hidden under plates and cloths but if ever I was stopped, it would easily be discovered and then I'd be for it.

But at least now I was free to drive miles from the farmhouse and I didn't feel so vulnerable when I needed to make contact with home. I stopped near a small duck pond and left the jeep. The grass was lush and warm and I sat down and ate my sandwiches of fresh bread and jam. I could have murdered a cup of tea but I had to make do with a bottle of home-made dandelion and burdock pop.

I lay back and closed my eyes and felt the warm May sun on my face. I must have dozed because someone was nudging me and I sat up anxiously. The figure was outlined against the sun; all I could see was a hat and a stick and the bent shoulders of an old man.

'What is it?' I demanded in German. He sat down beside me with difficulty and held out his hand towards the bottle of pop.

'We have to talk.' He spoke in French and I had a job understanding him. Also I was deeply suspicious and afraid.

'Speak German?' I said in my stuttering French. He shook his head.

'A little only.'

'Frau Euler, I have been watching you,' he said. 'You go out, you stop, you fiddle, you tap, tap, you go home. You spy I think.'

I froze.

'Your husband's mother was English.'

'No!' This man was dangerous. He was old and rambling, he looked as though he hadn't washed all winter.

'Go away,' I said harshly in strong German, 'you are mad.' I made a sign with my finger to my head and he laughed and then I noticed his teeth. They were straight and clean; this was no old tramp. I leaned forward and tugged his beard. It didn't move but grey grease came away on to my fingers. It smelt like goose grease.

'Who are you?' I demanded in German.

He was serious then, his face grave. 'Tell me, Frau Euler, why do you spy when you are a German lady? Is it because you come from somewhere else: Ireland, Britain – Wales, perhaps?'

I shook my head. I didn't speak; I had no idea what to say. He obviously had worked for some time finding out about me.

'I watched you from the time you were shipwrecked and my little boat followed the submarine and saw you landed at Saint Nazaire. One day you had a big round belly and then you were a slim, young, married woman. Who wouldn't be suspicious?'

'What has any of it got to do with you?' I still spoke German, cautious, wanting only to run away back to the farmhouse.

He delved into his pocket and brought out some papers. 'I could be tortured and shot if I was found with these.' He handed them to me.

The papers told me he was English, a high-up in the SOE – Special Operatives Executive; an agent. I handed them back.

'Papers can be forged,' I said.

'You should know.' He spoke in excellent English then. 'You are not Frau Euler but Miss Meryl Jones, isn't that so?' At least in this he was wrong, I *was* married – to Michael – and this at least gave me a great deal of courage.

'You are not so knowledgeable as you think you are.' My tone was scathing.

'We've been watching you closely,' he said. 'You have experience of codes and you have worked at the great Bletchley Park. We were going to train you up to join us but you pre-empted us and arrived in Germany in your own eccentric way and you have made an excellent cover for yourself if I may say so.'

'I am Frau Euler and I have never worked at Bletchley Park, you are confusing me with someone else.' I nearly said 'my sister' but that would have given me away at once. I still refused to speak English.

'I would advise you to be more careful with the radio equipment – that's the only concern I have – it could blow your cover. Once you were almost caught. Rhiannon died getting the radio here, or have you forgotten?'

I stayed silent. This man knew a great deal after all; if he wasn't what he said he was, I was finished.

'We need that radio,' he said. 'Where is it?'

'I have no idea what you are talking about.' I got up. 'Now I'm going and if you try to stop me I will scream and tear my clothes and you will surely be discovered and branded a molester, or worse. Now go away and leave me alone.'

'Meryl,' he said, 'please listen to reason.'

'Frau Euler, if you please.' My tone was icy. 'Why should I believe anything you say to me?'

'I will be here next weekend, say you'll come.'

'Don't count on it.'

'Then I will have to come to the farmhouse,' he said.

'That sounds like a threat.'

'Not a threat, a promise. I must have that radio. Big moves are being planned.'

'What moves?'

He shrugged. 'See you same place, same time.' He limped away, the image of an old man again.

'Wait,' I called. He turned back.

I caught up with him. 'Your teeth,' I said.

'What?'

'Your teeth are the only thing I have a concern about –' I aped his words to me – 'they could blow your cover.' I spun away and hurried back to the battered jeep.

I didn't sleep well that night. I thought every word of the conversation over and over and by morning was convinced the 'tramp' was a genuine English spy. It was, as I told him, his teeth: they were the thing that could give him away. The English, and the Welsh come to that, always brushed their teeth.

Fifty-Two

Hari sat looking at her transmitter. Should she let Meryl know about the plans for the invasion of the Normandy beaches by the Allies? It was certainly dangerous to attempt it.

'Overlord' was top secret, if the intelligence fell into the hands of the Germans, it would blow months, if not years, of planning. And yet Meryl would be in danger, the whole of Germany would be in danger; from the landing forces, from the bombers – that was the object of the exercise. She rubbed her forehead wearily. There seemed little she could do to help her sister who, to all intents and purposes, was a traitor to her country and her people. Undecided, she left the office and went home to Swansea; at least there she could try to put worrying thoughts out of her head.

Hari was invited to a meal at Kate's house that night and she made a special effort to look smart, to be cheerful, and most of all to allow Kate to talk about her problems. When she arrived, Hilda opened the door and gave a wry smile.

'Come in, girl, come and join the party.' And it was a party. The room was filled with cigarette smoke and the smell of beer. Hari was greeted with several wolf whistles and she forced a smile.

'I didn't know it was going to be so jolly.' She put her hand on Kate's shoulder. 'Who are these Americans you've brought home?'

Kate smiled. 'Sure you make me sound like some sort of siren maid calling sailors from the sea.'

'You're a beautiful girl, Kate, you make a good siren but what does Eddie think of it all?'

'Eddie and me have quarrelled, he's gone out.'

'And these airmen?'

'I went to the park, I got in trouble with the pram and these good fellows brought me home. Nothing to worry about, Hari, believe me, I've had enough of men to last a lifetime.'

Hilda bustled in from the kitchen with a pile of spam sand-wiches.

'Meat?' Hari said.

'The boys brought it with them, among other things.' Kate held up a pair of stockings. 'Bring back memories, eh? It all seems so long ago now.'

One of the pilots was standing in a corner. He seemed to be taking no part in the jollity. He held a cup and saucer in his hand instead of a glass or a tankard and Hari assumed he was drinking tea. On an impulse she went over to him.

'Hello, I'm Hari.' She held out her hand. After some hesitation he took it.

'Aldo,' he said, in his soft American drawl.

'You're looking very unhappy.'

'I'm feeling very unhappy. While I'm away fighting a war I've lost my girl to another guy. He just sits on his butt in an office safe and cosy, reliable you know. What's your excuse, you don't look too jolly either.'

'Same as you, I've lost my guy to another girl, he's married my sister. Ironic isn't it? Anyway, let's change the subject.'

'Shall we talk about the weather?' Aldo's eyebrow was raised.

'I suppose it's a serious issue with you pilots, the weather.'

'Aye, well that sure is true but there are other more important things to talk about – this feeling of being chucked wouldn't be a bad start. What's your story?'

'He ran away with my sister, married her and that's the end of it. I expect they'll start a family once the war is over, if they live that long. What about you?' Hari asked.

'We'll be moving out soon, special mission sort of thing, all very hush-hush.'

Hari knew at once what he was referring to but her expression gave nothing away. 'What a shame,' she said, and meant it.

'Look, let's walk a bit shall we?' he said, and Hari nodded.

'It is a bit noisy in here, isn't it?'

It was strange after the warmth and cheery atmosphere of the party at Kate's house to be reminded of the reality of war by the ravaged streets and jutting scars of the ruined buildings. Spirals of smoke issued from the devastation of the bombed sites. Torn pieces of blackout sheets fluttered limply in the night-time breeze and over all was an eerie silence as though the town brooded and waited, flinching from the next onslaught from the air. It wasn't long coming. The siren raked the streets and Hari's stomach turned in fear.

Aldo drew her into his arms and they hid in a doorway. Hari

closed her eyes remembering the last time she'd been held close to a man; Michael had held her, dearest Michael, she loved him so much. How could he turn against his own the way he'd done? And yet, she still clung to the belief that he wasn't a traitor, he'd been forced into joining the German Luftwaffe by his father.

Aldo tipped up her face and kissed her lips. She recoiled from him, knowing she would love only one man in her lifetime and that was Michael. Michael Euler.

'I'm sorry.' She pulled away from Aldo and began to run.

'I'm sorry too,' he called, 'can I see you again?'

'No.' Her voice was caught by the breeze and drifted away and by the time she got home, Hari was crying bitter, helpless tears that did nothing to ease her pain.

Fifty-Three

The next week I got into the jeep and drove to the spot where I met the 'tramp'. He was there waiting, snuffling away at a dry crust of bread. I handed him some sandwiches and he took them and began to gobble them greedily.

'I've had a big bloody breakfast,' he grumbled in a quiet voice. I stifled the urge to laugh.

'Tough! Eat the sandwiches.' I studied him. 'Your teeth look better now you've blacked some of them out.'

'Very observant.' He struggled through the sandwiches. 'I hate sausage,' he said.

'What's your name?'

'Fritz.'

'A likely story.'

'At least Fritz is a proper name. "Black Opal" is silly, too unusual,' he retorted.

'What do you mean?' I was indignant. 'I thought it was a good name.'

'For what, an adventure comic? You're going to be called Anna.'

'Who says?'

'I say. Our controller says too. Is that all right by you?'

'Our controller, what are you talking about?'

'You, my dear Meryl, are going to be a proper agent, not the silly, bumbling, dangerous amateur you've been so far.'

'I've been dangerous?'

'That's right.'

'How?'

'For one, as I told you last time, you were almost caught. At least you've the sense to travel about these days.'

'I don't want or need a controller thank you.'

'You are valuable to us. Your cover is perfect: your husband is half German; your father-in-law is a German officer; you even work in a German office. You are fully accepted, but you won't be much longer if you bumble around on your own.'

I folded my arms. 'I don't want to belong to anything, I told you. I'm Frau Euler, a respectable, married, *German* lady.'

'And I'm McDuff.' He foraged in the jeep for a few minutes and got the radio out of the picnic basket. 'Here. See how easily you'd be caught, you little fool! You're a liability.'

'I wouldn't be anything of the sort if you left me alone.' Just then the radio started making noises. I was receiving a message and it could only be from Hari. I hastily took down the message, most of it in coded Welsh, and gasped at the information, which was brief but to the point.

'What is it?' Fritz asked in a sharp voice.

I handed him the hastily scribbled message.

'I can't make it out,' he said, and appeared uncomfortable and confused.

'I relented. 'I'm not surprised, it's in coded Welsh.'

'See?' he said, 'see how valuable you are to us? Not many other people in Germany would speak and read Welsh; that's really clever. What does it say?'

I prevaricated, not sure if I could trust him. 'How do I know which side you're on, Fritz?'

He shook his head. 'You damn woman.' He undid the laces on his worn shoes and slipped them off. His socks were clean, confirming that he was no tramp. Gently, he took off his socks and showed me his disfigured feet.

'Your nails, they've been torn out,' I said in horror.

'Aye, the Germans suspected me of spying and took me in for "questioning". In the end I managed to convince them I was stupid and knew nothing.'

'Not too difficult a job for you.' My sarcasm brought a grimace to his face. He stared at me.

'The message, it could be urgent.'

I hesitated, instinctively I felt he was telling the truth but I couldn't be sure. He read my expression.

'If I'm the enemy why haven't I turned you in?' he demanded. 'You'd be a fine prize for the Germans I can tell you. Herr Euler is not liked by everyone, he has enemies who would like to see him disgraced. You would be the perfect excuse to discredit him.'

I capitulated; his words made sense. 'It's important,' I said at last. The Allies are going to invade several of the Normandy beaches at the same time.'

'You'd better tell me all about it, slowly and quietly.'

I decided I might as well trust him as I couldn't do a lot on my own. I told him the code names of the beaches: 'Sword, Juno, Gold, Omaha and Utah. The Americans and Canadians will be invading along with the British.'

I went over my notes again and explained several times and then Fritz took my piece of paper, lit a match and burnt it.

He gestured to the radio. 'Send an acknowledged signal and for God's sake switch the thing off. Come on.'

He climbed into my jeep and started to drive. He bumped over the grassy bank and on to the roadway and then we were heading away from the spot as fast as my poor old car could make it.

We stopped outside a tall building on the outskirts of Hamburg and he pulled to a stop. 'Thanks for the lift. I'll be in touch.' He took the radio and left me sitting there open-mouthed. 'I won't be Anna!' I said in a sibilant whisper. 'But I'll be Anwn if I have to be anything.'

I saw a movement in an upstairs window and instinctively looked up. A blonde woman was staring down at us, his girlfriend I supposed. When she saw me looking she let the curtain drop. Without turning, Fritz went into the building and closed the door. With a sigh of resignation, I shifted into the driver's seat and, seething, and not without difficulty, found my way back home.

Fifty-Four

Kate snuggled into Eddie's arms. 'I'm sorry about the row so I am.' She smoothed Eddie's lean jaw feeling a muscle jump and knowing with a dart of joy he loved her as she loved him.

'I didn't mean to quarrel,' she said pleadingly, 'but please, Eddie, accept that Stephen is the father of my baby and there's bound to be contact some of the time.'

Eddie was silent for a long time and when he spoke it was in a strangled voice that betrayed his feelings so clearly to Kate that she felt it like a knife thrust.

'But of all men, Stephen! He was the one who bragged that he took your innocence. He told me about all the men you'd had, he wanted to destroy us; how could you forgive him enough to take him back into your life?'

Kate was suddenly angry. 'I thought you were dead. I was about to give birth to a child with no name, "father unknown" on the birth certificate, what else could I do? Stephen stepped in at the last minute and gave our child respectability, even your mother was grateful. He kept us fed and clothed, Eddie, a roof over our head. He wasn't you but he was a good husband and father to our son. How dare you begrudge him a little bit of happiness? He's coming to see his own son later today so even if you can't be generous, sure you can just put up with it.'

A gentle tapping on the door interrupted her flow. 'That's Hari.' She sighed in relief. 'She's taking me and the boys to the park. Now Eddie, we must grasp what happiness we can get because who knows what is going to happen to us tomorrow?'

When Hari came into the kitchen Kate behaved as if no angry words had been spoken. Eddie helped to get the children ready and Kate knew he was contrite about his outburst. She smiled in his direction, loving him.

The weather was hot for May and the scent of blossoms drifted to where Kate was sitting on the warm wooden bench in the park.

'Everything all right, Hari? You're very quiet.'

'Just the usual, work and worry about Meryl.'

'And worrying and wondering about Michael,' Kate said.

'He's not mine to think about any more.' Hari's voice held a note of sadness mingled with anger. 'I slept with him, Kate, we made beautiful love, didn't that mean anything to him?'

'Learn a lesson, Hari, my love,' Kate said softly, 'making love doesn't mean a thing to some men; it's meaningful at the time, they think they love you just then but men can put things like feelings into different boxes. We women think it means they love us for ever, fools that we are.'

'Aye, wise words and I've heard them before but it doesn't make any difference,' Hari said.

Kate was glad to sit down in quietness while Hari took the boys on the swings. She could hear the excited squeals of her boys on the soft air, she could smell the spring flowers and for a time her sadness vanished.

Kate was sorry when it was time to go home but Teddy was crying; he was hungry and the baby grizzled incessantly.

'Let me push the pram.' Hari took charge. Kate held Teddy's hand and put her other hand on the pram handle for guidance. They walked in silence, the children quiet now they were on the move. Everything would be all right, Kate reasoned, Eddie would see sense, if not friendly he would at least be civil to Stephen and they would have tea together with Hilda, who was good at smoothing things over, and the hours of Stephen's visit would pass soon enough.

Kate would have liked to chat with Stephen, they had always been able to talk and, really, she was lucky to have two fine men in her life at a time of war when there were so many widows about. She made the sign of the cross quickly, her Irish roots surfacing. She heard Hari giggle.

'What evil thoughts are you thinking now, Kate, that you have to ask pardon of God?'

'You're a heathen,' Kate said mildly, 'you don't understand, not being Catholic.'

'Well, I'm a good chapel girl,' Hari said, 'nothing wrong with that is there?'

Kate pushed her friend's arm away. 'Go on with you! I'm not getting into all that, I've too much else to think about.'

As if to punctuate Kate's words, the wail of the air-raid warning wrenched apart the silence of the day.

'Hurry, Kate, we're nearly home.' She felt Hari drag her along the road and heard her push open the door and wheel the pram through the passageway into the kitchen.

There was the screech of a doodlebug. Kate froze. And then, after a long terrifying silence came a blast as the house fell apart. The glare penetrated Kate's eyes, for a long moment she was dazzled, her sight cleared and she realized she could see.

She cried out as she saw all around her the dead bodies of her family. Hilda, Eddie and Stephen were on the floor in a tangle of disjointed limbs. Teddy was flat on his face, his small body crushed by a huge piece of masonry. She crawled towards him to look at his face – he was the image of his father but he had her own dark curly hair and white skin.

'My boy, my boy,' she whimpered. She heard a small cry and struggled to where the pram lay overturned on the floor. The baby had tumbled out and his head was gashed and bleeding. Kate picked him up and snuggled him to her. He lay limp in her arms as slowly his little face became blue, waxen like a doll. Kate howled like an animal unable to bear the pain of it all.

She felt an agonizing pain in her legs, it spread slowly up her body and she realized the blood on her clothing was her own. That was all right, there was nothing left for her now, nothing to live for. She had got back her eyesight just to see her family die.

She saw a movement near the door. Hari was half in half out of the passage. She stirred and looked up.

'I'm all right, Kate,' she said, 'I'll help you to get out, don't you worry, my lovely.'

'It's too late, Hari, don't grieve for me.' Kate heard her own voice thin as a thread. There was no need for Hari to help her, she was going with her family to her maker. She put her youngest son on the blankets tumbled from the pram; any minute now she would lie down beside him and let the angels take them all together.

Hari managed to move a little way towards her.

'I can see you, Hari,' Kate whispered, 'just as lovely as you ever were.'

The dreaded sound of whining overhead, rushing downwards towards them 'Another bomb,' Hari cried, 'oh Kate, my lovely, don't die.'

Kate found the strength to move. She fell across Hari protecting her with her own body and waited. There was a smile on her face as the second explosion plunged her back into darkness and demolished what was left of the house.

Fifty-Five

I watched Michael come across the fields, German fields, but looking just like the fields of home. My heart fluttered and danced as though I was still thirteen years old. I loved this man and I anticipated the moment when he'd take me in his arms and hold me close.

He came close and when he kissed me I breathed him in, the man scent of his skin, the faint smell of shaving soap and fresh summer breezes. We held each other in the bright sunshine and then Michael took me upstairs to bed.

Our loving was deep, slow, almost as if we were saying goodbye. The thought frightened me. Afterwards, we lay together with just a sheet over us, the hot sunshine pouring in through the window, lighting on us like a benediction.

'I've only a few days' leave,' he said softly, blowing my hair with his breath. 'The mission, it's important; we have news of the Allies landing in France. We don't know where exactly, not yet, but I promise to try not to kill anyone.'

I put my hand over his sweet mouth to hush him. 'Let's not talk about the war.' I turned into his arms, his chest was hot, lightly dotted with gems of sweat. 'Love me again,' I begged.

The days passed like a honeymoon. I made the most of it. Perhaps this time was the only time I would own Michael, as if he was my husband only for now. We could not have been closer during the golden hours together.

When he left me I waved as happily as if my heart wasn't breaking and then I turned indoors, ran upstairs and flung myself on the bed and remembered every detail of our love and love-making, breathed in his smell from the pillows. At last I curled into a tiny ball and fell asleep.

It was early in the morning when I heard a thunderous knocking on my door. I knew instinctively I'd been found out – the Germans had come for me. It was Fritz.

Fritz came into the house and shared my breakfast – some weak tea and dry toast – every mouthful feeling like sawdust as I remembered Michael had gone.

'We have an assignment for you; it's dangerous.' Fritz toyed with a crust of toast.

'How kind, but I have to go to work or have you forgotten what you call "my cover"?'

'Not today, idiot, today you must plead sickness, take time off. Today you will not be surprised when you hear the invasion of the Allies is to take place in Calais although we know different.'

'So do the Germans, I thought that was part of the plan.'

'It is but the enemy must be fooled into confusion.'

'Germans are not that stupid,' I said thinking of my friend Eva.

'No, I grant you that, but lies and misinformation have been leaked through the right channels to convince the enemy that Normandy is just a sprat to catch a mackerel, you understand? We hope to send the enemy to Calais.'

'I'd worked that out. And what is this "assignment"?'

'You will help the incoming British troops to set up wireless signals at the bay now named "Sword".'

'I know that, I had the message, remember? In any case, the beaches are miles away.'

'You have the jeep and you will have plenty of time to get to the coast, Anna.'

'Anwn,' I said. 'I will not answer to anything but Anwn, it's an ancient Welsh name.'

'I don't want you to look ancient.' Fritz was just as stubborn as I was. 'You must plait your hair, wear childish clothes. You still have the roundness of youth in your face. How old are you, Anna?'

I closed my mouth firmly. He capitulated.

'How old are you, *Anwn*?'

'Old enough.' I was seventeen, a woman.

'All right. Here's a map. You will take the radio to "Sword" and there you will hand it over to a bona fide British radio engineer.'

'How will I know him?'

'He'll stop being shelled and shot and make a formal introduction! Don't be stupid. I will come there and take over from you.'

'So I'll take the risk of carrying the radio miles across the country and you'll have all the glory.'

'I'll probably end up with a bullet in my guts,' Fritz said.

'And if I'm caught with the radio before you come?'

'That's all part of the deal. You can say no if you want.'

How could I say no? I nodded.

'I'll meet you on the road on the fourth to the sixth of June. The invasion is scheduled to take place, hopefully about then, though it could be later. The weather might make a difference. Anyway, remember to start off early in the morning, it's a long drive.'

He went away and I sat over my cold cup of tea and wondered how on earth I'd come from the little town of Swansea to be a spy in Germany. I went to the window and tried to picture Michael, my last sight of him as he walked away from me. I was determined not to cry but I did anyway.

I arrived at work as usual and laid the groundwork for my 'illness'. I grimaced at Eva as I sat down. 'My monthlies are due, I've got belly ache.' My German was very good by now, I'd almost lost any Welsh accent I'd brought with me. Luckily none of my friends knew the difference between Welsh, Scottish, English or Neutral Irish and by now no one could tell me from any other German citizen.

'You look a bit pale,' Eva said, 'and your poor eyes are all baggy.'

I grinned. 'Michael's been home.'

Eva shot me a mischievous glance. 'I have no sympathy then you lucky slut.'

I rubbed my stomach. 'I'm paying for it now.'

'You are still a lucky slut! I haven't seen my man in months – I'm fancying anything in trousers these days. I foam at the mouth if Heinrich comes anywhere near me.'

Heinrich was a code maker and a code breaker and we all had great respect for him. He had bright eyes and pale gold hair and, as he rarely came into our little office, he was quite safe from Eva's desires. In any case, she loved her husband desperately, just as I loved Michael; in that we had a bond. And I was about to betray her and all my German friends. I bent over my radio unable to hide my shame. My brief happiness with Michael had evaporated and I was once more back in the real world.

Fifty-Six

Hari heard voices above her. She tried to open her eyes but they were gritty with dust. She felt an arm hanging lifeless over her face and her memory came flooding back.

'Kate!' Her voice was a whisper although she felt as if she'd shouted out the name of her friend.

They were all dead, the children, the two men, Hilda – and Kate? 'Kate?' Dust filled her mouth and Hari gagged on it.

Someone tapped on the masonry above her and Hari tried to lift her head. She felt Kate's body shift and tip sideways. 'Oh Kate!' Hari tried to move her arms but they were pinned by jagged pieces of bricks and mortar.

'Help us.' Her voice was faint but the tapping stopped. 'Help us,' she called again.

'It's all right, *cariad*, we're coming for you.' A face appeared in a gap above her grimed with sweat and dust. 'Be still, we're going to move the debris carefully, love, so not to hurt you.'

The work was painfully slow but the light above her became steadily brighter, the weight gradually lifting away so that she could breathe more easily. Hari tried to lift her head again but her neck was wracked with pain and with a sob she fell back against the bricks again. All she'd seen for her effort was a glimpse of Kate's hand with the wedding band shining golden in the light.

A lifeless, waxy hand smeared with blood. Her friend was dead, they were all dead. Hari couldn't stop the gasps of grief and pain escaping from between her swollen lips. Tears scaled her grazed cheeks as she let herself slip away into a fog of darkness.

A week later Hari was discharged from hospital with little more than cuts and bruises. The nurse led her to the entrance. 'You'll have two black eyes for a while but you got off lightly, my girl.'

Hari shook her head. 'Except that I lost people I love.' Her tone was disconsolate. The nurse touched her shoulder sympathetically.

'I see that here every day,' she said gently, 'we've got to keep telling ourselves we'll win this damn war, somehow.'

Hari stood on the pavement. She felt cast adrift on a blank sea; she had no sister, no Michael and now, no Kate.

'But you have father and Jessie and even poor old Georgie Porgie when he's home from the front so stop feeling sorry for yourself.' Her voice rasped as she scolded herself.

When she got home they all fussed around her. Jessie made her endless cups of tea, giving her a few precious aspirin and talking softly to her of the war being over one day. In the end, Hari went to bed worn out with tears, her head pounding, her eyes so swollen they were half closed.

She lay on her narrow bed and thought of the past, of before the war when she was free, of when she briefly had Michael in her arms.

Hari remembered when the air raids began, how Meryl had hidden under the table, peering out at them like a little animal from a lair and she began to cry again, the salt tears hurting her bruised eyes. But at last, too weary to stay awake, she slept and dreamed of peace.

Fifty-Seven

Somehow Fritz had got me enough petrol to get to the coast of Normandy. I knew he thought me a silly girl and dispensable. I tied my hair into plaits, wore no make-up and dressed as childlike as I could get away with. I looked at my breasts and grimaced, for all my efforts they were shapely and showed. Still, I could be well developed for my age I suppose. And then I began the long drive from Hamburg to the coast.

By the time I was close to the beaches of Normandy I was almost asleep. I slid from the driving seat and hid among some trees. I knew the beaches were still a few miles away but dare I take the radio any further? I sighed in resignation; if I put the radio down I might never find it again. I trudged on though the tough grass whipped my legs painfully. What was I doing here, in France, carrying a small but heavy suitcase with a wireless inside – proof that I was a traitor? I would be shot on discovery, nothing was surer than that.

I heard the noise while I was still more than a mile away: shelling, shots, screams and loud voices. For a moment I quailed. How was I going to get past German lines and how was I supposed to find Fritz?

I skirted the beach code-named Sword, a shell from seaward landing perilously close. I sank down into the grass and took stock of the situation. From my hole in the grass I peered out and I couldn't see anyone at all. Perhaps I was the wrong side of the bay, how would I know?

Fearfully, I looked across the wide expanse of beach; it would take me hours to reach the other side even if I wasn't killed on the way. Fritz had said the left-hand side but did he mean left facing the sea or left from the sea? Why hadn't I asked him more questions?

The truth was I didn't think I would be daft enough to do what he asked; he said I was a volunteer, didn't he? I peered out of my grass burrow again and I became aware there were German troops moving a huge gun forward, swearing and groaning at the weight. I lay close against the sharp grass and closed my eyes knowing it was a stupid thing to do, a childish thing to do, it was as if they couldn't see me if I couldn't see them.

I jumped as someone slid into the grass beside me. Dressed as an English soldier, Fritz grinned at me. 'Well done, kiddie,' he said and grabbed the case and disappeared over the top of the hole. 'Now bugger off home!'

Coward that I was, I crouched there for a long time hearing the sounds of battle raging around me. I wanted to pee and wondered if my knickers were already wet as they'd been when I was thirteen years old.

At last, I knew I had to get back to the jeep. I took a chance to peer out again and I saw the German army in retreat. I felt triumph, but only for a minute before I was grabbed by my plaits and dragged out of my hiding place.

'What are you doing here?' the German voice demanded.

'I wanted to see what was happening,' I replied in faultless German.

'You are a spy,' he said, looking around the hole as if for proof. There was nothing except a wet bit of sand where I had wet myself in fright.

'You are only a child, you are mad or stupid or you are a spy for the English. You will come with me for questioning.'

I cried out in pain as he tugged on my plaits. He released my hair and grabbed my arm and pulled me towards a truck. I was thrown inside and came down heavily on my knee. And when we were driving away from the beach I peered over the tailboard and saw the ducks, funny little ships with the fronts falling down, unloading yet more troops on to the Normandy beaches.

We travelled over bumpy ground at a fast speed while behind us mortars still rained and shots whizzed overhead. There were bodies of dead Germans everywhere and it looked as if the battle was going to the Allies; perhaps this was the end for the German army.

If the gossips were correct Herr Hitler was already losing his mind, getting more and more demanding every day, unable to believe the war was being lost because of his failure to believe in his generals. The road became bumpier; I was being thrown around like a rag doll. I tried to cling to the sides of the truck to steady myself but even though I was getting bruised and battered by the journey I guessed there would be worse ahead. At the very least I would be questioned, perhaps tortured, if what I'd heard of the SS was true.

At least I'd got rid of the radio before I was caught. The thought was not so much patriotism as self-preservation. With the radio as evidence I would have been shot where I lay in my bunker in the grass.

We travelled through the night. I tried to sleep but it was impossible with my head constantly banging against the sides or the bottom of the truck. The driver stopped at last and, getting to my knees, I peered outside. It was dawn, the sky was turning pink, the shrubbery coming to life.

The building was rising from a smelly marshland and I wrinkled my nose at the foul-smelling air; it was as though the scent of hundreds of unwashed bodies of prisoners hung around the building like a forbidding cloud. The truck stopped and I was dragged outside and led into the streets of the camp. I felt small and lost but my lips closed mutinously. I would tell the Germans nothing – now they really were the enemy.

I was put in a cell-like room and locked in and I knew deep in my mind that I was at the dreaded Ravensbruck camp, notorious for harbouring hardened traitors of the Third Reich. Surely I couldn't be considered that dangerous without even being questioned?

At least I could lie down on a hard, rough pallet but it took a while for the room to stay still – I felt as though I was still being thrown about in the truck. I thought about the day I'd endured,

I worried about my little, battered jeep left unattended among the trees. I thought of work and my colleagues. Would they be wondering where I was?

And then, at last, I thought of Michael: my darling, my lover, my man, my husband. I fell asleep at last, too tired even to worry what was to become of me and, when I woke, it was morning and the prison cell was a reality.

Fifty-Eight

Hari finished work with a sigh of relief; she would be glad to get home and put her feet up. The bus waiting outside the gates of the munitions factory seemed airless as she climbed up the steps and sank thankfully into a seat.

'Isn't it awful about Doreen?' A girl in a turban came and sat next to her and Hari could smell the explosive powder on her clothes. 'And I hear you lost your friend as well in a bombing raid, bloody awful war. Kate was a lovely girl.'

'Did you work with her?' Hari asked, grateful to talk about Kate to someone . . . anyone – at least she was remembered by some of her other friends.

'Aye, I worked with her, sometimes when we had no money we'd walk together to the station. A good girl was Kate, always a smasher, mind, even when she went blind in the explosion. I was told about the bombing of her house. Sad for them to all die like that and yet perhaps that's what she would have wanted, them all together as a family.'

She held out her hand and Hari couldn't help noticing it was stained yellow, even the girl's nails were yellow; she looked strange, as if she had been dipped in a dye.

'I'm Violet. I was trying to help Kate carry the powder when she was expecting but some of the other girls said she had to get along without help, that we couldn't afford to carry anyone.' She sighed. 'I suppose I wouldn't have been alive today if I'd gone with her. On the other hand I might have been able to push her out of the way or something. I'll never know.'

Hari shook her hand warmly. 'None of us will ever know,' she said comfortingly, 'I was in the same room as Kate and the family when the bomb fell and I was the only one to survive. An act of God, fate, a coincidence? We'll never know.'

'I lost my chap when the war started. About to lose my room too. The man of the house is coming home, too sick and old to stay in the war.'

The bus jerked to a stop at the railway station and Violet got up. 'Sorry to be morbid. I'm going to Swansea, you go to Swansea as well don't you?'

'We'll go together,' Hari said. 'It's not nice to be alone when you have worries on your mind. Got a family?'

Violet shook her head. 'No, they all lived in London, wiped out in the blitz. I was at college but when the war started I was sent to the munitions to work. I'll stay at the hostel tonight.'

'Come to tea with us,' Hari said. It was an impulse, but the way Violet's face lit up was a reward in itself. 'I warn you there are loads of us living together.'

'That will be a nice change,' Violet said. 'I'll wash and brush up first. What time shall I come?'

'As soon as you like,' Hari said, 'just as soon as you like.'

Violet proved good company and she made Jessie laugh. Georgie seemed taken with the girl in spite of her yellow skin toned down now with powder and sat close to her throughout the meal. Only Hari's father remained quiet, absorbed in the news on the radio. He'd left the table and sat in a chair with his ear up against the set, his face grave.

Hari didn't want to break up the happy atmosphere but at last she couldn't help but slip over to his side and crouch near his chair. 'What is it, Daddy?' she whispered.

He looked at her doubtfully and then glanced towards Jessie. Anxiety gripped Hari and she shook her father's arm. 'What, tell me?'

'A German plane has come down near Carmarthen; no news of the pilot.'

The group around the table fell silent at once. Hari cleared her throat and her eyes met Jessie's.

'It could be anyone,' she said quickly, 'there are bomber planes over the coast most nights, you know that.'

In spite of her usual reserve Hari broke down and cried, for Michael and Meryl, for Kate, but most of all for herself.

Fifty-Nine

I heard the key being turned in the door of my cell and got to my feet expecting the worst. A German soldier gestured for me to come with him and to my relief he wasn't holding a gun but his face was set in hard lines and he hardly glanced at me. I felt like I was a piece of furniture, a non-person, dehumanized.

'Frau Euler –' his voice was not kindly – 'what precisely were you doing on the beach at Normandy?'

For a minute I felt like being facetious, the word, 'bathing' came into my mind but I didn't think the jack-booted officer of the SS had a sense of humour.

'I had a day off work,' I said, 'I wanted to get away from the constant messages coming through my radio with intelligence about the hated English.' The words stuck in my throat and I coughed. I could see he didn't believe me; a young married woman cavorting around a beach where a fierce attack was taking place must have a few screws loose in her head. I suppose he wondered why the hell I didn't get out of there the moment I realized there was a battle going on.

I smiled in what I thought was a winning manner but I probably looked like an imbecile. 'It's my Irish ancestry, you know.'

He looked at me obliquely. 'We can make you confess your spying methods with very little trouble,' he said. 'Take your shoes and socks off.'

'What?'

A soldier moved from the door towards me and I hastily undid my laces. When my feet were bare we looked down at them contemplatively. The soldier took something like pliers from his belt and knelt down before me.

'You can't propose,' I said, and flashed my wedding ring at him. He didn't even look up but grasped my big toe in a painful hold. I yelped.

'Removing the nail will hurt even more,' the SS man said laconically. I began to cry. I was good at forcing tears out, big plopping drops that rolled down my cheek as though I were a baby. In that moment I felt like one.

'I honestly don't know what you want from me,' I gulped. 'I had a day off and I went to the coast. I didn't know all hell was going to break loose there did I? Please get in touch with my father-in-law Herr Euler, he will tell you I'm a simple girl. I don't know anything about being a spy. I live on my father-in-law's farm, I go to work at the office, I know nothing of any consequence.'

'Take her back to her room we'll find out more when she has calmed down.' Either my tears or my tone of voice convinced him I was harmless if not brainless, after all, the intelligence was that 'Overlord' would take place at Pas de Calais not the Normandy coast.

In my grey cell with the tiny window shedding in very little light I sat on the pallet and studied the calendar on the wall beside my so-called bed. The last dates marked off were the fourth, fifth and sixth of June – the previous occupant of the room had underscored it and must have known about the attack. And then it hit me, the date jogged at my mind, it was almost two months since Michael had been home, two months since I'd had my monthlies. Oh dear God, I was a prisoner and I was pregnant. A little curl of happiness unfolded inside me; I was having Michael's baby.

I slept a little and then I was brought some halfway decent soup. I ate hungrily wondering if the tiny being growing inside me would appreciate the nourishment, I hadn't eaten for many hours.

I slept some more, there seemed nothing else to do. Used to activity and company I was sometimes afraid but mostly bored. Staring at four walls didn't appeal to me one bit. And then I was brought supper, some sausages and hard bread with no butter. Still, it was sustenance and I needed it more now than I ever had.

I slept most of the night away but woke to the sound of blood-curdling screams, a woman's screams. I thought of the pliers and shuddered. I hugged myself; I felt cold and lost; and, opinionated and determined though I was, I could see little chance of getting out of Ravensbruck concentration camp. I'd heard women came here to confess or to die. My only weapon was my tongue. No, there was my wit, and now I had a baby to think of, my baby and Michael's.

'*Obersturmbannführer* Suhren himself wishes to see you, Frau Euler.' The stern-faced guard came for me and he sounded impressed.

'Oh, good,' I said. I wanted to talk to the commander as much as he apparently wanted to talk to me.

He was sitting behind a desk in his well-decorated uniform and he was younger than I'd thought he'd be, very young to be in charge of thousands of prisoners. I sat down meekly and pressed my hands together in what I hoped was an obsequious manner.

'Please, commandant, could I speak with my father-in-law Herr Euler. He will tell you I am the wife of his son, a pilot in the Luftwaffe, and I work in an office with my German friends.' I looked down modestly. 'I am also with child by my brave husband, I will bear Germany a fine son.'

'That is the only item of personal history I did not know.' The commandant spoke with precision. 'I have contacted Herr Euler, as you say, a respected German officer. I have also intelligence from your place of work.' He paused and smoothed his well-kept hands. 'Your friend Frau Eva speaks highly enough of you.'

'My friend Eva is not married, commandant.'

'Ah.' He looked at me. 'Quite right. You are expecting a child?'

I nodded and tried to look modest as though the conception had occurred through concourse rather than intercourse.

'You will see a doctor.'

'A lady?' I asked quickly. I had heard of the doctors at Ravensbruck, they experimented on humans with apparent relish and I didn't want their hands touching me. 'Please, commandant, I am young, a mere girl, the only male hands to touch me are those of my husband.' This at least was true except for the punching and kicking and rough fumbling I'd once got from Georgie Dixon.

'We will see.' He gestured to the guard and I was taken back to my cell, but this time I was not manhandled but led quietly along the road to my prison block.

I was given better food now, fresh sausage and crude, but fresh, bread. My talk with the commandant had done some good in spite of his attitude of indifference. I slept more easily that night, though I still heard the sound of women crying and the occasional scream. I closed my ears and hugged my stomach and thought of my baby.

In the morning, my father-in-law came for me and I was released into his charge. Herr Euler took me home to the farm and made a cup of tea and his face was a grey mask.

'What is it?' I asked fearfully, already guessing the answer.

'It's Michael –' there was a hint of a quiver in his voice – 'his plane has been shot down over enemy territory. I'm afraid my dear, Michael is missing, presumed dead.'

My heart froze and my hands went automatically to my belly, as though trying to comfort the baby inside me. It was a horror worse than prison camp, it was not possible that my beautiful Michael no longer lived or breathed.

'He can't be dead,' I gasped, 'I'm going to have his son.'

His father came towards me and cradled me in his arms. 'We must be brave, *Liebling*, we must be brave.' And then we cried together, despairing tears that could never wash away the anguish we both felt.

Sixty

Hari and Violet strolled together in the autumn sun; it was a hot day with the leaves beginning to turn red and gold, and the grass, in the open spaces, browned by the heat. Violet was pensive. At last she spoke. 'Sorry, thinking about the war and all that. By the way, have you heard from your sister?'

'Not a word –' Hari's voice was dull – 'I'm so afraid she's been killed, she's been leading a dangerous life, spying on the Germans, getting involved in goodness knows what. My independent Meryl was always up to something, was cheeky and lippy and so bloody courageous.' Hari realized she was speaking about Meryl as though she were already dead.

As they neared the rows of sheds, Violet began to move away from Hari. 'Shall I see you at break time? We could eat our spam sandwiches outside, it will give me a rest from that terrible stink of powder.'

'OK. See you about five then, the sun will have cooled by then but it should still be nice to sit outside and get some air into our lungs.'

'Aye, pity it's not fresh air!' Violet smiled. 'Even if it's gone misty by then I'll still see you, will I?'

Hari looked round the site of the munitions factory; it was usually covered in mist and that helped conceal the buildings from the bombers but she hoped that at teatime it would still be fine and the skies clear of enemy aircraft.

'I'll see you,' Hari said firmly.

The office was stuffy, the windows criss-crossed with tape. To one side hung a blackout curtain ready for the night workers to pull across when it grew dark. Hari longed to throw open the windows but even if she could the all-pervading dust would drift in and coat everything in malignant yellow powder.

She sat at her desk and listened for the Morse code to start chattering through her headphones but she couldn't concentrate. Her heart was heavy, Michael was gone from her forever, killed at the hands of his own people. If it was Michael who had been shot down, how was the artillery to know that flying a German plane was a Welshman, brought up on a farm in Carmarthenshire, raised by a good Welsh woman who happened to have had a German husband?

Hari felt helpless tears run down her cheeks and she brushed them away as the familiar tip-tapping came through from her radio. Her heart lightened a little. There was important news: 'Operation Overlord' had been a success. The message from a careless, frightened German operator told of the rout, the bad news phrased as diplomatically as possible so as not to alarm his superiors, who would pass the message to Hitler.

Hitler would take no notice; it seemed he never took notice of what his intelligence told him unless it suited him. But what of Meryl – was she alive or dead? Somehow Hari had the premonition that 'Overlord' had involved Meryl in some way. But how could it? Meryl was probably tucked up safely in bed by now crying her eyes out for her lost husband. With that thought, Hari clenched her fists into a tight ball and cursed love and all it stood for.

Sixty-One

With the success of the Normandy landings I thought the end of the war was nigh – silly me. The battle continued through the summer: the Allies made some headway and then the Germans made some headway; it was like the crazy dance of scorpions or spiders – it got soldiers killed but nothing achieved. And through my lonely days was the terrible knowledge that my darling, my

Michael, was dead. The one bright spot in my life right now was Eva. She was coming for the weekend and I could talk to her, tell her about my baby.

I made up her bed with fresh sheets; since my belly began gently to swell Herr Euler had hired a woman from the village to come and wash and clean for me. Frau Kleist was meticulous, a good, sensible woman. She was, inevitably, a war widow from the first time round and now she had white springy hair, a wry humour and an indomitable courage I admired very much.

We ate lunch together in the kitchen of the farmhouse. We ate the late vegetables from the garden, hers and mine, worked now by her disabled son with his one good arm, his weakened body hit by shrapnel, and the spirit inherited from his mother.

Eva arrived in a flurry, her boyfriend, a dazzling pilot, brought her in a car. In Wales we would have called him a 'toff' even a 'show off' but he was brave enough to risk his life fighting for what he believed was a worthy cause.

'Eva, come in and have some tea with us, it's all been done by my wonderful Frau Kleist, so no fear I'll poison you.'

Eva laughed and hugged me. 'I've missed your funny little ways,' she said, and then shyly, 'this is Erich, he can't stay long, he's got an operation tonight though he can't tell me where of course, you know, security and all that.'

Erich hogged the conversation – his German cultured, his talk all about himself. I was reminded of Stephen, Kate's boyfriend back home, before he was changed by war into a humble human being.

At last Erich rose and sauntered to the door. 'I'll have to go.' He was reluctant to give up his audience but I sighed with relief. I tactfully stayed behind as Eva saw her pilot to the car and Frau Kleist and I exchanged briefly raised eyebrows, a gesture that drew me to her and made us both smile.

That evening, sitting round the fire, just Eva and me, with a glass of good German wine courtesy of Erich, we relaxed into our old easy friendship.

'He's a bit full of himself –' Eva flashed her lovely smile – 'but he is generous with the goodies.'

'No rose-coloured spectacles then?' Strange how languages share clichés. Eva shook her head and her silky hair whispered across her cheeks.

'He's fun but that's all he is. My men seem to get killed as soon as I get fond of them so the lesson is, don't, get fond.'

'What happened after I left?' I had changed the subject abruptly and Eva grimaced knowing she'd touched a raw spot.

'Your desk was searched. The SS got very excited when they found your tin. You should have seen their faces when they realized it only held what it said on the lid, sanitary wear.'

She sobered, just a little because the wine was strong and taking its toll. 'I heard you were arrested all the same.'

'I was,' I said slowly. 'I was silly enough to go for a drive to the seaside just when the enemy landed.' I bit my tongue. I'd nearly said 'Allies'. And much as Eva liked me I couldn't afford to make any more mistakes.

'Well, you weren't to know the enemy had the gall to attack the coast, were you?' Her voice rose as if it was a question and I stared at her for a long moment.

'I worked on the same job as you, I heard just what you heard, we took down the same messages, how could I know about the invasion when you didn't?'

'Oh, I know that, I didn't mean to imply you did. It's just the rumour swept through the office that the authorities were looking for a radio set, the sort the resistance uses. You are so good at the Morse, so quick at the codes I suppose you were just being checked out. You wouldn't betray your own country, would you?'

'Of course not –' Eva would never understand the irony in my voice – 'and the SS had no evidence on me, that's why they let me go at last, that and the fact my father-in-law is a respected army officer. He came to get me out, thank God.'

'They didn't . . . touch you, did they?' Eva's eyes were round. I knew what she meant.

'No, nothing like that. My husband was a German pilot and I was already expecting his child; they showed me utmost respect in that way.' At least I could say that with all truth. I didn't tell Eva about the commandant and his threat to pull out my toe nails or about the screams of women during the night. She was a tender girl with belief in her country and the goodness of its leaders but I knew more than she did and I knew the truth would be unbearable to her once it all came out.

'Tell me more about your love life,' I invited. Eva's face lit up, she loved talking about herself, she was so young in the head.

We talked until midnight. As I locked up for the night, I peered through the curtains. The farm was quiet, the moon shining brightly outside across the garden, making a silver pathway in the grass. The Bombers would be out tonight, nothing was surer.

Eva and I kissed goodnight. I put out the lamps and candles – the generator needed fixing again – and climbed the stairs wearily. This was the time when I was filled with sadness, with doubts about living without Michael. Sometimes I could pretend he was on a mission but mostly there was this dreadful sense of emptiness and loss, of despair with no light for the future. I crept into my cold bed and rubbed my eyes, they were too dry for any more tears.

Sunday night a car came for Eva. There was an SS man driving it and as she left she fluttered her bright scarf at me. All I could see was Eva's white face as the car drew away from the farm and with a sinking heart I knew she was going to betray me.

Sixty-Two

'Your hair looks nice, Vi.' Hari touched Violet's bright curls. Violet had taken the only way out, saving her hair from the acid in the lead shells by dying her hair a proper blonde shade toned down from the garish yellow streaks made by the shell powder.

Vi's smile was grateful. 'I've put flour on my face mixed with a bit of the face powder my mam gave me, don't look too bad at all now, do I?'

'Very pretty, Vi, makes me feel like a frump in my low heels and thick stockings.'

Violet was wearing pretty shoes, second-hand shoes, shoes from a dead person. They were a perfect fit, and nice leather owned by someone much better off than Violet or herself. 'Classy shoes' Kate's mother would have called them. In some ways Violet reminded Hari of Kate.

The thought brought a lump to Hari's throat. There would be no more happy times round the table at Kate's place, no children laughing, crying, no Hilda, no tangle of men, two men, both of them in love with Kate.

A pain like a knife thrust turned inside her; no more Michael, no more strong arms to hold her, no more loving until she thought she would melt, her passion incandescent like the sun, her love glowing bright throughout their intimacy. She had found love and she'd lost it again. Even before Michael had died over the fields of Wales, trying not to drop bombs on his people, shot down in his German plane mistaken for the enemy, she had lost him. Lost him to Meryl and that was the sharpest cut of all.

'You're very quiet,' Vi said softly, 'thinking of your man were you?'

'I've got no man.'

'You never know, he could be alive, he could be taken prisoner, your Michael could still be alive.'

'I went to see where the plane crashed. It had landed on the common outside Swansea and buried itself in the ground and then it caught fire.' She swallowed hard. 'Michael is dead, there's no point in hoping he's alive.'

Hari noticed Violet stayed silent this time, there were no more protests. Hari felt tears in her eyes as she wondered why she wasn't glad Michael was dead – if she couldn't have him then no one would. And yet she knew that she'd rather Meryl had Michael than that he was gone from this world for ever.

'Shall we go out for a drink tonight?' she said at last. Violet agreed at once.

'I think we could both do with a bit of relaxation.' She shrugged her arm around Hari's shoulder. 'Look, love, there's other men out there, lots of girls are like you, their men taken by the war. We'll dance and sing and drink and let ourselves go.'

Hari shook her head. 'I won't be letting myself go, not in the way you mean, Vi.'

'Why not, you're not still . . . what do the posh folk say, "intacta" are you?'

'I'm not a virgin, no.' A thrill of joy went through Hari, she had given herself to Michael, he had made her a woman and she was fiercely glad she'd enjoyed his love if only once in her lifetime. She would never sully that memory by sleeping with another man.

'Don't sell yourself short, Violet,' Hari said. 'My dear friend Kate did that and I know she always regretted it.'

'I won't be selling anything –' Vi laughed – 'I'll be getting drinks and gifts and whatever I can from the Yanks but what they want I'll be giving free and with gratitude for the attention.'

'But you've never known a man, have you?'

'Not intimately, not in the biblical sense, Hari, but perhaps I should snatch at the chance. Tomorrow I might be dead, who knows?'

Hari smiled. Violet was all talk. She'd been tempted by more than one soldier, sailor or airman; she was a good-looking girl with deep black hair and brown eyes and her figure was perfect, her legs long and curvaceous; even in the baggy skirt and overall she wore to work she looked gorgeous, and she'd kept her charms to herself up until now.

'What I really want,' Violet said, her features softening, 'is the love of a good man. I want someone to care about me, me not my body; I want, just once in my life, some man to say he loves me. Am I asking too much, Hari?'

Hari kissed her cheek. 'Of course not. You just hold on to that thought, he'll come along you'll see, and it's a feeling worth waiting for.'

'I believe you,' Violet said, 'thousands wouldn't.' Laughing, she hurried back to the sheds, her feet dancing along the acid-yellowed boards, her curls bobbing, her hips swaying.

'You're incorrigible,' Hari called. Violet turned her head a little.

'Oh, is that what I am? I always wondered.'

Later, tired and heavy-eyed, Hari walked to the roadway and met Violet at the gate of the factory. The evening was dull, the clouds rolling overhead pushing aside the sun. She heard booted feet, the sound of marching and felt Violet draw her back against the fence.

'It's those Germans from the prison camp,' Violet whispered, 'I'll poke one in the eye if he dares to look at me.'

Hari stared, fascinated. The men were singing a German song; they looked well fed and well dressed in officers' uniforms. One was wearing a flying jacket, although it was still warm, and she stared at him.

'Oh, my God!' She put her hand to her mouth; she couldn't believe what she was seeing with her own eyes. 'Michael,' she said. The man looked at her but his eyes were dull. His expression didn't change. 'Michael?' she said, more uncertainly. He looked to the front and marched passed her and then he was gone jackbooting his way down the street towards Island Farm prison camp.

Hari sagged against Violet not knowing if she could believe the evidence of her own eyes. 'I think I've just seen a ghost.' Her voice was a mere whisper.

Sixty-Three

'Eva suspected me, father-in-law,' I said. 'She must have looked in my desk, found my tin box before I . . .' My words trailed away, I could see he didn't understand. I almost bit my tongue. I couldn't tell this honourable German officer that I was betraying his country, sending coded messages to Britain on my radio.

'I had secret papers in the tin,' I said hastily. 'They revealed that I was born in Wales not Ireland.'

'Indeed? That was careless of you. And what about my son, were there secrets about him also?'

'No, nothing about Michael,' I said with conviction, 'there was nothing to involve Michael in anything.' It was the truth. 'I think Eva searched my desk at some time.'

Herr Euler was leaning on the table, his brow furrowed. 'Then we must get you out of the country,' he said at last, his head rising from the palm of his hand. Now his eyes met mine. He looked so much like Michael that my heart lurched. 'I will arrange it.'

I knew better than to ask him how. My father-in-law could be very kind but he was a formidable officer and it would pay me to remember that.

'You are past the three-month danger period with the child?'

'Yes, Father-in-law.' I was almost five months gone but I was still slim, my muscles, hardened by cycling, held my stomach like a girdle.

'Good, then you will be able to walk, to hide, to run if necessary, though I hope that will not be necessary. I will make your departure from Germany as comfortable as possible, trust me.'

'I do, Herr Euler.' I meant it.

'At least I will have a grandson even if I have lost a son.' He patted my arm. 'After the war I will see you both and we will toast the new Herr Euler together.'

'It could be a girl,' I pointed out. He shook his head and tapped his finger to his nose.

'I know it is a boy.' He smiled his charming smile and I wondered how Jessie could ever have left him behind in Germany and gone home to Wales. He answered my unspoken question.

'I was a young buck at Michael's age,' he said, shaking his head, 'like most men I was eager for experience. I never realized what a good wife I had by my own fireside until she packed her case and left me.'

I made a wry face and he smiled again. 'Michael is not like me, he is a faithful man, he loves you daughter-in-law. He would never stray.' He sighed. 'Now he is dead no woman will have him.'

We stood and looked at each other for a long, silent moment. 'But you will have something no one else can ever have; you have his son growing inside your young belly. Take him back to the farmlands my little girl, bring him up to be a good Welshman but also to remember his German forefathers, promise me.'

Tears stung on my lashes, my lips trembled. 'I promise but you will see him, you will hold him in your arms, one day, when all this silly war is over.'

'I hope and pray so. Now I must go and set the wheels in motion. You put together a few things, only what is necessary, we will begin the journey to the Belgian border tonight.'

He went and I was alone in the farmhouse. I made some tea, the silence pressing round me. I wondered through the long lonely hours if the SS would come and find me. I felt sure that Eva, my once dear friend, would think it her duty to tell the guards where I was. If Herr Euler didn't move quickly I would be back in Ravensbruck and this time there would be no mercy for me.

We were on the move before it was light in the morning. The fields around the farmhouse were dark, the trees made forbidding shapes and behind every one was a trooper waiting to shoot me.

Even though 'Overlord' had been a success there was still trouble, the Allies couldn't penetrate into the German territory itself and I wondered how my father-in-law could take time off from the war to see me safely on my way out of the country. But he was there beside me in the staff car driving the vehicle himself, big and reassuring, my dear Michael's father.

I put my hand over his on the steering wheel and he smiled briefly but his jaw was tense. And then, for the first time, I realized that Herr Euler was putting himself in danger by trying to save me.

'Father-in-law,' I said softly, 'go back to your post, you will be missed, your fellow officers will think you've deserted them.'

'I will go back when you are safely over the border,' he said, his tone brooking no more argument.

'We came to a checkpoint and Herr Euler waved away the guards impatiently. 'Let me through, I am on urgent business for the Beloved Leader,' he commanded. At once the barrier was lifted, the men saluted him, and I knew my father-in-law was a very important man, highly respected, and he was risking everything for me. Shame rushed through me, I felt my face burn. I had been betraying this dear man and all he stood for to those he regarded as his enemy, the British.

We drove for hours before we stopped for a rest. In the end I had to beg Herr Euler to let me out of the car; I needed badly to pee, one of the pitfalls of pregnancy I'd learned.

He opened a flask and we drank hot, sweet coffee without the benefit of a cup, but it was the best drink of coffee I'd had in a long time. I was hungry but now my main bodily needs were satisfied I felt ready to go on. I slid into the car and leaned my head, for a moment, on my father-in-law's shoulder.

'Thank you Father,' I said softly.

Sixty-Four

Hari sat in her bedroom, the only place in the full house she could be alone, and thought of yesterday's events. Now she doubted the evidence of her own eyes, she thought she'd seen Michael but she couldn't have seen Michael; he'd crashed his plane into a Welsh field – ploughed it into the rich earth; No pilot could survive such a crash and yet . . . and yet.

She heard the siren cut into the night; she heard the scramble from downstairs as Jessie, Father and Georgie, who was home on leave, made for the shelter. Violet was out somewhere, she'd long ago found a little flat she shared with several of the girls from the munitions.

'Come on Hari, get to the shelter, there's a good girl. 'Jessie's voice rang up the stairs, anxious and with a touch of panic in it.

'I'll be there in a minute, I want to make some tea; you lot go on ahead of me, keep me a decent place to sit.'

The door slammed and Hari wondered about the folk who kept the door open all day, leaving the house open to anyone; perhaps they felt that in a raid it was best in order to secure the property – as though the bombs would make a polite entry into the place through the door instead of plunging, screaming as though in agony through the walls and roof, blowing everything, including the door, to tiny pieces of meaningless rubble.

Unhurried, she went downstairs and made a canteen of tea, spooning some glutinous tinned milk into a screw of greaseproof paper. Then she cut some bread and cheese and wrapped them carefully, putting them neatly into an old biscuit tin.

She heard bombs crash around the house, the street outside, heard the voices of the Home Guard as the men, too old for war, rushed about bravely doing the work of putting out fires, saving those they could save and commiserating over those they couldn't. She didn't hurry, by now she knew that death was arbitrary, if your name was on the bomb or the bullet you would die wherever you were.

At last, she stepped out into the street in the same manner as if she was slipping out to the shop for bread or potatoes. No use looking back, trying to preserve memories. In any case, foremost in her mind was the face of Michael, or the man she thought was Michael, marching, German-fashion down the street in Bridgend, on his way back to the Island Farm prison camp.

'Thank God you've come at last.' Jessie sat in the dimness of the shelter hugging her. '*Duw, cariad*, I thought the buggers had got you.'

'Don't worry about me, Jessie.' She put down her bag. 'Tea and bread in there if you get hungry.' She hesitated.

'Jessie, do you think Michael might have survived the crash?'

Jessie's jaw dropped. 'What a question, girl, you saw the hole in the ground the same as I did. I loved my son dearly but in my head I've buried him so let the dreams go, girl, right?'

'You're right –' there was a catch in Hari's voice – 'of course you're right, I'm being silly.' She didn't tell Jessie she thought she'd seen Michael in a line of prisoners, it would have only upset her and she was upset enough as it was.

At last the all-clear sounded and Hari, arm in arm with Jessie, and Georgie limping behind, left the shelter.

Everything was flaming; pieces of roof lay across the road burning fiercely, windows were smashed, glass was strewn across the road. An ARP worker lay moaning, clutching his torn stomach, trying desperately to put his innards back in place. One of his friends bent over him.

'Can I help?' Hari said. 'I'm not a nurse but I know some first aid.' The ARP man shook his head at her and then spoke to the dying man. 'We're getting you to hospital Tom, the ambulance is on its way, you'll be all right, mate.' There were tears in the man's eyes as he looked down at his friend.

Hari closed her eyes in pain and caught up with Jessie. She bit her lip trying not to cry.

'Gonner, him,' Jessie said flatly, 'no creature can live, not with his guts hanging out of his belly.'

Hari swallowed hard, wishing Jessie's comment wasn't so graphic. 'When will this war ever end?' To her own ears, Hari's voice was like the bleat of a lamb.

'Now girl –' Jessie's voice was hard – 'self-pity never did anyone any good. There's a war on and that's all there is to it. We endure it till it's over, girl, and we try to smile into the bargain, right?'

'Right,' Hari said with renewed vigour – the last thing she wanted was to lower Jessie's spirits. But a thought had entered her head: tomorrow she would take an hour off from work and have a look at the prison camp for herself, see if Michael really was there.

Her spirits lightened, she would spend the night planning her approach to the building. Should it be covert, like a spy, or should she brazen it out and pretend to be an official of some kind?

The next morning was bright, a sunny, early-September day. A little mist lay above the area but then it was always misty over the munitions factory as she'd observed many times before.

Hari wore a jacket with a nipped-in waist and a peplum that rested on her curvaceous hips over a pencil skirt. She wore dark stockings and plain, heeled shoes and carried a clipboard. A brightly coloured chiffon scarf and a dash of precious lipstick completed her outfit.

She walked boldly up to the sentry on duty; his eyes lit up.

'Morning, miss,' he said. 'I can't let you into the camp, you know, those German men are dangerous rascals.'

'*Bore dda.*' She said good morning back to him in Welsh and smiled at him, curling a red hair around her finger. 'I've been sent from the Department of Prisoner's Rights –' she spoke in her most girly voice – 'I must just tick off some boxes, look at the men, see they are not being ill-treated and all that. It won't take long. A good soldier like you will have everything in order I'm sure.'

He looked doubtful. 'The senior British officers are all in an important meeting in the town,' he said. 'I suppose I could call Sergeant Beynon to talk to you, miss.'

'My name is Angharad, what's yours, officer?' He preened himself. He clearly wasn't an officer but he enjoyed her apparent admiration.

'I'm James, miss, I suppose I could show you round myself if you don't take too long.' He looked round him; there was no one in sight. 'I really should make a check on your papers, though.'

Hari had thought of that; she had typed up a letterhead with an impressive-looking seal made by candle wax and red cochineal and impressed it with a worn coin that would not stand too much inspection. But the soldier hardly glanced at it; he was watching as Hari hitched up her stocking.

'Come on then, I suppose it's all right. What harm can a little dainty Welsh girl like you do?'

The huts were laid out in serried ranks. The soldier glanced across at hut nine, which lay a little back from the barbed wire fencing. His brow furrowed for a moment.

'Anything wrong?' Hari looked up at him from under her eyelashes. James shook his head worriedly.

'I don't know, Miss Angharad, something is going on in there but do you think the big-headed officers will listen to me? '

'Do you mean . . . an escape attempt?'

'I've thought of that but there's no way the Germans could get out – and where would they go? They got it cushy in here: good food, sitting around gassing to each other in that foreign tongue – yet something's going on I know it is.'

The first hut smelled of sweat. The prisoners lounged around a table idly chatting but they sat up as one when the saw Hari. Some were wearing old jumpers provided by the camp, some were in worn uniform. Hari stood there smiling and looked around her at the men. The whistles were deafening and then James shouted in a sergeant major's voice.

'Shut up you clowns. Treat a lady with respect if you please.'

Eyes roved over her with blatant lust and Hari felt as though she was being undressed.

'I have some questions,' she said. 'Do you all speak a little English?'

'Not a word,' one grinning prisoner said in German.

'In that case some of your friends will explain I'm sure,' Hari simpered, longing to put her fist into his face. She asked a few questions about food and about sanitary conditions and jotted down replies. Meanwhile, she listened to the conversations, understanding just enough of the language to make out what they were saying.

In the corner of the hut were some young men. They were hardly bothering to look at her and she moved nearer. Her heart almost stopped beating as she heard the word 'escape'. She didn't look at the men but pretended to look at a painting on the wall. It was of a woman, a girlfriend, wife – or mother perhaps – and she suddenly felt sorry for the foreigners. But as soon as she got outside she would tell James what she'd heard, that his instincts were correct; there was an air about the camp, something in the attitude of the men. It was clear something dramatic was going to happen. She made a few more notes and then left, smiling at James as he led the way out of the camp. Of the man who looked like Michael there was no sign.

Sixty-Five

The journey seemed endless as Father-in-law's car bumped over the rough ground. Clutching my stomach, as though I could absorb the shock and spare the baby, I think I must have dozed.

'Halt!' A harsh German voice shook me awake and I reluctantly opened my eyes to see a guard standing behind a barrier with a gun pointing at me.

Herr Euler spoke in rapid German his tone cold, precise, commanding. The soldier at once lowered his gun and muttered an apology, holding his arm out in a 'Heil Hitler' so stiffly, I thought, absently, I could hang a line of washing on it.

I had seen newspapers and propaganda films about Hitler and to me he just seemed to flap his hand in rather an effeminate way, but this 'guardian of the gate' was determined to impress.

Herr Euler grunted and we drove on. 'How far now?' I asked mournfully. I needed to pee again and a bite of food in that order of urgency.

'Have patience.'

I crossed my legs and prayed, and closed my eyes against the blossoming dawn. At last, when the light was brightening and trees were jumping into focus and colour, and the grass was showing a bit of green instead of soft blue, my father-in-law stopped the car.

'This is a church.' My voice was accusing. 'I'm not going into any nunnery.'

He laughed and patted my belly. 'In your condition I should think not. This is a monastery, my dear.'

He pulled my arm and urged me from the car. 'I suppose that's marginally better than a place full of pious women,' I grumbled.

'The front of this monastery is in Germany, you see?' He waited for a reply and I nodded none too patiently.

'But . . .' He grinned and suddenly I wanted Michael.

'God, you're like your son.'

'Anyway, as I was saying –' he looked pleased – 'the back door is in Belgium, do you realize what I'm telling you?'

I beamed. 'Father-in-law, you are a genius.'

Inside the monastery it was not as gloomy as I expected; soft early light slanted through the arched windows giving a rosy tint to the hallowed halls and the stone floor.

Quietly, a monk appeared as if from nowhere and greeted us warmly. Herr Euler rapidly explained that I needed to leave the country. The Father smiled and nodded to me. 'I speak a little German,' he said. 'God and I will be making you comfortable while you stay with us.'

'Stay?' I looked at Father-in-law in dismay. He put his arm around my shoulder.

'Arrangements have to be made,' he said gently, 'it will be a matter of one night, two at the most, we can not afford to have you here any longer. The Belgian resistance, they will come for you, don't you worry your pretty head.'

I knew then the enormity of what Father-in-law was doing for me. I turned into his chest and began to cry. 'Go back now, please go back. I don't want you to get in any trouble, Father-in-law.'

'Give me a fine healthy grandson.' He smiled sardonically. 'At least he will be good Aryan stock as the Herr Hitler desires all people to be.'

The monk showed me to my bed, in a small cell; it was spartan but it was quiet and cosy, and to my relief a lavatory was adjoining it. The bricks, warmed through the day by soft sunlight, were almost glowing. The cell was lit by a single candle and, in the distance, I could hear the chanting sing-song of monks at their worship.

Inside me, the baby moved as if in response to the singing. I wrapped my arms around my growing stomach and hugged my child as best I could. And I prayed. Then, at last, I slept.

The early morning chanting woke me. I washed in the cold water from the little tin bowl and dressed quickly. It was cold now, the sun was not yet showing its face and from the look of the sky it was only about four or five in the morning. Still night-time to my mind.

I was brought a breakfast of bread with a slight scraping of margarine and a grizzled piece of bacon and in its glory, topping the bread, was a precious egg. I felt tears well in my eyes; the good men of the monastery had given their all to look after me.

Herr Euler was ready to leave. He clicked his heels and bowed and then I hugged him and he laughed.

'Don't suffocate me child!' He stepped away from me and made for the car. Soon he would be back in his heartland, his Germany, where with mixed feelings he would fight Herr Hitler's war.

I caught a glimpse of a shadowy figure among the trees outside the gates of the monastery. I saw the gleam of a rifle barrel. I shouted a warning as my father-in-law climbed into the car. A shot rang out and Herr Euler fell to the ground.

I ran to him and knelt beside him and the good Father knelt beside me.

'He has been shot by one of the resistance or maybe he was followed by his own soldiers, we will never know.'

I cradled Father-in-law's head in my arms, holding him to my more than ample bosom. His eyes were open but he was dead and I couldn't even say goodbye. I looked at the monk for help.

'Father-in-law gave his life for me, how can I ever bear the guilt?'

'Dear little girl, be proud, Herr Euler saved you and his grand-child. Now come away into the safety he wanted for you and, remember, this good man gave his life for freedom and for the future of the human race.'

Carefully, I took off my coat and padded it behind dear Herr Euler's head. Then I closed his eyes. In repose, he was so like his son, and I touched my father-in-law's still-warm hand to my rounded stomach.

'I will tell your grandson about his father and his grandfather, I'll teach him to be proud of his heritage, I promise you that. And then I left him to the monks and, dry-eyed with grief, I went back into the monastery.

Sixty-Six

Hari tugged Violet's arm. 'You're getting very friendly with Georgie Porgy.' They were on their way home from work and Hari noticed that Violet had taken to putting cream on her face to prevent the yellow powder sinking into her skin. Just like Kate used to do. Hari felt a sudden pain squeeze her heart.

Violet grimaced. 'Don't call him that, he's a grown man now, not a little kid.' Her tone was even but Hari could see Violet was rattled.

'Sorry!' she said, 'it's just that I've known George since he was a little boy. He used to bully Meryl unmercifully.'

'Well, from what I hear of Meryl she could well look after herself.' Violet's good humour reasserted itself. 'Sounds as if your sister could take on the whole German army and beat them to death.'

Hari closed her eyes for a moment. 'She might have to.' Her voice was quiet.

'It's my turn to say sorry now, I didn't mean it nastily,' Violet said, 'but don't worry, your Meryl will be all right. Anyway, changing the subject, what were you doing up at the German camp?'

Hari was startled. She wasn't aware that she'd been seen near the camp. 'I just went to look at the men – the Germans – to see if they were the monsters the papers make them out to be.'

'And?'

'And they were ordinary men, like ours, but foreign. I felt quite sorry for them really.'

'And did you see that special one, the one who made your face turn pale when they all marched past us that day? Handsome bloke he was too, looked more Welsh than German.'

'I don't know what you mean,' Hari said. 'Yes, I looked, I've got blood in my veins and with no men of our own around of course I looked.'

'All right, all right, don't get so heated about it, I'm only teasing. You can dish it out about George but you can't take it, Hari, where's your sense of humour gone these days?'

'I think I lost it somewhere in the war,' Hari murmured.

'Ta-ta for now then, I'm making tea for George.' Violet smiled happily. 'See you tomorrow.'

That night Georgie didn't come back at all. Hari didn't mind, let him make Violet happy while he could. George would always be the fat little boy who teased Meryl but Hari recognized he was much changed. Discharged from the army because of wounds he sustained in the last battle at the front, he worked in Swansea now, in the munitions factory making the shell cases that were sent to Bridgend for filling; his job was dangerous if only because the German bombers saw Richard Thomas and Baldwins as a factory in need of blowing up.

It was a relief to settle to a new day of work in the quietness of her office; to listen to the messages being sent across the airwaves and try to decipher them. By now she could tell the difference between various German signallers: they all seemed to have their own 'signature' their own hesitancies, their own rapidity, all different and identifiable. Some Germans were careless, believing no one would be listening or at least understanding the messages they sent. At Bletchley they had been just as careless, not realizing that their codes could be broken.

Once she thought she recognized a woman's hand, the staccato beat of the Morse seemed to be handled less forcefully, but there was no message from Meryl, no Welsh language words mixed in with the coded message.

When she returned home that night, it was to find Violet and George sitting snugly together on the sofa. There was no sound from the kitchen, no boiling kettle on the stove.

'Where's Jessie?'

Violet giggled. Your dad's taken her to the pictures. They've gone to the Plaza to see some sentimental picture or something.'

I didn't know Jessie was sentimental, or Father either.' Hari sank into the armchair. 'How about a cuppa for a working girl then, Vi, you've had the day off remember?'

Violet obligingly made tea but she treated herself and George to some home-made wine. It looked and smelled revolting.

'Come on then, George, I thought you were taking me for a walk,' Violet said. George responded with alacrity, putting down his unfinished drink and trying to wipe the grimace of disgust from his face at the taste.

'See you later then.' Violet grasped George's arm, winked at Hari and then they were gone, leaving Hari sitting alone in a cold, empty and unfriendly house.

She had the fire glowing in the grate and a pile of toast and jam ready when Jessie came bustling into the house with Father in tow.

'Something smells good.' She beamed at Hari. 'How did you know what time we'd be back?'

'I made a guess,' Hari said dryly. 'Actually I consulted the paper and read what time the show was ending.'

'*Duw*, I haven't been to the pictures in years – well you don't, stuck out on a farm in the country, do you?'

Hari saw Jessie glance at Father with a look of affection and felt a wash of something very much like envy. Everyone had someone to care for except her. She made a fresh pot of tea and then went up to her bedroom. She washed in cold water and climbed into bed and hugged herself, feeling lonely and unloved.

The Sunday bells were ringing when she woke. The sun was shining into the bedroom and with renewed energy Hari got up to face the day and dressed quickly. After breakfast she would take her bike and ride to Bridgend and watch the prison camp. Some of the German prisoners went to St Mary's church for Sunday worship and if Michael was alive he would most certainly go with them.

It was a fine day, the autumn sun warming her back as she rode towards Bridgend. Questions reeled through her head: could Michael have survived? Was it another pilot who bore a resemblance to him? But no, it was Michael she'd seen, she was sure of it, but he'd looked at her without recognition. Had he lost his memory when his plane crashed on to Welsh soil? She wished all her questions could be answered. But today she would make sure she saw Michael even if she had to question every guard in Island Farm.

When she arrived at Bridgend she parked her bike and waited outside the church, glad to sit down on the warm stone wall. Her legs ached and her head ached through tension. And then it began to rain.

Hari unpacked her cape from the saddlebag and draped it around her shoulders. Soon her red hair curled into damp tendrils but, doggedly, she waited until the church bells rang out at the end of the service.

The Germans came filtering out of the church, the senior officers first and then a few non-commissioned men. There was one pilot at the rear of the trail of men and behind him a British guard. Hari recognized him.

'Morning, James, been to morning worship I see?' He stopped, but the pilot walked on without looking at her. 'Is that the man who came down in the German plane?' she asked.

'Aye, that's the bastard who came to bomb us trying to send the munitions and the whole of Bridgend up in flames, pardon my French.' He stared at her bedraggled appearance. 'What you doin' here, work on a Sunday do you?'

Hari improvised. 'No, but it was a lovely morning when I started out, I thought I needed some exercise and fresh air after being cooped up in an office all week and then it started to rain on me.' She pushed back her wet hair.

'Anyway, I can see the prisoners are allowed to attend church, that's very good.'

'Aye, more than they'd do for us I dare say.'

Hari ignored James's hostility. 'How did that pilot survive the crash? I surveyed the site of the crash – no one could have got out of that.'

'He baled out, what do you think? Cowards all of them. But at least he'd got rid of his bombs before he came down. We're just lucky they fell before they got to us.'

Hari's eyes followed the party of prisoners and, as if Michael sensed her gaze, he turned briefly and looked at her. His hand moved in a small gesture and she felt a rush of joy, her heart began to race. He *knew* her, it was *Michael* – he was well and strong and, hopefully, he would live out the rest of the war in the safety of Island Farm prison camp.

Sixty-Seven

I heard the chanting in the early morning and woke up with my heart thumping. For a minute I thought I was back in Ravensbruck prison camp – the cell I was in was just as small – and then I listened to the monks praying in song and knew I was safe. I ran my hands over the small swell of my stomach. The baby kicked and I smiled.

'We're going home,' I whispered in English. 'I'm taking you to Carmarthen. On the farm that will be your land, we'll remember your father and your grandfather and I will tell you all about the bravery of the men whose name you will carry.'

I cried a little and then one of the monks brought me a breakfast of warm, thick brown bread. 'Today they will come, the resistance men from Belgium, they will take you to the coast and put you on a ship to Ireland.'

I felt a dip of disappointment; somehow I'd imagined I'd be flown straight to Britain but I could see it would be a long time before I was home again. I thanked the good man and slowly ate the fresh bread. There was a scraping of home-made butter on it melting into the warmth and nothing had ever tasted so good.

I was ready when the brother came for me. I had no possessions, only the papers Father-in-law had given me, my marriage certificate and a fake passport in the name of Katherine O'Brien.

He had told me that if the Belgians were caught taking me out of the country I was to show my marriage certificate and make up a story I'd been taken hostage. 'You're good at that sort of thing,' he'd said, with a smile. I bit my lip but the tears welled in my eyes anyway. Biting lips was supposed to bring control but for me it only hurt without any benefit at all so I immediately stopped digging my teeth into my lip and continued to cry.

We went down a long passageway towards the back of the monastery where the kitchens were situated. There sat four men eating breakfast, one of them was Fritz.

'Hello, in trouble again,' he sighed heavily. 'I'll be glad to be rid of you, young lady.'

That remark did more than any biting of lips to stiffen my shoulders. 'Trust you to be the one to come to my rescue –' my tone was full of sarcasm – 'you nearly got me killed last time you "helped me". I'm perfectly capable on my own, you know.'

Fritz bit into his brown bread and a dribble of butter ran down into his beard, only the beard didn't look grey now it looked black. His disguise as a tramp had been a good one but now he was just a young man, albeit a brave young man.

'We'll be making a move in half an hour,' he said, his mouth full of bread. He ate as if he was ravenous and I suppose he was.

The others, Belgians, smiled at me once, all of them taking in my round belly and the wedding ring on my finger, and looked away giving attention to their breakfast. I watched them masticate slowly, mentally urging them to hurry up. I wanted to be on my way home as soon as possible.

At last, Fritz wiped his mouth indelicately with the back of his hand. He saw me looking and spoke defensively. 'We don't often get fed and when we do it's always on the run so forgive our lack of napkins and dinner table manners.'

'I never said a word.'

'You didn't have to.'

'You're good for me, you stop me feeling afraid and vulnerable,' I said. He shook his head.

'You, vulnerable? Don't make me laugh.' He got up and thanked the brother who had served the food. Fritz was fluent in several languages, obviously, and under my breath I said, 'Clever clogs'. He heard me but made no reply.

The brother led the way along a winding passage towards the rear, through some unused rooms and to a small door in the thick back wall. He opened it with difficulty as if it was seldom used, but it was a ploy to fool the Germans. I knew prisoners escaped from Germany this way practically every month or so.

We were out in the fields then and I looked round: this then was Belgium, land of the free except that it wasn't; the country was awash with Germans and we filed away into the nearby trees in silence.

I noticed that the men, all four of them including Fritz, wore rucksacks; I was spared, so I thought, until Fritz handed me a bag.

'What am I supposed to do with this? I'm pregnant if you hadn't noticed.'

'It's food – if we all get parted or some of us killed you'll need to make your own way home.' His dark eyebrows were raised. 'You are perfectly capable or so I understood.'

I sighed. 'You're right of course.'

He helped me on with the bag. 'You're not bad you know, for a girl.' He led the way through the forest where there was a pathway already worn by many other feet. I knew we had days of travelling before us before we reached the coast and I wondered if I, and my baby, would survive the cracking pace Fritz set.

That night we stayed at a farmhouse. The young lady was obviously smitten with Fritz and after a plain supper they disappeared upstairs. The other three men gave a ribald laugh joking in their own tongue, but I didn't have to understand the language to know what they were saying.

Later, when Fritz reappeared, he went out to the yard and I could hear the sound of a pump and the sound of spraying water. When he came in his hair was wet and he shivered a little, his shirt sticking to the dampness of him. The men had a beer and I looked enquiringly towards the lady in charge.

'Come with me.' She recognized my look of weariness and led me up the rickety stairs to a tiny loft room. But there was a bed and I looked at it gladly. She patted my arm. 'You share it, with me.' She laughed and threw back her dark hair. 'But I no like girls, I like strong men like Fritz so you are safe with me, little one.'

I knew I was blushing. 'I don't care if I have to share with the entire Highland Regiment so long as I can lie down.'

It was luxury to stretch out, though fully clothed in case we had to move swiftly, and soon, exhausted, I fell asleep.

The next morning, we had transport, at least some of the way. Gladly I climbed on the back of the lorry and crouched down under some scruffy potato sacks. I heard kisses and a playful slap and I guessed Fritz was saying a fond, if unromantic, farewell to his lady love, one of many if only she knew it.

The dawn came, the earth warmed and so did the creatures in the sacking. The fleas or ticks or whatever they were bit me and stung, but at least I wasn't having to walk and I was getting nearer the coast all the time and soon, perhaps sooner than anticipated, I would be home.

Sixty-Eight

Hari stood in the register office in Swansea holding a tiny bouquet of flowers. She was witness to her friend Vi's marriage to Georgie Dixon and she could hardly believe it. Alongside her was one of Georgie's workmates looking uncomfortable in a shabby suit with a white scarf instead of a tie.

It was over very quickly. The registrar tried to make the ceremony sound meaningful but there were many hasty marriages made in time of war and usually they ended in a disaster of some kind. Hari could tell he knew that by the sadness of his tired blue eyes.

Vi was excited and happy and her pretty face was flushed. Even the yellow had been toned down by the application of powder. She clung to George's arm as if she would never let him go and he seemed to have blossomed under her love, his smile happy but his eyes full of tenderness as they rested on his new wife's face.

Jessie had given them leave to use the farm during their honeymoon; Carmarthen was where George grew up and where he would probably want to live after the war. Vi would find it strange and quiet after the town and the company of the people in the munitions works but she would soon adapt to country life Hari was sure.

Outside in the late sunshine Hari kissed her friend and hugged her close. She smelled sweet, lavendery, her hair shiny and curling on her shoulders. 'I know you're going to be happy,' Hari whispered, and Violet's smile was radiant.

'I've never been in love before, not with anyone. I really didn't know what love was till I met George –'Vi's voice was breathless – 'isn't he so handsome and proud in his best suit?'

He did look handsome, a far cry from the 'porky pig' of Meryl's childhood memories and Hari felt a pain like a stab wound as she thought of her sister. The thought led to Michael and grief and confusion engulfed her. Hari fixed a determined smile on her face.

'So long as he's good to you everything will be just fine.' She glanced at George and raised her voice. 'You be a good husband to my dear friend now George, or you'll have me to deal with.'

He grimaced. 'I don't want that, not if you're anything like your sister Meryl.' He put his arm around his wife. 'She was a little devil, mind, we used to fight like enemies. She whacked me where it hurt most one day, not that I didn't ask for it.' He smiled wryly. 'But then none of us are kids any more, war makes a man grow up and realize that violence achieves nothing.' He wandered away to talk to some friends and Hari and Violet watched as Jessie finished making flat Welsh cakes with a little margarine and tiny bits of fruit, mainly bits of apple and dried figs. The cakes steamed hot from the griddle and the spicy aroma filled the kitchen.

'They smell nice,' Hari said.

'Should have currants and raisins in and a nice bit of sugar but they're the best I could do,' Jessie grumbled. 'She smacked George's hand away as he reached for one. 'Go and have the spam fritters first, fill your belly with potatoes and then you can have Welsh cakes, right, my boy?'

Hari had acquired a bottle of gin from her friend up at the German camp – she had kept in touch with James hoping to learn more about the German prisoners. She knew Michael was alive, had been in the camp, but she never saw him again and the fear was he had grown sick and ill and had been shipped off elsewhere.

After the meal she raised her glass. 'A toast to the bride and groom,' she said, sipping a little of the gin spiced liberally with Jessie's home-made pop. 'May you live happily ever after and have many little ones.'

Violet blushed and Hari stared at her in concern. 'Violet you're not, well . . . you're not, are you?'

Violet looked puzzled and Jessie put it more bluntly. 'Was this a shotgun wedding, girl, that's what Hari means?'

Violet's blush deepened. 'Of course not, we haven't done anything like that – how mean of you, Hari. Don't you think George married me because he loved me not because he "had to" as they say these days?'

'Sorry, Violet, very sorry,' Hari said hastily, 'it happens to so many people.'

'Well, not to me and George.'

'Well, be happy.' Hari hugged her and Violet relented and smiled.

George shuffled his feet and glanced anxiously at Violet. 'We're taking it steady, aren't we love?'

'Yes, of course we are George, anything you want.' She sounded uncertain and Hari wondered if Violet knew the facts of married life. Would Violet lie dazed and fainted with love and delight in her husband's arms? Would she be raised on a glowing cloud to heaven the way Hari had been when Michael made love to her? She pushed the thought away. All that was over, a thousand waters had flowed beneath the bridges since then. Michael was a married man now and, what's more, was a prisoner considered an enemy of the British people, spat on and hated by the inhabitants of Bridgend and all the world for all Hari knew.

Later, she drove the newlyweds to their country retreat. Violet stared out of the back of the jeep Hari had borrowed and looked in awe at the darkening countryside.

'It's a bit lonely isn't it? No lights . . . nothing.'

George put his arm around her. 'You'll love it like I do, you'll see.'

Hari left them at the door of the farmhouse and drove away, a lump in her throat. She could picture Michael there; his hair blown into a mop by the wind, his face tanned, his eyes very blue – and she wanted him.

It took her hours to drive back through the gloom of the blackout and, sometimes, when the moon appeared from behind the clouds and the roadway was a ribbon of light, she thought the bombers would spot her and drop their load on her. It was a relief to enter the familiar streets of Swansea and park the jeep at the curb outside her house.

Inside, the kitchen still had the scent of fruit and cake but Jessie was sitting at the table, her apron screwed up between her hands, her face white. 'They've got out. The prisoners – they've got out.'

'What do you mean?' Hari's mouth was dry.

'A man called James came here, told me to tell you, "report to you", he said. The Germans have escaped, girl, run away. Dug a tunnel they did, made the place all tidy like with milk tins and lights and such. Anyway, over seventy of them have got out, gone, God knows where, we could be killed in our beds.'

Hari wished she could faint, be out of the grip of fear and pain and the thought of Michael on the run with police and army and men with guns chasing him. But she just slumped into a chair and stared into the fire. How could she tell Jessie that her son, the boy she believed dead, was alive and probably with the other escaped prisoners on the run?

Sixty-Nine

It was days now since the escape and Hari had heard nothing about the prisoners. Outside the camp the guard had doubled and even though Hari managed now and again to talk to James he was more tight-lipped than he'd been previously.

She saw him now outside the fence and waved and to her relief he came over to her. He took her in his arms and to her surprise buried his face in her neck.

'For Gawd's sake pretend you're my girl,' he murmured, the other fellows are getting a bit suspicious like.'

Hari felt uncomfortable as she put her arms round James's neck but she could see the sense of his words. A warning bell sounded in her head, even James must be suspicious the way she kept standing around the camp. She put a bit of enthusiasm in her hug and James responded, kissing her soundly.

She drew away and forced a smile. 'I'm sorry, James, it's early days yet but I do like talking to you.' She hated herself for the deception but it was necessary; she had to hide the fact that one of the German prisoners was in fact brought up on a farm in Carmarthen by a Welsh mother.

The Welsh guards might be sympathetic but the Germans would manage to do away with Michael because they would most certainly think him a spy.

'Where do you think they are, the prisoners I mean?'

James looked dour. 'One of them has got out of Wales, I know that, he was seen on a train, pretending to be a Welshman, could even speak Welsh. Wonderful what these chaps have picked up in here. Intelligent blokes these Germans.'

Hari's heart pounded. 'Was he caught, this man?'

'Aye, he's been caught, don't know what state he's in, mind, might have been shot or something or at least given a good hammering, don't look right for prisoners to escape from our camp in Bridgend.' He looked even gloomier. 'So far this is the first escape ever of German prisoners, they don't want to go back to war, most of 'em, havin' a fine time doin' nothing but lying around being treated like lords. I can only hope our boys are bein' treated half as good in Germany.'

Hari handed James an apple she'd stolen from Jessie's store, the orchard behind the farm in Carmarthen, which, though neglected now, had still yielded some fine apples. She and Jessie had brought them to Swansea and Jessie had 'set them down' in the cool larder in the back kitchen of Hari's house.

'A little treat for you James.' Hari wished she could give it to Michael but of course that was impossible, especially now. Hari bit back a sigh. Where was Michael? Was he still alive or had he been shot attempting to escape? Fear was like a cold knife in her heart but she tried to smile as James took the apple, his features softening.

'You're like that there Eve in the Bible, girl,' he said softly, 'but I don't need any tempting, see?'

Hari moved away from him. 'I'd better not stay too long, don't want to lose my reputation now, do I?'

'You won't do that, Hari, everyone can see you're respectable. We only been inside the camp once and then we weren't alone, like. No, you won't lose your reputation as a nice girl, don't you worry.'

Hari walked back to the munitions gate and settled down to wait for the next bus. She missed Violet's company but Vi was on her honeymoon, enjoying life as a new bride.

As she waited, Hari remembered the way George had fought with Meryl. But they were children then and war had changed George: he'd seen violence and death on the streets; he'd done dangerous work; he was honed now into a good man. Violet had done well for herself.

When Hari at last got home, she saw her father sprawled in a chair, a steaming meal of hot pie on a tray on his lap. Jessie as usual was fussing over him. To be fair, with Violet and George away, Father was the only one Jessie had left to fuss over.

'Jess has made us a delicious pie for our dinner, Angharad.' Her father put down his knife and fork. 'It will put some meat on those thin bones of yours.'

'Precious little meat in that pie,' Jessie said, in her usual blunt way, but her eyes gleamed at the praise. 'Mostly veg from the farm and a bit of offcuts of lamb, bits and pieces, and pastry mostly made from lard.'

'Still, it's delicious.' Father was in a good mood though lines of pain from his leg etched his face. He caught Jessie's hand and held it for a long moment. She blushed and Hari hid a smile; her father and Jessie were clearly very fond of each other. She supposed they weren't really that old. Father was fifty-two and Jessie was an indeterminate age, perhaps fifty, maybe younger, but her hair was white and long and always coiled into a bun which might make her look older. Anyway, they both appeared transformed, happy. Could there be love in the air?

Suddenly, Hari felt upset. She went outside into the tiny back garden, planted now with vegetables which were tended mainly by Jessie, and forced back the tears. Everyone had a loved one: Violet, even Father, and of course Meryl, who had the best love of all, married to dear darling Michael, who had once loved *her*, had lain with her, made a woman of her.

'Don't be so melodramatic!' she said aloud. 'You're acting like a Victorian maid. Grow up, Angharad Jones, for God's sake.' She felt ashamed of herself, her little sister might be dead for all she knew.

'Taking the Lord's name in vain now, then, girl?' Jessie stood beside her, her voice was anxious. 'You're upset. Is it me and your father? We're not rushing into anything if that's what you're worried about. I just find I care for him.' She was pleading for Hari to understand.

'No, it's not that.' Hari decided it was time to tell Jessie the truth. 'It's about Michael.'

'What about Michael – has anything happened to him?' Jessie clutched her arm. 'There's me thinking about myself, acting like a girl again, and not thinking about my son.'

'It's all right, Jessie, at least I think Michael is all right, but you've heard the news about the escaped prisoners from Bridgend?'

Jessie shook her head. 'Of course, but I didn't think too much about it. But what's that got to do with my Michael?'

'He crashed as you know, Jessie, but he lived and was a prisoner in Island Farm. I wasn't sure at first if it was him then he looked at me and gave me a sort of signal.' She took a deep breath. 'He escaped but they've got him again. God knows what state he'll be in when they fetch him back.'

'No love, you're mistaken, Michael is dead, you're dreaming, wanting him to be alive. Don't fool yourself girl, what would Michael be doing in a prison with a lot of Germans? You're just being plain daft.'

Jessie hugged her. 'Forget my Michael, Hari, he was never for you; find another man; you're young, beautiful and you're alive. Michael is dead; dead; do you understand?'

Hari nodded. 'I understand Jessie, go back to Father, he needs you. I'll just calm myself before I come in.' But how could she be calm when her thoughts were a confusion of doubts and hopes and her every sinew yearned for one man only, and that man was Michael Euler?

Seventy

The days and nights passed without incident, that is until Fritz got us near the coast. We were emerging from a small forest when suddenly shots were fired, whizzing overhead like a swarm of bees. German voices shouted the order to 'halt' and Fritz accelerated away into another group of trees. He stopped among thick brush.

'You get out,' he said, almost gently, 'for your sake and for ours. I'll try to come back to pick you up. If I don't, you're on your own.' He drove away and I wished him luck with all my heart.

I must have waited hidden in the trees for hours but no one came for me. At last, as it was growing dark, I knew Fritz wasn't coming back and I began to walk. I was so tired I wanted to cry, to give myself up to the Germans, tell them everything and let them shoot me. And then I thought of the baby, my baby – Michael's baby – and I knew I had to make an effort to escape.

My legs were aching and my belly grumbled with hunger by the time I saw the lights of a dockyard. I knew it was dangerous to go any further but I had to bluff my way back home, live by my wits as I'd done since I left British shores.

I could see German uniforms everywhere. I dug out my German papers. They were all in order, German and Irish, thanks to my dear father-in-law.

I walked into the dockyard and my heart lightened. I might get a passage to Ireland from here if I was lucky. It didn't occur to me I didn't know where 'here' was. Head high, I was stopped at a barrier and showed my German papers.

'What is your business at the docks?' The guard spoke in heavily accented German and I barely understood him.

'I think I'm lost.' It was all I could think of on the spur of the moment.

'From Berlin, eh?' He looked me up and down.

'Hamburg,' I said at once.

'Berlin has been attacked again by the British and the Americans.' He stumbled for the right words. 'Soon be burned like Dresden.' I could swear there was a touch of glee in his voice; he must be Belgian or Dutch I decided.

'Why you leave Hamburg?' He almost shouted the question and I jumped.

I am leaving for Ireland,' I said, in German, 'Sick mother to visit.' I patted my rounded stomach. 'Tell her about my baby, too.'

'No ship from this port to Ireland. You go somewhere else.'

I stood there with my little bag in my hand feeling abandoned. 'I don't know where to go or what to do, my husband, a pilot, is lost over enemy territory.'

That was as much of the truth as I wanted to tell him. I hoped he wouldn't probe too deeply. If he did he might discover who I really was and he'd soon find out I had been wanted in Germany as a spy. He looked at my bag and I held it out to him. He shook his head.

'Please help me.' I perched uncomfortably on a bollard and put my case on the ground.

He was silent for a long time and then he sighed in resignation. 'Wait here.' He disappeared.

I sat uncomfortably on the uneven surface feeling the cold from the pewter, oily water of the docks chill my bones. I sat there for at least an hour unnoticed. Then he was back.

'You stubborn.' He smiled suddenly. 'Must be Irish in you. Show papers again.'

I showed him my papers and he nodded hesitantly. 'You Catolic, then?' It seemed to please him. 'I speak to wife Ella, she Catolic as well, say you can stay in my house.'

I didn't bother to tell him I was Welsh Baptist down to the bone. 'I don't want to put you to any trouble,' I said, just to be polite.

'No trouble, it is all right.' He took me to the edge of the dock and pointed to the house.

'Oh, thank you.' I stepped from one foot to the other not knowing what to do.

'You sit on bench,' he said, pointing. 'I relieved of duty in only few minutes. I am Freddie, I take you.'

Relieved, I sat on the bench; it seemed if you were small, young, pregnant and alone every man wanted to take care of you.

About an hour later I was seated near a warm fire with Freddie's wife, Ella. She was Belgian too and brought me a hot drink of chocolate. It was a treat and though I knew that the tin of powdered chocolate was probably pinched from one of the ships on the dock, I drank with relish.

I slept on the sofa tucked into a warm blanket, the fire burned low in the grate but the embers gleamed comfortingly and out of sheer fatigue I fell asleep almost at once.

In the morning, Freddie had to go to work and Ella and I poured over a map. I wondered if I could hitch a lift into France which, to my delight, had been liberated some months ago by the British army. It was miles away, but if I could hitch a lift to Calais I would surely find a way to go to Ireland and from there to Britain.

Ella told me I was in Antwerp where the Germans had command of the dock and the seas beyond.

'But the Allies will come soon; the Germans haf lost. You good married girl, you haf ring on finger,' she said softly, her hand over mine. 'You are soon to haf child?'

I smiled widely and she nodded sagely. 'You stay us till Allies come.'

Christmas came and went. It was cold, the water in the docks looked like ice. Ella made little dolls for her two daughters and Freddie made a wooden train for his son. I just grew fatter.

One morning in February I awoke to the sounds of shooting and my heart turned over, I had grown comfortable, safe. But now I realized the war was not yet over.

Seventy-One

It was a momentous time at the beginning of the year 1945. The Americans had come to the Ardennes, the whole country was celebrating and I began slow labour at the unearthly hour of twelve o'clock in the night.

I got up and dressed and packed my little bag and then I woke Ella and Freddie. 'I'm going home to have my baby,' I said firmly. I knew Ella would argue and she did.

'Not now,' she said, 'wait till baby come.'

'That won't be for a few weeks.' I was lying through my teeth but Ella didn't know it and she nodded.

'I understand, you want your child to be Catolic like us.'

'That's right, Catholic,' I said. It was the only way she would allow me to go. She frowned.

'But at least wait till morning.'

'I will go now.' I kissed her and hugged her and then kissed Freddie. 'Thank you for all you've done, I'll write to you when I'm home.'

I set out, well wrapped in Freddie's scarf, to the edge of the docks. There was a battalion of British soldiers and one American pilot.

'What you doing here lady?' The American pilot stood looking at my round figure with surprise.

'I must get home,' I said, trying my best to hide a small contraction.

'You an English lady?' He was even more surprised.

'I'm Welsh,' I said stubbornly. 'My husband was a pilot, shot down a few months ago. I'm having his baby and I don't want to have it here.' I didn't mention that Michael was flying for the Germans.

'What do you expect us to do?' one of the other men said, frowning at me.

'I've been spying for the British,' I volunteered, 'I've put myself in danger to help my country and now I want to go home to have my child. Is that asking too much?' I demanded. No one replied.

'Look, I was supposed to be taken out of the country by the resistance but they had to leave rather hurriedly if you get my meaning and I was left to fend for myself, but now I'm asking, begging for help.' I looked directly at the American pilot.

'You got a plane?'

'Of course I got a plane, lady, so what?'

'My name is Meryl,' I said sharply, 'yours?'

'Aldo,' he said reluctantly. 'You got a sister in Swansea, a girl called Hari?'

'Yes, you know Hari?'

'I met her, fine girl, lovely red hair.'

I was a little piqued, everyone admired my sister. 'Well, Aldo, you can take me home. It will only take an hour or so, won't it?'

'There are fuel checks – you can't just take an aeroplane, you know, mam.'

'Why not, who is to know? I thought you pilots were dare-devils.'

The men talked among themselves, one or two argued, and then Aldo grinned. 'All right, for your cheek and because your sister was so nice, I'll risk it. Tom, you drive us to the field and see about refuelling, OK?'

I breathed out a huge sigh. I didn't think I was going to get away with it. Every bump of the jeep threatened to break my waters. I'd seen enough birthing on the farm to know more or less what happened. I knew the mother ewe delivered the lamb sometimes alone in a field and if a dull sheep could do it so could I.

It was an ordeal climbing into the plane but, by lifting up my heavy belly, I succeeded, managing not to moan with the pain.

Thankful, I sat down and closed my eyes. Incredibly, I must have dozed and then I woke up sharply to the rat-tat-tat of guns.

'Gerry on my tail,' Aldo said, 'some cloud to the right, I'll hide in there.' Through his windscreen I saw nothing but grey fog and I knew we would be in trouble if he couldn't get out of the clouds again, but at least the enemy plane had given up and gone away. That was until we slid out of the clouds and then the shooting, alarmingly close, began again.

I pressed my palms together and like a child recited the Lord's Prayer in English and in Welsh. *'Ein Tad*, Our Father' – the words whispered out like molten silver between my lips. Aldo ducked and dived and turned the plane and fired his own guns. I saw the German plane begin to smoke and then it screeched down towards the sea. 'Good shot!' I said, then, *'Diolch yn fawr'*, as I looked up towards heaven.

'What damn language are you speaking now?' Aldo asked.

'Welsh of course,' I said huffily as if he should know. 'By the way, you can drop me on the Welsh coast, Carmarthen, it will be nearer for you and there are plenty of fields to land in.'

'Thank you, mam.' Aldo's tone was dry. 'At least I made another kill on the way so it wasn't entirely a wasted journey,' he said.

The landing was scary but, following my directions, Aldo landed within about a mile of the farmhouse.

'You didn't bother to tell me about the hills,' he said. 'Now go before I'm taken for the enemy and arrested.'

I flung my bag out of the plane and dropped it to the ground. Then I had to drop myself because there were no steps. I landed with a bump and *my* bump protested by squirming frantically to get out of this uncomfortable belly.

'Good luck, Meryl, and love to that sister of yours.' Aldo winked, looking every inch the dashing pilot. I waved back in the rose dawn and watched him lift his plane into the sky with great skill and aplomb. And then I walked to the cold, empty farmhouse that still held the scent of Jessie and my darling Michael and prepared for the birth of my child. Alone.

Seventy-Two

Hari stood with James outside Island Farm Prison and looked at his face, dark with anger, in dismay. 'How many of them have been caught?'

'A few.' He stared at her. 'You seem very interested, sure you didn't have anything to do with it all, Miss Jones?'

'How could I?' She stared at him aghast, she couldn't lose his trust, not now, when she needed to know where Michael was. 'I warned you they were talking about a tunnel didn't I?' she said defensively.

'Aye, so you did Hari, I'm sorry, *merchi*, that was a daft idea of mine but you're up at the camp so much, girl, I wonder what's behind it all. I don't flatter myself it's my charm.'

Hari thought quickly. 'But James, you know I'm writing a report about the prison –' she paused – 'it's all good, mind, you've treated the prisoners with every respect, you've looked after them very well indeed.'

He seemed mollified. 'Aye, too bloody well, pardon my language, we were all so sure they wouldn't run back to the war we got too easy with them.'

Hari kissed James's cheek. 'You're a good pal, James,' she said gently, 'I'm sure they'll all get caught, they can't get out of the country, can they?'

'I told you one of the blighters got all the way to Birmingham. They're bringing him back as we speak.'

'Oh, do you know his name?'

'If I did I couldn't tell you, miss.' James's voice was hard. 'By the way, I didn't have a good look at your papers, did I?'

'It's top secret, James, I work for the government.'

He looked dubious.

Hari sighed. 'All I can say is I work at the munitions here in Bridgend but it's special work. I used to work for Colonel Edwards until he died.'

James's face cleared. 'Everyone has heard of the old man,' he said respectfully. 'But why are you watching Island Farm Prison Camp? If it was because of me you'd go out with me.'

Hari hesitated. 'There's someone special here, someone who might not be the true German he seems to be.'

'His name?'

'If I knew, I wouldn't tell you.' She imitated his tone and he smiled.

'All right, Hari, I'll believe you.' He came a little closer. 'But you do like me, just a bit, don't you?'

'Of course I do James, I wouldn't spend so much time talking to you if I didn't – I'd just march in here and get on with my job.'

He touched her hair. 'So lovely, *cariad*.'

Hari smiled and after a moment moved away. 'Look, James, I'd better get back to work.'

'Euler,' he said suddenly, 'the man we caught at Birmingham, his name is Michael Euler.'

Hari's heart lifted. 'Is he unhurt?'

'Aye, except for the injuries he got when he crashed, some leg wounds and minor burns, lucky bas—. Sorry, Hari.'

'I can tell you this, James,' Hari said, suddenly happy, 'we're going to win this war. I can't tell you how I know but I do, all right?'

He grinned. 'Come back tomorrow, I'll see if you can interview this man Euler.'

'Really, you can do that, James?'

'I'll do my best for you, Hari *fach*.'

'I'll see you tomorrow then James and thanks for all your help, you certainly make my life easier.'

Hari rode home on the bus and then caught the train – missing Violet's happy chatter. She was worried about Violet. Since she'd married George and moved out to Carmarthen she seemed more subdued, not her usual happy self and, when she visited Swansea, she looked around with nostalgia, clearly wishing she was back home.

'Vi –' Hari hugged her friend's arm – 'if you don't like the country, ask George to bring you back to town.'

'We've moved into his mam's home, that's what I don't like,' Vi said, 'but George is doing the house up, he hopes to sell the place and buy a house of our own.' She brightened. 'At least I've got a man I love – I'm better off than most girls – and we'll make the move soon, I'm sure.' But there was a glint of tears in her eyes and Hari promised herself she'd have a word with George as soon as the opportunity arose.

Seventy-Three

I'd managed to put up the black-out curtain and I lit the lamps, glad of the warm glow in the old farmhouse. Wincing with pain I lit the fire, I'd always been good at fires, and then I fetched some towels and spread them on the old, sagging sofa.

I wished Jessie was here; she'd be warm and comforting and would tell me what to do when my baby was born. I felt the pain of my contraction encircle my body and tried to squeeze the baby out, the way I'd seen the animals do but I realized my baby wasn't ready to come yet – or my body wasn't ready to push – so I went with the wash of pain and let the moans bubble from my lips without restraint.

The hours seemed to pass slowly and painfully and I felt a sense of relief as the waters broke, washing down like a puddle, reminding me how I'd peed my pants when I was thirteen. Here I was at seventeen about to bring a child into an uncertain stormy world where nation killed nation and Michael was dead.

I began to cry with self-pity. What had I done to God to be treated like this I demanded in a loud voice. And then the door opened.

'Jessie?' My voice wavered as I lifted my head but it was George who came into the room, a huge stick in his hand. I thought he'd gone mad and wanted to kill me. Right now I didn't care, I just wanted to be out of my pain.

'*Iesu Grist*,' he gasped. 'Jesus Christ, Meryl, you're alive and you're *here*. I thought we had burglars – do you know there's a light showing?' He jerked the curtain close to the window.

'Damn the curtain, you're obtuse as ever George, can't you see I'm about to have a baby!' I moaned again, 'Can you help me?' I asked more humbly.

George dropped the stick and washed his hands; at least his

awful mother had taught him to be clean. He came to the edge of the sofa and undid my skirt. 'Your knickers are sopping wet, you haven't got a clue about birthing a baby have you, a cow about to calf got more sense than you.'

I felt a growl begin in my throat. 'I think I want to push,' I managed. The feeling of burning was almost a relief from the contractions that seemed to tear me apart. 'George, I'm scared.'

He grinned and winked at me. 'Think yourself to be a young healthy animal and remember I've delivered more beasts than you can count, so just stay calm and we'll be alright.'

George was gentle, his capable hands guiding my baby into the world with unerring skill and assurance. 'You're not as easy as a cow,' he said, 'I've got to cut the cord. Why can't you be an animal and bite it with your teeth?'

He did the job without any trouble and then put the baby on my already full breasts. 'You've got a son,' he said, 'he's got a big, strong you-know-what; his father, whoever he is,' he said, under his breath, 'would be very proud.'

I hugged my boy, who looked like an unfurled petal and felt his pleasing weight against me. I was crying again as George carried on with the business of the rest of the birth. Then he gently washed me, found me a clean blanket, wrapped me in it and took my boy out of my reluctant arms.

I watched as he washed my son with infinite care, wrapped him in a clean towel and put him back into my arms.

'Thank you, George,' I said gratefully.

'Drink of brandy to wet the baby's head and help you sleep.' He boiled up some water, something he hadn't done for the birth, and made me a syrup of brandy, sugar and hot water. I sipped it delicately – it was very strong on brandy.

George went upstairs. I heard him bang about a bit and then he returned with a drawer from one of the dressers. He had lined it with a pillow and some white sheets from Jessie's cupboard. 'The *boy bach's* bed.'

I felt my eyelids begin to droop as George took my son and laid him carefully in the home-made crib. With George there I felt safe. I snuggled down thinking absently that this morning I was in a different country and then, weary, slept the sleep of the dead.

It was morning when I opened my eyes, alerted by the sound

of the baby's cry. I sat up remembering, frantic to go to my son but there was George bringing the boy to me, placing him in my arms.

'Try to give the child suck,' he said. I looked at him feeling dense.

'Put your teat into his mouth!' George was irritated.

'I know what you mean, I just don't know how to do it.'

He pulled aside my clothes and put the baby against my nipple. 'Let him clamp on, he won't get much milk yet but he will have goodness and comfort.'

Clamp was the word. The baby grasped my nipple in rosy lips and immediately began to suck. I winced.

'If the beast's teats get sore, I put Vaseline on them between times suckling the young 'uns,' George said. He peered over the baby's head. 'You're not doing bad for a townie,' he said.

'Townies have babies and . . . anyway, stop looking, I'm embarrassed.'

'I don't need to look at you,' George said reasonably, 'I've got a lovely wife in Vi, she's good and loyal but I know in my heart she can't stand it in the country. She wants to go home to Swansea and I want her to wait till the war is over.' He laughed. 'The old horse bit her arm a few weeks ago and Vi ran away screaming. The demented horse began to gallop and Vi was convinced the creature was after her. I don't want her to go back to Swansea, I couldn't bear it if I lost her.'

I thought hysterically about Mrs Dixon and longed to make some insulting comparison between her and the horse. I restrained myself.

'George,' I said softly, 'the war is almost over, the British and the Americans are taking control, there are rumours that Herr Hitler is dead.' I shook my head. 'I don't really know what's happening but look, perhaps it would help if Vi came to help me with the baby, stayed for a few days, perhaps that would lift her out of her gloom.'

George held my hand. 'Thank you, Meryl. I once thought I loved you and I suppose I did in some boyish way but Violet is my blood, my bones, she's part of me and I'm grateful to you for doing your best to help.'

'And I'm grateful to you, more grateful than I can say. I don't know what I'd have done without you, George.'

He turned red. 'I'll slip back home, bring some food and things and bring Violet, we'll be together just like a family, at least for a while.'

When George had gone, the farmhouse seemed empty. I glanced down at my son and kissed his curly, wispy hair, red, like my sister's. 'You are going to be called Harry after your aunt and Michael after your daddy.' My son opened his eyes and looked at me, and a smile, maybe wind, curled his mouth and I began to cry. Again. I began to realize that's what babies and their mothers did: cry, a lot.

Seventy-Four

The war was over, officially, at last. Troops were still fighting in Burma but they would be home soon. The Japanese had surrendered after the huge bombs were dropped on Nagasaki and Hiroshima and I was a woman who was still a wife, not a widow as I'd believed for so long. My regret was that Herr Euler never could know his son and his grandson were alive and well.

When I visited Daddy in Swansea I learned that Michael was being held in Island Farm; he'd escaped and been recaptured and I had very little idea when he would be released. Hari and I didn't speak.

As I trudged now across the grassland towards the prison, I hoped yet again to catch a glimpse of him. That's all I could hope for, he was still a German prisoner of war and I'd be risking his life if I said anything different.

This time he was there. My heart leapt as I saw Michael looking at me from beyond the fence, a smile on his face.

'Hello wife.' He spoke in German and I understood it was his cover. If the truth was known about his background the other prisoners would lynch him. 'How are you keeping?' His tone was jocular, I still had no idea how he felt. I wanted to ask if he had made his choice between us, between me and my sister Hari, but we couldn't talk intimately. Even as we stood looking at each other a British soldier came along and pointed a gun at Michael. 'Move!' he ordered.

'We're being sent back to Germany any day now.' Michael spoke quickly. When I'm discharged I'll come back and . . .' He didn't finish his sentence, the soldier jabbed him and moved him on giving me a filthy look.

I caught sight of Hari, her red hair flying in the wind, but I was too sick at heart to stop. I hurried away as if I hadn't seen her. She was visiting my husband and I wondered if he had made her any promises.

I caught the bus to the station and sat staring sightlessly out of the window wondering if making love, even having a child by a man, was enough to hold him.

It took me forever to get home. I had settled back into the farmhouse with George of all people – no longer my enemy but my dear friend – and his devoted wife Violet, living with me while they decided if they would move to Swansea or turn one of the barns on the farm into a cottage. For the time being they would work the farm for me and George had plans for when Michael came home.

'We'll build this place up, Meryl, you'll see.' George was sitting at the kitchen table when I got in, his wellingtons full of the good earth of Carmarthen, his eyes alight with enthusiasm. 'Vi has settled now she knows we won't be living in Mam's house very much longer.'

'Thank goodness for that!' My words were heartfelt.

'We'll restock the animals and grow potatoes and root veg and soon we'll all earn a good living from Jessie's farm.'

The door was pushed open. 'It's only me, Mrs Jones.' The girl from the village who cleaned for me came into the kitchen and eyed me with suspicion as she always did, especially when I forgot myself and spoke in German. She refused to use my married name, Frau Euler, and insisted calling me by my Welsh maiden name.

'Morning, Glenys, how's the goat?' This was our one line of conversation: Glenys's goat Smuttie. He was so wild I thought he should be called 'Paddy Murphy's Goat', but the two loved each other like lovers.

'Eatin' my home up as usual, Mrs Jones.' She tickled the baby's cheek briefly and the baby grinned toothlessly. This courtesy over, Glenys rummaged under the sink for her cleaning things.

'The bedrooms today, is it?'

'That will be lovely, Glenys, thank you.'

'I saw him today: Michael,' I said to George, 'they're sending him back to Germany soon.'

'That's good,' George said.

'How can it be good?'

'Well, he'll be discharged and then he'll come back to Wales. The Jerries have got nothing against Michael, mind, he served his country, so as far as they know he's been a good German, crashed in "enemy" land, held in a prison camp till the end of the war. I wouldn't mind betting he'll get a medal.'

I brightened up. 'You're not as daft as you look.'

'I've told you to stop saying sweet words to me, my wife will be getting jealous.' George grinned as Violet came into the room with a tray of cocoa and some biscuits.

'You two arguing again?' She smiled lovingly at George.

I shook my head. 'George is talking a lot of sense,' I said, 'he's made me feel better now.'

Violet kissed George fondly on the brow. 'You're a good man, George, *my* man.' She hugged him round the neck and he blushed like a schoolboy.

I got up quietly, picked up my son and went to help Glenys with the bed linen.

Seventy-Five

Hari stood in the grass outside the prison camp looking out at nothing at all. Then she glimpsed her sister again; she seemed to be here almost every day. Meryl was still tiny, her slim figure showing no signs she'd had a child. Hari watched as Meryl walked towards the barbed wire fence. She saw Michael come towards the other side of the wire and her heart leapt with love for him.

And then anger like a black angel beat in her temples as she saw him, unaware of her, standing there in the shadows. He was talking with Meryl so sweetly, looking down at her from his great height with such love and tenderness that Hari gave an involuntary sob and then a guard came and shouted at Michael to go back inside. Since the escape the guards had to be more vigilant.

Meryl, her face white, saw her and, after a moment, came towards her, her baby wrapped in a Welsh shawl.

'Hari –' Meryl spoke tentatively – 'Hari, I love him.'

'So do I.' Hari heard the hard edge to her voice. 'You have him and I don't. You have his son, you've lived with Michael, married him, had the approval of his mother and his father, what more could you ask?'

'I want your approval, Hari, I want your love. We're sisters; blood of blood, just as the baby is blood of your blood. Look at him, Hari, please.'

Hari felt a red-hot anger sear through her head. She wanted to lash out and beat her sister senseless, obliterate any barrier to her love for Michael. She deliberately ignored the child.

'Well, if Michael wants you he can have you and good luck to him, but remember this, little sister –' Hari was appalled at her own bitterness – 'I had him first.'

'You may still have him,' Meryl said humbly. 'I don't know who he wants, I never did. Herr Euler said we should marry, for safety's sake, so we got married.'

'And then you slept together, obviously,' Hari said, 'so there was no immaculate conception was there?'

'Of course not.' Meryl's cheeks were red. 'We grew close; we loved together; it's difficult not to when you lie in the same bed, but I never did know if I had his love, really had his love, or if he still pined after you.'

A tear slipped down her cheeks. 'Even now he remarked about your lovely red hair and how the baby was so like you.' She hung her head. 'I can't fight you, Hari. I've fought for my country, I've fooled the Germans and fought like a cat for my freedom and for my son, but I can't fight you.'

Hari bit her lip. This was her little sister and all she said was true; she had been brave beyond the call of any young woman. Suddenly, she drew Meryl into her arms.

'Oh Meryl, of course Michael loves you.' And yet the few words her sister had just said about Michael heartened her, perhaps he still loved her, still wanted her, still cared. She looked down at the sleeping face of the baby and knew her hopes were selfish and vain.

As they stood there, the noise of banging and loud orders from the prison caught Hari's attention. She drew a sharp breath. The prisoners were being lined up, the British guards were shouting orders. A German officer, clearly high-ranking, was drawing a cart with his possessions packed.

'He's being sent to another prison, or else sent back to Germany, if he's lucky.' Meryl had dried her tears and was looking anxiously at the other Germans in the group.

'Why send him away at all?' Hari asked, 'I thought the men would be kept here long after the war.'

'Some will.' Meryl sounded tired, worldly-wise. 'Von Rundstedt has committed no war crimes; he'll go to Nuremberg and then go home. Less important prisoners, like Michael, will be sent back to Germany.'

She stared Hari in the face. 'Then neither of us will have him. He might choose to live out his life in Hamburg.'

'What are you saying?'

'I'm saying we might never see him again – don't act duller than you are, Hari.'

'But of course he'll come back, he'll want to see Jessie. Surely he'll come home for her and his son, and you, of course.' The words stuck in Hari's throat, but the prospect of never seeing Michael again was too awful to contemplate.

'Perhaps you're right. Come on, take me back to Swansea to see the family and then I'm going back to the farmhouse.'

'You'll be alone.'

Meryl stared at her meaningfully. 'I haven't seen any of you come rushing to Carmarthen to see me or the baby.' She sounded hurt. 'Thank God for Vi and George.'

Meryl laughed suddenly, tearfully. 'Poor George, seeing my private parts when he was bringing baby Michael into the world. You should have seen his face; he was redder than me and I was doing the pushing.'

Hari hugged her. 'Come on then little sis –' she gulped back the sob in her throat – 'let's take you home.'

Together both girls walked away from the prison camp, unaware of a pair of anguished eyes staring after their receding figures.

Seventy-Six

I stood outside the church and watched as Father and Jessie came out into the sunshine, she looking like a young, beautiful girl in love. She clung to Father's arm and her homely, weathered face was radiant as are the faces of all brides I suppose.

Even I, with Herr Euler standing over me and the official – cold, hurried, anxious to get back to the safety of his office – thrusting a page at Michael and me to sign, even I, when I had the gold ring on my finger and I was Michael's wife, even I had had a glow in my eyes and I knew it.

Perhaps it was the pink flowers Jessie held in her hand, or the soft pink dress she was wearing or it could have been the sheer happiness in her eyes, but she looked wonderful. Like a radiant young girl.

From my experiences in Germany and now, the vulnerability of my motherhood, I realized fifty wasn't very old these days. Women of near that age had been killed as spies, proper spies, not amateur bunglers like me.

They were going on honeymoon but only to the farm in Carmarthen, so for the time being I was to stay in the Swansea house with my sister Hari. I was apprehensive; what if Hari was hostile to my baby? I needn't have worried. When we got home Hari smiled and took the baby from me and kissed his fuzzy head.

'Thank goodness you're here,' she said. 'They've all gone: Georgie and Vi, Father and Jessie; from a full house I find an empty one.'

'Hari,' I began. She waved her hand.

'Don't talk about it, it won't help,' she said gently.

'But you loved Michael and I . . .' I stopped, prevented by the turn of her shoulders that begged me to say no more.

'"*Love*" Michael, present tense,' she said, almost in a whisper. 'I will always love Michael.' She visibly pulled herself together.

'Want something to eat, gannet?'

'What have we got?'

'Eggs, some cheese, a tiny bit of butter. It's still rationing in town, you know, we're not overflowing with milk and honey like the country.'

I stopped myself saying the 'milk and honey' had to be worked for, the chickens fed on bran and mash and potato peelings, the butter endlessly churned until my arms nearly fell out of the sockets.

'I have to keep up a good supply of milk for baby gannet,' I said, pointing at little Harry, 'so I'll have eggs on buttered toast and hope it doesn't give the baby too much wind.'

We talked after the meal and as I fed the baby, hoping he wouldn't clamp too hard on my poor nipples, Hari went to wash up, singing as she swished the dishes through the water, hoping, I think, to drown out the sound of my baby, Michael's baby, suckling at my breast.

And then, for the rest of the evening, we talked about anything but Michael and we drank a little home-made wine, and we avoided each other's eyes. I was glad to go to bed in my old childhood room, staring at the pictures of fairies on the walls, at the cut-outs of Rupert Bear, Bill the elephant and Podgy, who still reminded me of George Dixon – George, who had changed now into a good man and who had brought my son safely into the world; and then I was lonely for Michael and began to cry.

Hari left for work early the next morning. I heard her creep downstairs. I changed the baby's sodden napkin, washed my hands and took him back to bed. I snuggled him into the warmth of the pillows and gave him the comfort of my milk. We both fell asleep.

The sun was shining when I woke again and I felt well and happy even though the word 'repatriation' was being talked about at the prison camp; this repatriation of the German soldiers would take months yet, there was plenty of time to act.

I would go and see Michael, I would give him Fritz's name and what I remembered of his contact code. I felt confident that the resistance movement would get Michael back to Wales even if Fritz had to get Michael forged papers.

The train was full and stuffy with body smells. Harry didn't like the journey; he wriggled and moaned. The woman sitting next to me in the small carriage tutted her disapproval.

I turned and smiled falsely at her. 'Do you serve in the forces?'

'No,' she said shortly.

'The munitions?' I persisted.

'Well, no.' Her arrogance was fading.

'Too old, I expect,' I said in mock sympathy. She looked abashed and stared out of the window. 'Excuse me.' I brushed past her and held my baby fast as I climbed from the carriage, ashamed of my burst of spite.

When I arrived at Bridgend, to my shock and anger, my sister Hari was standing outside the barbed wire fence of Island Farm Prison Camp talking to one of the soldiers. Hari was plainly dressed and carried a clipboard as if she were in a position of authority.

Always the actress, I went close to the soldier and looked up at him with limpid eyes. 'Excuse me, officer –' I knew very well he was no such thing – 'you've seen me before I'm sure. I've got a baby by one of the prisoners. Please let me see the father for just one minute, would you? Please, sir.'

He stared at me in disgust. 'Yes, I've seen you and heard you talking to him in German, you traitor. Us British aren't good enough for you, eh?'

'I fell in love; I'm just seventeen.' I said. 'Please, sir, the German should take some responsibility for his baby, shouldn't he?'

He caught my chin and turned my face up to his. 'When did all this happen?'

'Please, officer, it was when the prisoners were allowed out in town for church or something.'

He shook his head. 'I don't know what young girls are coming to these days. In my time they . . .'

'It's the war, sir, tomorrow we could all be dead,' I murmured. 'Please, sir, let me see him. I'm afraid he'll be sent back to Germany soon.'

'Aye, and then you'll never see hide nor hair of him again my girl. Saddled with a bastard kid you'll be for the rest of your life.'

'I expect you're right sir,' I said meekly.

'What's his name?' he asked at last.

Michael was fetched and came to the fence watched by the other German soldiers laughing and jeering, saying vulgar things in German all of which I understood all too clearly.

'You don't look well,' I said in concern. He was pale, sweating, he'd lost weight. 'Hold my hands,' I ordered Michael, resenting his quick look in Hari's direction. He did as he was told.

'It's a contact for one of the Belgian resistance people,' I said in hurried, whispered German – in case you're sent back.'

I showed him his son and simpered, aware of the soldier watching us. Michael looked at his small image amazed, properly aware now that his son was beginning to look like him.

'My code name is Anwn, remember that.' I stared at him as he leaned against the fence. I glanced up at the barbed wire lacing the top of the fence and knew there would be no escape that way. In any case, Michael would be tracked down and fetched back to prison again.

'See you soon, *Liebling*,' he said in mock, halting English.

I turned away then as the soldier hauled an unresisting Michael back to the huts.

'You deserve a good kicking for despoiling one of our young girls,' he said fiercely.

I didn't speak to my sister. I don't know why – ashamed or choked with tears I suppose. I made my way back to Swansea with tears in my eyes but there was a glimmer of hope in my heart.

Seventy-Seven

It was three weeks since Hari had last seen Michael and then Meryl had been there, her son cradled in her arms, whispering sweet nothings through the fence to Michael. Well, she would see him now, alone; well, as alone as they could be with a fence between them. She would confront him about his feelings for her and for Meryl.

Had his marriage to her little sister been one of expediency, what the Victorians would have called a marriage of convenience? Of course it must have been, it was a cover so they would both be safe. But the baby, how could she explain the baby, even to herself? There must be an explanation, there had to be; had Meryl seduced him, had he given in to her in a moment of weakness?

Hari made her way from the munitions to the camp and waited for about an hour, hanging about among the trees until she saw James come out of one of the huts. 'Evening, James.'

'Hello there, *cariad*, you're looking very pretty today if I may say so.' James smiled, obviously happy to see her again. 'Where on earth have you been, I thought you were supposed to make regular checks up here?'

'My job is nearly over now,' Hari said, 'in any case I had to go away for a few days.'

'Well, I must say you look well for it, girl, red suits you.'

Hari looked down at her new coat, red, like poppies, like blood, like dear dead Kate's shoes.

'Thank you, James. What are you going to do now that the war is over?'

'I'll have to stay here; important officers are being shifted into Island Farm, Hari, men like Field Marshal Von Rundstedt. He's a real gent, not a war criminal, but he has to go to Nuremburg in Germany as a witness. In the meantime I'll be guarding him and the other high-up officers.'

'And what will happen to the ordinary officers?'

'They are being shipped back to where they belong,' James said fiercely.

Hari's heart sank. How would Michael manage in the chaos there must be in Germany, right now? The Russians and the Allies were occupying the place and Hitler was alleged to be dead, but no one knew the truth of that. It would not be safe for any German returning to the Fatherland. In any case, Michael belonged here, in Wales.

'And what about that girl who was here a few weeks ago, a silly girl with a baby – will her chap be sent back to Germany?'

'Haven't seen the poor creature at all, though the other guards say she hangs around like a stray cat, but she's wasting her time.'

'What do you mean?' Hari asked.

'That fellow, the German she was daft enough to . . . well you know, he's already gone.' He nodded in satisfaction at a job well done.

'Gone where?'

'He was sent back to Germany quick, sharp. Fell sick, see, and we got enough problems without keeping sick enemies here.'

Hari hid her feelings of shock. She wondered if Meryl knew. She would have to make the journey down to the farm, see her sister and find out what was happening. It was a bitter taste in her mouth that she had to ask Meryl anything about Michael. He was *hers,* she'd seen him first, lain with him, lost her virginity with him.

'And are you staying at the munitions place, Hari?' James's tone was anxious.

'Oh, yes, it will take years to sort everything out and at least I've got a job to keep home and hearth together, for now.' Her tone was wry.

Hari didn't want James to ask any more questions. 'I've got to get back home.' She blew him a kiss. 'See you soon, James.'

She had a car now, an old clapped-out van someone had fitted windows in. She drove home to Swansea trying to wipe away the mist in her eyes. The streets were empty; the shelters still looked the same; the home guard roamed the streets; the blackout curtains were still in place; it was as if no one believed yet the war was over.

Later, the dark crept in and even the electric lighting didn't dispel Hari's gloom. What was she going to do with her life when she eventually left Bridgend? She might get a job as a telephonist or a typist even or perhaps work in Marks and Spencer's. Yet none of those jobs appealed.

She might meet a man, as Violet had pointed out. Another man she could love as she loved Michael? She didn't think so. She indulged herself, remembering their love-making, the one and only time they'd been intimate together. She had melted into Michael, her love obscuring every other emotion. They had become one being together forever, at least that's what she believed then. Would she ever trust another man?

She sat alone in her bedroom, the bedroom of her own house, her empty house, and knew she felt bitter and sorry for herself. She'd taken them all in: Jessie, Father, George and Violet, and even allowed Meryl to stay with her child. And now they had left and she was alone. She sat before the fire, her toes pointed close to the flames, and though she was grieving, her eyes for once were dry as if all her tears were gone.

Seventy-Eight

I saw Hari coming towards the farmhouse and prepared myself for – well I didn't know what, but I realized the meeting would be difficult, perhaps even hostile. She didn't knock, but opened the door and came straight to where I was sitting near the window, Michael's hastily scribbled note, reread a hundred times, on my knee.

'You know,' I said, and heard the challenge in my voice. She stood over me, Hari, my sister, her cheeks flushed, her red hair tossed around her face. She looked beautiful. How could I compete with her?

'Jessie had the kindness to tell me.' She shook back her hair. 'How could you tell Jessie and not me, Meryl, how could you?'

I stood up to face her, determined not to get angry. 'My husband is coming back from Germany, he's coming home and if I chose to tell his mother that's my business.'

'Michael would expect you to tell me.' She sounded sure and my heart nearly failed me.

'Why didn't he write to you then, and not just me?'

'He had your contacts to help him, didn't he? They would hardly expect him to write to anyone but his wife, would they? They probably stood over him to make sure he wasn't going to betray them.'

It sounded sense to me and the sense of euphoria that swept over me whenever I held the paper Michael had written on vanished.

'Yes, they would expect him to write to his *wife* and not his "one-nighter".'

'He told you we only had one night?'

'Of course he told me, one night when we lay half asleep after making love; he told me it was the biggest mistake of his life.' So he had but not in the way I said it. Michael regretted taking Hari's virginity with so little thought for her future, he felt he'd taken advantage of her innocence. I hammered the nails home. 'He wished he'd never done it.'

Hari's cheeks were suddenly pale and I felt sorry for her. I nearly took her in my arms but then she spoke.

'At least I had him first.' It wasn't the first time she'd told me and it hurt like hell.

I retaliated like a child. 'Aye, and he made all his mistakes with you, experimented with sex as boys do. He came to me a man full grown, knowing his own mind and his own body.'

'I could have had his child.' Hari was losing now, her lips trembled and like a tiger I went for my weakened enemy.

'But you didn't have his child! I did, his lawful wife, I had his son, carried him in my womb, brought him safely back home – a legitimate child of a true marriage.'

Hari retreated to the door. 'I won't give up, Meryl, Michael is mine, he'll want to be with me. We can have children too, lots of them, you don't have the monopoly on motherhood you know.'

She slammed out of the house and I sank back into my chair near the window, hating myself, hating Hari, and unwilling to feed my now-crying child until all the pain and venom had drained from my trembling body.

A week later I stood on the platform at Swansea Station and waited for the train to puff into sight. It would poke its sparking, shooting nose round the curve of the land and pull up beside me, and Michael, my beloved Michael, would step out. And then what?

I'd left the baby with Jessie, who had a few cryptic words to say to me before I left, words that did not reassure me. 'He'll decide where his future lies,' she said sagely, 'Michael is a man now and only he knows where his heart is.'

I heard the clip-clop of heels and saw Hari coming along the platform. She was wearing a red coat and new, shiny red shoes identical to those Kate had worn that day, so far away now when I'd sat under the table and stared out at the world in fear of dying under a bombers' moon. My sister and I didn't look at each other but she stood resolutely at my side as though asserting her rights.

The gush of steam alerted us both and the train steamed round the bend spitting sparks into the grass at the side of the rails and setting up little fires. I felt one of the sparks had ignited in me too. I longed for Michael to be in my arms, safe and well and mine. But would that happen?

People gushed out of the train, disgorged on to the platform and then drifted away to disappear like the smoke from the train. And there he was.

Michael stood for a moment, staring along the stretch of platform between us. I thought of a film I'd seen: sand, blue seas, lovers running to each other, arms wide. But it was Hari doing the running.

I was unable to move, still watching a film unwinding as Michael's arms closed around my sister. His head bent and he was kissing her. I noticed he looked bedraggled, his hair was too long, too thick, his jacket was threadbare, his feet were shod in shabby shoes. One of the soles flapped like a tongue as he came towards me.

He was coming towards me. Hari, I saw, was standing with her head sagging on her chest and she was crying.

He held me close. His lips were warm and searching on mine. 'My darling wife,' he said, 'I'm going to spend the rest of my life telling you how much I love you and I do love you, you funny little thing, so efficient, so straight, so brave. I've loved you since that night in the barn when I cuddled you and you slept in my arms. Then you were only a child and I didn't acknowledge my feelings, I was afraid to confront them. I fear I made Hari a substitute for you and I'll always regret that.'

We clung together for a long time and a great glow of happiness filled me. And then I remembered my sister. I looked at her; she was so smart in her red coat and red shoes and the thought flitted through my mind that red shoes never were lucky.

Hari came towards us, bravely forcing a smile, and I loved her so much in that moment. 'Thank you, sis,' I said, my eyes full.

'Come on then you love birds.' Hari spoke cheerfully. 'Michael, aren't you going to offer your sister-in-law a cup of tea before you take your wife home?'

She squeezed my arm and together we left the platform – me, my beautiful sister, and the man I loved more than life itself. My war was truly over.